Praise for the Mysteries of Janet Dawson

"Dawson's extensive research into train life is translated into a moment-by-moment account of life on the *California Zephyr*, and we are privileged to see every aspect of being a Zephyrette. ...Train lovers will love this glimpse of a life spent riding the rails on this unique streamliner."

—*Historical Novels Review* [on *Death Rides the Zephyr*]

"*Death Rides the Zephyr* is an entertaining tale of spies, counter-spies, and intrigue which also captures nuances of a transcontinental train trip in the early '50s."

—*Railfan & Railroad* Magazine

"*Death Rides the Zephyr* is an engrossing murder mystery with enough suspicious people to provide multiple suspects. A late-in-the-story catastrophe raises the stakes and the suspense. The book is also an unapologetic paean to railroading, recreating the train travel experience of the 1950s. The pace of the narrative matches the pace of a train trip."

—*Gumshoe* Magazine

"Dawson knows how to blend real history and real crime into an intriguing mystery about a missing man and the people, and the land, he loves."

—*Mystery Scene* [on *Cold Trail*]

"Exciting... Dawson keeps the suspense high as Jeri seeks to find her brother before it's too late."

—*Publishers Weekly* [on *Cold Trail*]

Death Deals a Hand ————————————

MYSTERY FICTION BY JANET DAWSON

Death Deals a Hand

A California Zephyr Mystery

JANET DAWSON

2016

PERSEVERANCE PRESS / JOHN DANIEL AND COMPANY
PALO ALTO / MCKINLEYVILLE, CALIFORNIA

A Perseverance Press Book
Published by John Daniel & Company
A division of Daniel & Daniel, Publishers, Inc.
Post Office Box 2790
McKinleyville, California 95519
www.danielpublishing.com/perseverance

Distributed by SCB Distributors (800) 729-6423

Cover art © Roger Morris, Two Rock Media. All rights reserved.

CZ car diagram: From plans originally drawn by Julian Cavalier. Used by permission. Copyright White River Productions, 1974, 1999

Book design by Eric Larson, Studio E Books, Santa Barbara, www.studio-e-books.com

10 9 8 7 6 5 4 3 2 1

LIBRARY OF CONGRESS CATALOGING-IN-PUBLICATION DATA
Dawson, Janet, author.
 Death deals a hand : a California Zephyr mystery / by Janet Dawson.
    pages cm
 ISBN 978-1-56474-569-9 (pbk. : alk. paper)
 1. California Zephyr (Express train)—Fiction. 2. Railroad travel—Fiction. 3. Murder—Fiction. I. Title.

PS3554.A949D425 2016
813'.54—dc23

                        2015028933

To Mom, as always

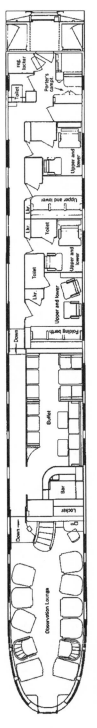

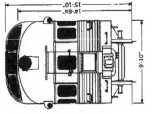

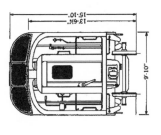

California Zephyr
Dome–Observation
Plans not to scale

Dome arrangement

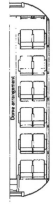

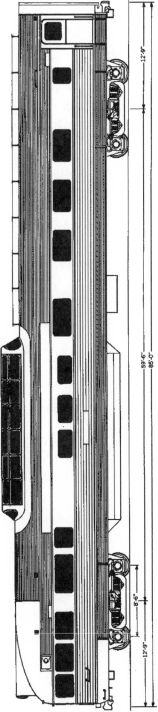

Death Deals a Hand ———————

Chapter One ────────────────────

THE WESTBOUND *CALIFORNIA ZEPHYR* sped across the high plains of eastern Colorado, the train's headlamps piercing the early morning darkness. In the cab of the first diesel engine, the engineer blew a warning signal as the train approached a crossing—two long blasts on the horn, followed by one short, then one long.

Jill McLeod had just entered the Silver Banquet, the dining car. She paused in the corridor that ran alongside the train's kitchen and turned toward the nearest window, her face reflected in the glass. Then, outside the train, twin headlights glowed. Silhouetted in the lights from a nearby building was a pickup truck, stopped at the crossing. Then the lights, building and vehicle disappeared as the train passed.

Breakfast service aboard the *California Zephyr* started at six o'clock in the morning, and it was a quarter after the hour. Jill walked down the corridor past the kitchen to the main part of the Silver Banquet. This early in the morning, few of the tables were occupied. Jill nodded to several early risers. Some of them she recognized as passengers who'd boarded the train the previous afternoon and evening, in Chicago and at other stations across Illinois and Iowa. At one table were two people Jill hadn't seen before, a mother and her young son. They must have boarded the train late last night, after Jill had gone to bed.

Near the center of the car, the steward, Mr. Taylor, stood behind a curved counter, its base decorated with a mural of carved linoleum. Behind the steward, a doorway led back to the kitchen, a hub of activity this morning, as cooks in white uniforms, aprons and caps moved between the shiny stainless steel counters, opening cabinets and reaching up to remove pots, pans and serving pieces from shelves.

The dining car crew consisted of the steward, a chef and three cooks, as well as six waiters. The *California Zephyr* was the joint operation of three railroads—the Chicago, Burlington & Quincy; the Denver & Rio Grande Western; and the Western Pacific—and each railroad operated a segment of the run. The dining car was staffed for the entire trip by a crew made up of employees from one of these railroads. For this westbound run, the dining car crew was from the CB&Q.

Before the train left the rail yard and moved to the platform at Chicago's Union Station, the kitchen and pantry had been loaded with supplies from the commissary. The train—also known as the *CZ*—carried enough food and beverages to feed the passengers and crew during the two-and-a-half-day westbound run. The pantry also carried supplies—crockery, glassware, silver service and kitchen equipment, and the linens used to cover the tables.

Jill greeted the steward, who smiled and waved a hand at the tables. "Good morning, Miss McLeod. Sit anywhere you like."

She took the window seat at a table for four, facing toward the train's engine. The table was covered with a crisp white cloth with matching napkins and set with heavy silverware. It was set with china bearing a pattern of violets and daisies. Each table held a full water bottle, a bud vase containing a fresh carnation, and a heavy silver stand holding the breakfast menu and meal checks on which passengers marked their menu choices. Jill didn't need to look at the menu. She marked her meal check, choosing a favorite breakfast.

There were six waiters in the dining car, all of them wearing white jackets. She knew many of the waiters by name, having traveled with them before. Jill was the Zephyrette, the only female member of the train's onboard crew.

A waiter approached her table, carrying a silver coffeepot. "Good morning, Mr. Gaylord," Jill said. From the conductor on down, the crew were expected to keep their communications with their fellow crew members on a "Mister and Miss" basis.

"Good morning, Miss McLeod. Coffee?"

"Yes, please."

He smiled as he poured a steaming cup of black coffee and took her meal check, though he didn't have to give it more than a glance. The waiters aboard the train were adept at reading the passengers' tastes, the better to serve frequent travelers. After many trips on the CZ, they knew what the crew members liked to eat as well. "I'm guessing you want your favorite. French toast and bacon, crisp but not burned."

Jill smiled. "That would be a good guess."

"Coming right up." Mr. Gaylord moved away from the table, heading for the kitchen.

Jill reached for the heavy silver pitcher and poured cream into her cup. Then she raised it to her lips. Ah, the coffee tasted good. And the caffeine jolt was most welcome.

She usually slept well on the train, but she'd had a restless night. Yesterday, Jill had reported for duty an hour before the *California Zephyr*, designated train number 17, was due to leave Chicago's Union Station. She'd been in the Windy City for two nights, a layover following her eastbound run from Oakland to Chicago on train number 18. Now she was returning home, to California.

When Jill arrived at Union Station, she stowed her suitcase and first-aid kit in her compartment at the end of the Silver Chalet, the buffet-lounge car. Then she began her pre-departure routine. She walked through the train from beginning to end, checking the washrooms for cleanliness. Each car had a card holder, and in these, she inserted cards identifying her as the Zephyrette.

The train's consist—the rail cars that made up the train—began with three diesel locomotives owned by the Chicago, Burlington & Quincy Railroad. Following the engines were cars built by Pennsylvania's Budd Company, a mix of equipment from all three roads. The legend CALIFORNIA ZEPHYR decorated the sides of each car and the gleaming stainless steel cars all had "Silver" in their names. This was why the *California Zephyr* was known as the Silver Lady.

For this trip, the baggage car was the Silver Buffalo. Behind this were three chair cars—the Silver Scout, Silver Mustang, and Silver Ranch. Each of these cars had seating for sixty coach passengers, as well as an upper-level Vista-Dome, a glass compartment with seating for twenty-four coach passengers. The Dome rose out of the car's roof, accessed by stairs in the middle of the car. Underneath the Dome, two steps on either side led down to the depressed floor, which contained the men's and women's restrooms.

In the middle of the train were the Silver Chalet, the buffet-lounge car, and the Silver Banquet, the dining car. Following these were the sleeper cars, the Silver Quail, the Silver Falls, the Silver Maple, and the Silver Rapids. At the end of the train was the dome-observation car, the Silver Crescent. Both the Silver Chalet and the Silver Crescent had depressed floors and Vista-Domes, for the use of the sleeper car passengers.

Before the train's 3:30 P.M. departure from Union Station, Jill and the Pullman conductor, Mr. Winston, stood at the check-in tables inside the station, greeting passengers and directing them to their cars. Jill also made dinner reservations for people traveling in the sleeper cars. These she charted on a diagram which she later turned over to the dining car steward. Once the train left the station, Jill went to the public address system in the dining car, where she'd made the first of several announcements she would make during the westbound journey. After that, she'd walked forward through the train to the three coach cars, where she began making dinner reservations for those passengers.

She'd made another announcement as the train crossed the Mississippi River at 6:30 P.M. and headed into Iowa. After the dining car closed later that evening, Jill made her last announcement of the day on the train's PA system, which was located just opposite the steward's counter.

"May I have your attention, please. Before retiring this evening, you may wish to move your watches back one hour, as we will enter the Mountain Time Zone at McCook, Nebraska at about four A.M. Good night."

After making her announcement, Jill walked through the train once more, stopping to talk with passengers. Many were settling down in their seats and sleeper berths, ready to turn in for the night, although seats were still occupied in the Silver Chalet's coffee shop, which served hot food, snacks, and beverages. There were a few people in the lounge, where a waiter served liquor and non-alcoholic drinks. Both venues would be open until 10 P.M.

Jill went back to her compartment at the rear of the Silver Chalet. The narrow space contained a bench seat that folded down into a bed, as well as a toilet and sink. The washstand pulled down from the wall and pushed up again when not in use.

Inside the compartment, she took her suitcase down from the overhead rack and opened it, reaching for her soft blue cotton pajamas. She undressed and put on the pajamas, then stowed the suitcase on the rack. She pulled the sink down from the wall to wash her face and brush her teeth. She pushed it back up, letting the water drain into the pipes in the wall. Then she converted the seat into her bed, climbed under the blanket, and plumped the pillow.

Jill didn't go to sleep right away, though. First she worked on her trip report, which she was required to file at the end of the train's fifty-one-hour journey. The report was an account of each day's activities, a journal of the ordinary things that happened on the run, as well as anything out of the ordinary. It included information about any complaints from passengers, or problems that arose during the journey, such as difficulties with the dinner reservations, accidents, or late arrivals and the reasons for delays.

She prided herself on the details in her trip reports, and she kept a small notebook and pencil tucked in the pocket of her uniform, making notes during the day. Her trip reports usually included comments about the number of dinner reservations she'd made the first day out, any troublesome or special-attention passengers, children traveling alone or any baby-sitting that she'd done for passengers with small children, medicine she had administered, although that was limited to giving passengers soda mints to relieve motion sickness, or treating minor scrapes and cuts with supplies from her first-aid kit. It seemed that no matter which run she was on, there was always a child who stumbled on the stairs or got a finger caught in a door.

Jill finished this first day's portion of the report, adjusted her pillow and settled back into bed. The hardbound book propped on her lap had a white cover showing a hat, an umbrella and an ax in black, with a bunch of flowers in the lower left corner, and the author's name in black letters in the upper right corner. It was the newest Agatha Christie novel, *Funerals Are Fatal*, and Jill was eager to start chapter one.

She read for a while, absorbed in the workings of Hercule Poirot's little grey cells, accompanied by the steady and familiar *click-clack* of wheels on rails and the occasional burst of laughter coming from the lounge in the middle of the car. Finally she yawned and put down the book. It was half past nine. The train was due to stop at Creston, Iowa, at 9:45 P.M. After that came Red Oak, Iowa at 10:30 P.M. This wasn't a regularly scheduled stop for the *CZ*. The train paused briefly in the small Iowa town only if passengers were getting off or boarding. In the latter case, the passengers would let the stationmaster in Creston know ahead of time that a stop was needed. After that, the train would leave Iowa, crossing the Missouri River at 11:15 P.M., heading into Nebraska.

Jill set her own watch back an hour, ready for the move from the Central to the Mountain Time Zone. Then she turned out the light.

Tired after a long day, Jill dozed off almost immediately. Then she woke up, not sure how long she'd been asleep. What had awakened her? Raised voices, just the other side of her door.

She sat up in bed, turned on the light, and looked at her watch. It was just after ten. She listened to the voices, trying to make out words. A man and a woman, and they were having an argument, though Jill couldn't figure out why. The man's voice became louder, more insistent, and there was a thump, as though someone had bumped against Jill's door. That was followed by the sound of flesh striking flesh.

Now the man's voice was clear, just the other side of the door. "Bitch!"

Jill threw back the blanket and swung her legs out of bed, her feet scuffling around on the floor, searching for her slippers. She unlocked and opened the door of her compartment, peering out. Whoever they were, the people who had been out in the corridor were gone.

Jill closed and locked her door. She ran a hand through her short blond curls, worn in an easy-to-care-for style known as a poodle cut. Yawning, she stretched her arms overhead. Then she turned out the light.

She woke again sometime later. The sound of the wheels on tracks changed and she knew they were on the bridge crossing the Missouri River. She confirmed this by looking out the tiny window in her compartment and checking her watch. It was 11:15 P.M., on the dot. She yawned again and returned to her blanket and pillow.

She slept for half an hour, then woke up again as the train rolled into the station at Omaha, Nebraska, at 11:45 P.M. The pattern of interrupted sleep was repeated all the way across Nebraska. She woke as the *CZ* arrived at stations in Lincoln, Hastings and McCook. She fell asleep again when the train resumed its motion.

When she woke yet again and looked at her watch, it was a quarter to six. Might as well get up, Jill told herself.

She threw back the blanket and got out of bed. There would be no shower until she got home the following afternoon, at the end of the train's run. She made do with a sink bath, then dressed and put on her makeup before turning her bed back into a seat. She stowed her suitcase on the shelf above and left the compartment, heading back to the next car, the Silver Banquet.

Now, as Mr. Gaylord set her breakfast on the table, Jill looked at her watch. It was 6:30 A.M. The train's next stop was Denver, at 8:20 A.M., an hour and fifty minutes from now. She thanked the waiter as he refreshed the coffee in her cup. Then she drizzled syrup over the French toast and cut into a thick slice with her fork. It tasted wonderful, as usual.

The tables in the dining car filled up as passengers awakened and went in search of breakfast. Outside, the darkness changed from black to gray as the sun rose in the east. Here and there, houses and barns showed lights as farmers began their work day. As daylight crept over the landscape outside the train's windows, she saw snow in the crevices of hills and the rims of ponds, left from the last snowfall. It was early April. At home in California it would be sunny spring weather, perhaps with rain. But Jill had grown up in Colorado and she knew that the state's weather was changeable. It might be spring on the calendar, but snow could fall all through April and sometimes into early May. And there would definitely be snow on the ground once the train climbed into the Rocky Mountains.

April 1953, Jill thought. She had celebrated her twenty-sixth birthday in March. That month was also her second anniversary as a Zephyrette.

She was eager to complete this run and get home, for several reasons. She wanted to see her family, of course. Since graduating from college, Jill had lived with her parents, her younger sister, Lucy, and younger brother, Drew, in an old two-story house in Alameda, the island city across the estuary from Oakland. Her mother's birthday was coming up at the end of next week, and Jill had found the perfect present for Mom during her layover in Chicago.

The other person she looked forward to seeing was Mike Scolari. She'd met him on the train during an eastbound run last December, when he was traveling to Denver with his elderly grandfather. Mike was a veteran of the Army Air Corps in World War II. Now he was using the G.I. Bill to get a degree in sociology at Jill's alma mater, the University of California in Berkeley. She and Mike had been dating for three months now. Her relationship with Mike had gone a long way toward banishing the specter of her fiancé, who'd been killed in the Korean War two years ago.

She took another sip of coffee and smiled, thinking about Mike and her family. She already had a date scheduled with Mike for the coming weekend. And she was supposed to meet someone for lunch in San Francisco, later in the week. That appointment was with Mrs. Grace Tidsdale. She'd met Tidsy on that same eventful December journey and the two women had stayed in touch.

"May we join you?"

Jill looked up. The woman wore a flowered shirtwaist and a green cardigan sweater. She and two children, a girl and a boy, had entered the dining car from the direction of the coach cars. She had stopped at Jill's table, one hand on the back of a chair.

"Of course." Jill set down her coffee cup. "Please sit down."

"I'm Mrs. Saxby," the woman said, pulling out the chair next to Jill. "These are my children, Maureen and Bruce."

Maureen took the window seat, opposite Jill. Her hair, worn in pigtails, was the same light brown shade as that of her mother. She was about ten, her sturdy body clad in a pink nylon blouse and a green-and-blue plaid skirt. Her brother, settling on the aisle chair, was a few years older, perhaps thirteen. His hair was darker, worn in a crew cut, and he wore gray slacks and a striped shirt.

"You look so pretty in your uniform," Mrs. Saxby said as she reached for the menus and meal checks, distributing them to her children.

"Thank you." Jill's uniform was a tailored teal blue suit worn with a white blouse. On the left breast pocket of her jacket, a monogram read ZEPHYRETTE. There was a similar monogram on her garrison cap. The blouse under the jacket also had a *CZ* monogram, standing for *California Zephyr*, and she wore a *Zephyr* pin as well.

Maureen stared at Jill. "Are you a train hostess?"

"Yes, I'm the Zephyrette for this run. My name is Miss McLeod."

"What do you do on the train?" Maureen asked.

"I do lots of things," Jill said. "I greet passengers and answer questions. At the station in Chicago, I was there with the Pullman conductor, meeting passengers as they arrived and directing them to their cars. One of my duties is making dinner reservations. This afternoon, I'll walk through each of the cars and ask passengers what times they'd like to have dinner."

"We got on the train in Omaha," Mrs. Saxby said. "It was midnight when we left. So we had dinner at home before my husband drove us to the station."

"That was a long time ago. That's why I'm so hungry." Bruce looked up from the breakfast menu and marked his choices on the meal check. "Bacon, eggs and toast, that's what I want. Milk and orange juice, too."

Maureen was more interested in Jill than she was in the menu. "What else do you do? Gosh, it must be interesting to work on the train."

Jill smiled as she cut off another piece of her French toast. "Yes, it is. I enjoy it. What else do I do? Well, there's a public address system here in the dining car, so I make announcements, pointing out some of the sights to see along the train's route. I keep a first-aid kit in my compartment, just in case. Sometimes I babysit so that parents can have some time to themselves. And I collect postcards and letters to mail at the stations. I send wires, too."

Mr. Gaylord returned to the table, coffeepot in hand. "Oh, there you are, Waiter. Coffee, please, and plenty of it," Mrs. Saxby said. The waiter poured coffee for her and then looked up as Mrs. Saxby finished marking her meal check. "I'll have apple juice and the corned beef hash with a poached egg and toast." She handed the check to the waiter, and Bruce did the same with his. "Maureen, you haven't even looked at the menu. What do you want for breakfast?"

The girl had been staring at Jill. Now she dropped her gaze to the menu. She grabbed a pencil, marking her choices on the meal check. "Ham and eggs, with the eggs over easy. And I'd like a muffin instead of toast. Milk and orange juice, too."

"I'll get these orders in right away," Mr. Gaylord said. Meal checks in hand, he turned away from the table.

"I do love eating in the dining car on the train." Mrs. Saxby stirred cream and sugar into her coffee. "It's such fun to sit with other people and chat. On my last trip I met a couple from Manchester, England. And the trip before that, some people from Italy."

"Where are you headed?" Jill asked.

"We're visiting my sister in Fruita, Colorado," the woman said. "The children are out of school this week and so are hers, so it's an informal family get-together."

"You'll be getting off the train in Grand Junction, then," Jill said. "We're due to arrive at the station at three-forty this afternoon."

Mrs. Saxby smiled. "You must have the train timetable memorized. How long have you been a Zephyrette?"

Maureen leaned forward, peppering Jill with questions. "How did you get to be a Zephyrette? Did you have to go to school to learn how? How many trips do you make every month?"

"For heaven's sake," her mother said, "let Miss McLeod answer one question before you throw another at her."

"Don't worry, I'm used to it," Jill said with a laugh. "I've been a Zephyrette for two years now. The requirement is that you must have nurse's training or a college degree, which I have. As to how it came about, well…" She paused, and then went on. "After I graduated from college, I was debating what I wanted to do with the rest of my life."

There had been a reason for that debate. A few years ago, Jill thought she'd already answered the question about the rest of her life—marriage, family, a teaching career. But something had happened to alter the original road map.

Jill was going to marry Steve Haggerty, the man she'd met during her junior year in college. They'd both graduated from the University of California in the spring of 1949. Steve was in the Navy ROTC, though. He owed the military a tour of duty. Given a choice of the Navy or the Marines, he'd picked the latter and gone into training at Camp Pendleton in Southern California. As the months went by, Jill worked as a receptionist in her father's medical office, saving her money and preparing for the wedding, which was scheduled for a Saturday in August 1950.

But North Korea invaded South Korea in June 1950. Steve's unit was scheduled to go overseas. So the wedding was postponed. Then Steve was killed in December of that year, in a battle at a place called Chosin Reservoir.

Jill went through the next few months in a haze of grief. She wasn't sure what she wanted to do. Teaching had lost its appeal, and she didn't want to make the job in her father's office permanent. In March of 1951, Steve's Uncle Pat, a conductor for the Western Pacific Railroad, proposed a solution.

"Someone I know suggested that I might like being a Zephyrette," Jill said now. "I thought that sounded like a good idea. So I applied for the job and got it. I didn't have any formal training, like school or a class. I accompanied another Zephyrette on a run, and then I was on my own. I make two or three round-trips a month. I live in California, so I do the eastbound run to Chicago, then I lay over at a hotel for a couple of days before taking a westbound run to the Bay Area."

"Then you're going home this trip," Mrs. Saxby said. "I'm sure your family will be glad to see you."

"Yes, they will."

Jill talked with the Saxbys a while longer as she finished her breakfast. Then she excused herself and stood. As she stepped toward the aisle, she met two passengers coming from the sleeping cars at the rear of the train. One was tall and cadaverous, with brown hair receding from his forehead, his navy blue suit hanging on his thin frame. The other was short, about Jill's height, maybe an inch or so taller, with a square face and threads of gray salting his thick black hair. His frame was compact and muscular inside his charcoal gray suit. He had an expansive, authoritative manner that commanded attention.

"Good morning, Mr. Geddes, Mr. Fontana," Jill said.

Mr. Geddes, the taller of the two, mumbled a greeting, looking as though he would be unable to communicate until he had a cup of coffee. Mr. Fontana smiled at her, lines crinkling the corners of his brown eyes. "Good morning, Miss McLeod. You look lovely, as usual."

"I hope you both slept well," Jill said.

Mr. Geddes shrugged without saying anything. Mr. Fontana's voice boomed, audible over the dining car chatter. "I always sleep like a baby on the train. Now I'm hungry enough to eat a horse." He laughed and rubbed his hands together.

Mr. Fontana was a Chicago businessman. Jill had met him shortly after the train left Chicago yesterday afternoon. As the train moved through the rail yard, heading for the outskirts of the city, she had walked back to the Silver Crescent, the dome-observation car at the very end of the *CZ*. There were four sleeper berths there, and Mr. Fontana was traveling in the largest of these, the drawing room. She'd also talked with him later in the day, when she walked through the train making dinner reservations for passengers.

His associate, Mr. Geddes, was traveling aboard the transcontinental sleeper, the Silver Rapids. The car was owned by the Pennsylvania Railroad and had made the journey from New York City to Chicago as part of a Pennsy train. Then it was attached to the *California Zephyr* for the westbound run.

The two men took vacant chairs at a nearby table. Mr. Geddes wasn't much of a talker, Jill thought. He nodded briefly to the other people at the table and stuck his nose in the breakfast menu. Mr. Fontana, on the other hand, introduced himself to his dining companions. His voice carried, and Jill heard him talking to the others as she made her way along the aisle, heading forward toward the engine. Something nagged at her. Then, at the end of the car, she realized what it was.

Mr. Fontana's voice. That booming voice, the manner of speaking, the cadence of his words. That sounded like the man's voice she'd heard outside her compartment last night, arguing with a woman. Angry words, she thought, from those she could make out. And then that loud noise, the one that sounded like a slap, followed by a man's voice saying "Bitch."

He was traveling with Mr. Geddes, as far as she knew, but not with a woman. It was possible, though, that Mr. Fontana had met the woman in the lounge car last night. She'd seen him there, drinking and talking with other passengers. Or maybe he'd run into someone he knew on the train.

That would explain the woman. As for what Jill had heard in the corridor, she could guess. She'd seen it happen many times on the train. A man bought a drink, or two, for a woman in the lounge. As the evening wore on, the man made assumptions about what would follow.

Sometimes what followed was a slap on the face.

Chapter Two ───────────────

JILL WALKED UP THE CORRIDOR past the kitchen, then stepped to one side to let two coach passengers pass her. Behind them was the train's conductor, Mr. Evans. He was a burly man in his forties, wearing a dark uniform, a white shirt and a vest. His billed cap had a badge that read CONDUCTOR C.B.&Q. R.R., indicating that he worked for the Chicago, Burlington & Quincy Railroad. In Denver, the three CB&Q diesel engines at the front of the train would be switched out for five Denver & Rio Grande Western Railroad diesels, the extra motive power needed to pull the train over the Rocky Mountains.

Unlike the dining car crew, which would stay the same for the entire westbound run, the engine and train crews switched out frequently during the trip. From Chicago to Denver, the crews were made up of CB&Q employees. From Denver to Salt Lake City, they would be D&RGW employees. Then crews of Western Pacific Railroad men would take the train all the way to Oakland, where San Francisco-bound passengers would board the ferry at the Oakland Mole.

Jill and the other Zephyrettes, who numbered about a dozen, were considered Western Pacific employees. And there was only one Zephyrette per run.

Mr. Evans consulted his pocket watch, then glanced at Jill. "Good morning, Miss McLeod. Looks like an on-time arrival in Denver. I'd better get some food before we get there."

"Enjoy your breakfast," Jill told him. She stepped through the vestibule into the Silver Chalet, walking past her own compartment and the one used by the dining car steward, Mr. Taylor. Next was a door leading to the crew dormitory, which had a shower and toilet, used by the waiters and cooks. Inside this area, bunks were stacked five high.

A curved stair just next to the dormitory door led up to the car's Vista-Dome, a glass compartment rising out of the roof, with seats for passengers. The front, rear and side walls of the Vista-Dome were glass windows providing a three-hundred-sixty-degree look at the scenery. It allowed the passengers to "Look up, look down, look all around"—the line frequently used in the *California Zephyr*'s advertising brochures.

Just beyond the stairs leading to the Vista-Dome, two steps went down to the depressed floor under the dome. This area contained a small kitchen and a lounge, where the waiter-in-charge, on this trip Mr. Peterson, was scooping oatmeal into several bowls. A toaster popped up golden-brown slices of bread. The breakfast menu in the coffee shop was more limited in food choices than that in the dining car; however, as Jill entered the coffee shop, every table was taken. The shop buzzed with people's voices, the words overlapping, as Jill picked up the threads of several conversations.

"I can teach you to play canasta," an older woman said to her younger companion. "It's easy. I've got some playing cards in my bag. We'll just find a table in the lounge after we finish breakfast."

At the next table, two men rehashed last year's World Series as they spread jelly on toast and drank coffee. The 1952 Series had seen the New York Yankees best the Brooklyn Dodgers, and the men's voices grew louder as they argued about the merits of Yankees Mickey Mantle and Yogi Berra compared with Jackie Robinson and Duke Snider. "If it hadn't been for that catch by Billy Martin—" the man on the left said. The coffee cups rattled in their saucers as he slapped the table for emphasis.

Two women, blond and brunette, were talking about movies. "That one with Marilyn Monroe and Joseph Cotten," the blonde said. "It was really good. *Niagara*, that's the name of it. I saw it at the Bijou with Frank." The brunette leaned closer and said something, and the blonde laughed.

Jill smiled, too. She'd seen the movie with Mike, and they'd both enjoyed it. As she left the coffee shop, she heard another conversation, this one about politics.

"Now that McCarthy is heading up that Senate Committee on Government Operations, we'll see some action on Communists in the federal government," a man said, leaning across the table toward his woman companion. "And it's about time they get around to executing the Rosenbergs. They were spying for the Commies, for crying out loud. And the Supreme Court turned down their appeal. Enough with all these delays. I say it's time to get it over with."

"I think he's guilty," the woman said, "but I'm not sure about her."

Jill had heard similar sentiments concerning Julius and Ethel Rosenberg. It had been over two years since the couple had been convicted of espionage and sentenced to die in the electric chair. The couple's execution date had been set for January of this year, and delayed yet again.

Jill headed forward, into the coach cars. She walked through the train on a regular basis, every couple of hours, making sure that passengers knew who she was and that she was available to assist them. She did so now, walking through all three chair cars until she reached the first coach car. As Jill walked through the cars, she stopped to chat with passengers, answering questions and assuring several people that the train would arrive in Denver on time. She checked with the coach car porters, who pointed out new passengers who'd gotten on the train during the night.

A middle-aged man and woman sat next to each other, a small chess set balanced between them. Across the aisle, a young woman worked a crossword puzzle, chewing on her pencil eraser as she studied the clues. Next to her, in the window seat, a girl sat with an open book on her lap, but she wasn't reading. Instead, she stared out the window, a dreamy look on her face.

A woman in an aisle seat on the Silver Mustang beckoned to Jill. "How late is the dining car open?" The woman tucked a strand of hair behind her ear. "I haven't missed breakfast, have I? I could certainly use some coffee. I got on the train in Hastings, Nebraska, a little before three this morning. I did manage to get some sleep." The woman had used her coat as a blanket. Now she sat up and folded the coat, putting it at the small of her back. She smoothed her skirt and straightened the collar of her blouse.

"No, you haven't missed breakfast," Jill said. "The dining car is open. You have plenty of time. Lunch service will start around eleven-thirty. You don't need reservations for breakfast or lunch. But you will for dinner."

"I won't be on the train for dinner." The woman stood up. "I'm getting off in Grand Junction. Thanks, I'll head back to the diner."

"Enjoy your breakfast," Jill said. She continued her walk through the coach cars, greeting new passengers and old. "The coffee shop? Yes, sir, that's several cars back. You can get food there as well. Cereal, toast, things like that. If you want something heartier, I would suggest going to the dining car. Yes, ma'am, you will need reservations for dinner in the dining car. We have several seatings, including the Chef's Early Dinner for families traveling with children. I'll walk through the train this afternoon making reservations."

When she reached the Silver Scout, the first car, Jill went up to the Vista-Dome. A number of passengers had staked out places in the seats upstairs. In the distance, Jill saw the Rocky Mountains rising to the west, dark blue against a light blue sky, with white at the peaks.

She turned to go back downstairs. In the last seat on the left was the boy she'd seen earlier in the dining car, having breakfast with his mother. He waved at her and she stopped to talk. He was six or seven years old, towheaded with freckles scattered across his face. The woman seated next to him had the same blond coloring, but fewer freckles. She was reading an older Agatha Christie novel, *The Moving Finger*.

"That's a Miss Marple book," Jill said. "She's my favorite."

"Oh, I love Miss Marple," the woman said, marking her place in the book.

"I'm reading the new Poirot. It's called *Funerals Are Fatal*."

"I like the Poirot books, too. But Miss Marple is the best. I'm Betsy Shelton, by the way."

The little boy wriggled in his seat, unable to sit still. "Hi, I'm Timothy."

"I'm Miss McLeod, the Zephyrette. Nice to meet you, Timothy." Jill held out her hand and the boy shook it.

"You must have gotten on the train late last night," Jill said. "I don't recall meeting you yesterday."

"We got on in Lincoln," Mrs. Shelton said. "It was after one in the morning, so we settled into our seats and went to sleep. But Timmy has been awake since it started getting light outside."

"We had scrambled eggs and bacon in the diner," Timothy said.

"Very early." Mrs. Shelton laughed, rolling her eyes. "We were there as soon as it opened."

Jill nodded. "I saw you in the dining car when I came to breakfast."

"We saw you," Timothy said. "Breakfast was pretty good. I love scrambled eggs and bacon."

"I do, too," Jill said. "But my favorite breakfast is the French toast."

"I'll try that next," the little boy said. "I like eating in the diner. It's really fun to eat breakfast and look outside the window at the same time. We saw the sun coming up."

"He loves trains," his mother added. "He's always excited when we take a trip."

"Me and Mom are going to visit Grandma and Grandpa," Timothy chimed in.

Mrs. Shelton nodded. "That's right. I grew up on a peach farm in Palisade, Colorado. Mom and Dad are still farming there."

"Western Slope peaches are wonderful," Jill said.

"I'm gonna help Grandpa on his farm," Timmy said. "We take the train, but it doesn't stop at Palisade."

"No, it doesn't," Jill said. "You'll get off the train in Grand Junction. That's about ten miles from Palisade."

"That's right. Grandma and Grandpa will pick us up at the station. But we stop in Denver first. What time do we get to Denver? Pretty soon, I hope."

Jill glanced at her watch. "We're due into Denver at eight-twenty. It's a quarter after seven, so that's another hour."

"How long will we be there? Can I get off the train?"

"I think we'd both like to stretch our legs," Mrs. Shelton added.

"We'll be in the station for twenty minutes, departing at eight-forty," Jill said. "You can get off the train, but don't go very far. Make sure you get back on as soon as the conductor calls 'all aboard.' If you walk to the front of the train, you'll be able to see the yard crew switch out the engines. We need extra engines to pull the train up the Rocky Mountains."

The boy bounced up and down in his seat. "How many engines?"

"We have three on the train now," Jill said, "and we need five to take us over the mountains."

"That sounds neat." Timothy turned to his mother. "Can we watch them change the engines, Mom?"

Mrs. Shelton nodded. "Yes, we will. I'd like to see them. That should be quite a sight."

Timothy looked up at Jill. "So after Denver, what time will we get to Glenwood Springs?"

"At one fifty-three this afternoon. You can eat lunch in the diner, too. And enjoy the scenery. We'll be traveling through the Rocky Mountains. You can see them up ahead," Jill added, pointing to the west. "It's beautiful country. We go through lots of tunnels when we get into the mountains."

"And there's hot springs in Glenwood Springs," the little boy said. "Grandpa says we'll go there sometime. We can soak in a big swimming pool, even in the winter, and we won't get cold unless we get out of the pool."

"I know. I've been there."

Jill said good-bye, leaving Mrs. Shelton to her book and Timothy with his nose pressed to the glass. She went down the stairs to the main floor of the car. She retraced her steps, heading back through the cars, asking passengers if they had any letters or postcards to mail in Denver. She had a supply of stamps in her pocket. At the rear of the Silver Mustang was the conductor's small office. When she glanced inside, Mr. Evans was there, drinking a cup of coffee as he conferred with the brakeman. Jill continued through the next chair car, collecting several more postcards. In the Silver Chalet, she made a brief stop in her own compartment. In the dining car, most of the tables were occupied. Jill walked down the aisle, heading for the four sleeper cars.

The train wasn't carrying any "specials" this trip. These were "special attention passengers," usually prominent people who had come to the notice of the railroad when they'd booked their accommodations. "Specials" were singled out for extra attention from the crew and might be traveling anywhere on the train, usually in the sleeper cars.

Jill crossed the vestibule and entered the Silver Quail. It was a six-five sleeper, so-called because it contained six bedrooms and five compartments, all designated by letters. The compartments were larger than the bedrooms, and each contained a toilet and sink, as well as sleeping space for two passengers.

Mr. Winston, the Pullman conductor, stood in the passageway near the middle of the car, looking fit in his tailored uniform. He was a short man with chocolate-colored skin and a head of close-cropped gray hair visible under his cap. He had charge of all the sleeping cars, and oversaw the porters, who were employed by the Pullman Company rather than the railroads.

The car's porter, Joe Backus, was visible just beyond Mr. Winston. He was coming from the linen lockers at the end of the car, judging from the armload of towels he carried. Mr. Backus was a head taller than Mr. Winston, and several years younger, his light brown skin as yet unwrinkled. Jill thought he was a new porter; at least, she had not traveled with him before now.

Both men greeted her as she approached, and she said good morning in return. "Getting ready for new passengers?"

"Yes, Miss McLeod." Mr. Winston consulted the list he carried. "This car had three empty berths coming from Chicago. But we'll be full once all the Denver passengers board."

"Yes, ma'am, and we'll be ready for them," Mr. Backus said with a smile. He stepped into compartment C.

Jill continued down the corridor, past the linen lockers that held sheets and towels. At the end of the car was a small seat where the porter sat during the trip, although the porters were quite busy for the entire run. There was also a toilet here, for the porter's use, and another locker as well as a water cooler.

She crossed the vestibule and entered the Silver Falls. This car was a different configuration, a ten-six sleeper. At this end of the car were six double bedrooms, designated A through F. Then the corridor jogged to the right and went down the middle of the car, where there were ten roomettes, five on each side, with space for one passenger. The roomettes contained toilets and sinks as well.

The porter for the Silver Falls was Frank Nathan, a tall slender man with high cheekbones and a dark coffee-brown face. Jill had traveled with him before. He stood near the door of bedroom E, talking with a man and a woman. The young couple, Mr. and Mrs. Mays, were on their honeymoon, as they'd told Jill yesterday when she took their dinner reservation. They planned to spend a few days at the Brown Palace Hotel in Denver before visiting family in Colorado Springs.

"You have plenty of time for breakfast," Mr. Nathan told them now. "It's almost an hour before we get into Denver. Isn't that right, Miss McLeod?"

Jill looked at her watch as she approached them. "I make it fifty-three minutes. Yes, you should have time. The dining car crew is quick."

Mrs. Mays smoothed her shoulder-length brown hair and adjusted the collar of her herringbone tweed suit, which was a shade lighter than the brown serge suit worn by her husband. "We slept later than we'd intended. I do sleep well on the train. Now I really need coffee and something to eat before we get into Denver."

"We're packed and ready to go," Mr. Mays said. "Except for one small case that's open. We'll have that ready as soon as we get back from breakfast."

Frank Nathan nodded. "Soon as we get near Union Station, I'll carry your bags to the vestibule."

"Thanks. I appreciate all your help during the trip." Mr. Mays reached into his pocket. He took out his wallet, opened it, and slipped several dollar bills into the porter's hand. Mrs. Mays took her husband's arm and they walked in the direction of the Silver Banquet. The porter pocketed the money Mr. Mays had given him.

The door to bedroom F opened and a dapper, white-haired man stepped out, dressed in a natty gray suit. Mr. Poindexter had boarded the train in Chicago, and he was traveling all the way to San Francisco, to visit relatives. "Good morning," Jill said. "I hope you slept well."

"Good morning, my dear." He gave her a jaunty smile. "I slept like a baby, which is good for someone my age. Now I'm off to get some breakfast. I am partial to the French toast."

"So am I. In fact, that's what I had for breakfast." When Mr. Poindexter had gone, Jill turned to the porter. "How's your trip so far, Mr. Nathan?"

"Uneventful. And that's the way I like it." He gave her a wry smile. She knew he was thinking of an earlier trip, just before Christmas, that had far too many events, quite a few of them unplanned and in some cases, deadly.

"How's your mother?"

"She's fine. She got a new job, working as a housekeeper for another family there at the Naval Air Station in Alameda. Those Navy officers, they just come and go. I expect I'll go over to see her as soon as we get into Oakland. I'm ready for some of her good home cooking."

"Same here," Jill said with a laugh. "Dining car food is good, but it isn't the same as the food my mother cooks."

"I've been meaning to tell you," the porter said. "I saw your brother down in West Oakland. It was on a Saturday night, a couple of weeks ago, at Slim Jenkins's club there on Seventh Street. They do get a lot of white folks there listening to music. I noticed him because he's so young, and he looks like you. I heard somebody call him Drew and I know that's your brother's name."

"He's only seventeen, still in high school." Jill frowned. "He's also underage and he shouldn't be hanging out at a place that serves liquor. But Drew is absolutely music mad. He loves jazz and blues. He plays guitar and piano, very well, I must say. Mom and Dad want him to go to college, but all he talks about is being a musician, playing in clubs and going on the road. My parents are afraid he'll turn into…" She hesitated, aware that the man she was talking with was a different color.

"A black sheep," Mr. Nathan finished. "Maybe he just needs to go his own way and figure it out for himself."

"Like I did, when I became a Zephyrette," Jill said, half to herself.

A young man appeared, rounding the corner in the middle of the car. "*Bonjour*, Mademoiselle McLeod."

Florian Rapace was an attractive young man from Paris, with wavy brown hair and bright blue eyes. In his early twenties, he was a graduate student at Northwestern University in Chicago, heading west to visit a friend who was studying at the University of California in Berkeley. He was traveling in roomette ten, farther back in the car.

"*Bonjour*, Monsieur Rapace." Jill enjoyed practicing her French. In her two years working on the trains, she had encountered people from all over the world. She had an ear for languages and prided herself on picking up enough phrases to answer questions and give directions. French, German, Italian, Spanish—she even managed a smattering of Chinese, Japanese, and Russian.

They talked for a moment longer, discussing the landscape of eastern Colorado and the early spring weather, then Monsieur Rapace excused himself and continued forward, going to the dining car for "*le petit déjeuner.*"

"So you speak French."

Jill turned. Miss Grant was in the doorway of bedroom C. She had boarded the train at the next stop after Chicago in Aurora, Illinois. At dinner the night before, Jill had overheard Miss Grant telling her dining companion that she was a librarian. Indeed, she looked the part, buttoned up in her dowdy long-sleeved wool dress, the color of tea that had steeped too long. Her hair was dark brown, caught up in a severe bun at the nape of her neck. Her eyes, behind oversized cat's-eye harlequin frames, looked like two tarnished pennies. A thin scar marred her cheek, stretching from the outside corner of her left eye to her jaw, noticeable despite her expertly applied makeup. Miss Grant appeared to be in her forties. At one time, she might have been quite pretty. But now her mouth had a sour twist that made Jill wonder if life had treated Miss Grant badly, or whether the woman was under some sort of strain.

"Yes," Jill said now, with a polite smile, "I do speak a little French. It really helps with the international passengers. How are you this morning? I hope you slept well."

Miss Grant allowed herself a tight little smile as she shrugged. "As well as I ever sleep. I take it we are almost to Denver?"

Jill nodded. "We'll be at the station in about forty minutes."

"Thanks." Miss Grant fiddled with the catch on her large brown leather handbag as she stepped into the aisle. Then she stopped, her head tilted to one side. Someone else was coming this way, two men from the sound of the voices. "Hmm, forgot something," Miss Grant said. She turned and stepped back into her bedroom, shutting the door.

Jill glanced back as the men entered the car, coming from the direction of the dining car. Victor Fontana was in front, with Mr. Geddes bringing up the rear. "We meet again, Miss McLeod," Mr. Fontana said in his loud, booming voice.

The two men passed her, heading around the corner to the roomette section of the car. Then Miss Grant opened the door of bedroom C and stepped out again, tucking a pack of cigarettes and a lighter into her large handbag. She snapped the bag shut and turned to face Jill. "Guess I'd better get some breakfast." She left the roomette and walked forward, heading for the dining car.

The door to bedroom B opened and a woman stepped out. Jill smiled at her. "Good morning, Miss Margate."

The other woman returned the smile as she checked the small gold watch on her wrist. "Good morning. It's a lovely day. I'm sure it will be even better once I get some breakfast. Oh, you can make up the bed, Porter."

"Yes, ma'am." The porter stepped into the vacated bedroom.

Jill watched Miss Margate as she walked up the corridor, heading toward the dining car. She was tall and curvaceous, with hazel eyes in an oval face, her dark brown hair worn in a short bouffant style. Today she wore a wine-red dress made of silk shantung. The fitted bodice was set off by round gold buttons. Her high-heeled pumps matched the dress and so did her large handbag, made of soft buttery leather.

When she checked in the previous afternoon, at Chicago's

Union Station, Miss Margate had been wearing a wedding ring. Jill's attention had been drawn by the stylish black-and-white jersey dress and black velvet hat the passenger wore, set off by a black wool coat with a fur collar. Jill had watched as the woman in line removed her wide gold band and slipped it into her black leather purse. When she stepped up to the counter where Jill stood with the Pullman conductor, she'd given her name as Miss, not Mrs.

It was none of Jill's business, of course. She'd seen it too many times to count, really. But she just hadn't seen a woman do it till now. It was usually a married man who decided to be single during his trip on the *California Zephyr*. Often the man was middle-aged and looked around furtively, to see if anyone was watching, then removed his wedding band and tucked it into his pocket, to be retrieved when he reached his destination.

These were the wolves who put the moves on Jill and other Zephyrettes. Jill had become adept at getting out of the way when such men tried to back her into a corner. She was also quite good at politely declining suggestions to head back to the passenger's compartment for "just one little drink."

She walked past bedroom A, and then turned as the corridor jogged to the right, facing the soiled linen locker, where the porter put sheets and towels he'd removed from the sleeping accommodations. Then she turned left again, into the aisle between the roomettes, stopping to say hello to Mrs. Obern in roomette nine. Farther along the row of roomettes, Miss Larkin emerged, at the same time as Mrs. Baines. The two women hadn't known each other when they'd boarded the train in Chicago the day before, but they'd hit it off during the trip, discovering a mutual passion for gin rummy. After dinner the previous evening, they'd headed for the lounge of the dome-observation car, playing into the night. Now Jill stepped aside to let them pass as they headed forward, toward the dining car.

The next car to the rear was the Silver Maple, a sixteen-section sleeper. The semi-private seats on this car converted into berths, curtained off at night. The first two berths in this car were six feet eight inches long, designed for use by tall passengers. Now that it was morning, the porter, Mr. Mack, had converted the berths back into seats. The women's washroom was at the front of the Silver Maple, and as Jill entered the car, she encountered a woman and her daughter coming out of the washroom.

"Good morning, Mrs. Kelso," Jill said. "I hope you and Helen slept well."

"I did," Mrs. Kelso said, shifting her train case from one hand to the other. "Helen was a bit restless."

The girl, who was about fifteen, shrugged. "The man across from me was snoring something awful."

"Well, never mind," her mother said. "It looks like a beautiful day, and we'll be in Denver soon. You can take a nap when we get to Aunt Sarah's house."

"I can manage without a nap," Helen said. "I want to go up to the mountains. It sure looks different than Iowa."

Jill made her way through the car, asking passengers if they had any postcards or letters to mail. She was given several postcards, which she tucked into her pocket. In the middle of the car, two teenage girls were chatting. The first girl shook her head. "I like Patti Page, but that song about the dog in the window is just plain silly."

"That's for sure," the other girl said. "I'd rather listen to Joni James any day. And Perry Como. He just sends me."

At the end of the car, a man sat with a newspaper on his lap, dealing himself a hand of solitaire. Across the aisle from him, two women were deep in conversation. "Well, he told me, he wasn't going to run for city council. Next thing I know, he's thrown his hat in the ring." She chuckled. "He's stealing 'I Like Ike' and turning it into 'I Like Mike.'"

Jill continued down the aisle, masking a soft chuckle. "I Like Mike" made her think about Mike Scolari, and how much she was looking forward to seeing him this coming weekend. She passed the door of the men's washroom at the rear of the car and nodded at the Pullman porter, Mr. Mack. Then she made her way to the transcontinental sleeper, another ten-six sleeper.

The prices of the sleepers varied according to the size and capacity, the departure and arrival city of the passenger, and how many passengers occupied the space. A compartment occupied by two people from Chicago to San Francisco cost $59.15, while the same compartment from Denver to San Francisco would be $43.30. The double bedrooms were less: Chicago to San Francisco for two people would be $46.15, while the Denver-to-San Francisco run would cost $33.95. The roomettes, designed to be used by one person, were $29.40 for the entire run and $21.55 from Denver to San Francisco.

The least expensive sleepers were the sixteen-section cars like the Silver Maple. The cost for a lower berth from Chicago to San Francisco was $21.00, and an upper berth was even less, only $16.00.

Making her way through the transcontinental sleeper, Jill nodded to the Pullman porter, Mr. Jessup, who had just come out of bedroom D, which was occupied by Mr. Geddes. The porter was carrying some towels over his arm. He headed around the corner to the soiled linen locker. Then the door to bedroom C opened and the occupant of that berth stepped into the corridor. She was a woman in her forties, her short salt-and-pepper hair a match for the soft tweed of the suit that she wore. "Good morning, Miss McLeod," the passenger said. "Splendid morning, isn't it?"

"Good morning, Miss Brandon. Yes, it is."

"I'm so enjoying the trip. These wide prairies, and the mountains in the distance. We simply don't have this sort of terrain in England."

"The climate is certainly more arid than England's green and pleasant land," Jill told her.

Miss Brandon's blue eyes twinkled as she smiled. "Ah, you've read Blake. One of my favorite poems, and songs."

"Yes, I've read Blake. We studied his poetry in college. Speaking of authors, how are you and Agatha Christie faring?" When Jill had met Miss Brandon the day before, the Englishwoman had been reading *Mrs. McGinty's Dead*, an Agatha Christie novel. Discovering that they both enjoyed mysteries led to a discussion on Hercule Poirot and Miss Marple.

"Oh, I've quite finished that one," Miss Brandon said now. "Started the next one, called *Funerals Are Fatal*. I picked it up in

New York City. It's the latest, you see. Hasn't been published at home yet, of all things."

"I have the new book, too," Jill said. "I started reading it last night. But I didn't get very far. I got sleepy. Not because of the book, of course."

"I shouldn't wonder you're tired in the evenings," Miss Brandon said. "What a schedule you must have. You certainly get your exercise, walking up and down the train. Well, I'm off to the dining car for breakfast."

Jill watched Miss Brandon head toward the front of the train, then she continued her walk through the Silver Rapids. She paused to collect a postcard from a passenger. Then she went through to the last car on the train.

The Silver Crescent, the dome-observation-sleeper, contained four sleeping berths, three of them bedrooms with space for two passengers each. The first two bedrooms, A and B, were occupied by a family of four, the Hamiltons, who had boarded the train in Chicago, heading for Denver. Bedroom C was occupied by a woman, Miss Larch, who'd also gotten on the train in Chicago. She was heading for San Francisco. The last berth was the drawing room, which could accommodate three people, now occupied solely by Mr. Fontana. At a fare of $62.95 from Chicago to San Francisco, the drawing room was the most expensive berth on the train.

At the front of the car was a small compartment for the porter, opposite the electrical locker and a toilet. A passageway led past the doors to the four sleeping rooms, then two steps went down to the depressed level under the Vista-Dome. Here a glass partition separated the passageway from the buffet, where passengers could get beverages and a limited menu of food items. There was a small bar here, with a curved counter similar to that in the dining room.

Two steps led up to the main level, where another set of curving stairs led to the car's Vista-Dome. They were edged with Lucite that glowed at night. On the other side of the stairs was a writing desk stocked with stationery and postcards for the passengers' use. Here, too, were the Chicago newspapers that had been delivered to the train before it left the station. More newspapers would be delivered in Denver and Salt Lake City.

The back half of the dome-observation car was a lounge, with big comfortable chairs upholstered in sandalwood and brown. There were five on one side, and four on the other, leading back to the rounded end of the car, which was called a "fish tail." The carpet was flowered, and the windows were covered with Venetian blinds and curtains. Here and there in the middle section of the lounge were round metal tables with recessed holders for glasses and ashtrays in the middle. Two settees, big enough for two people each, faced the car's rear door. Small tables were built into the sides of the car, on either side of the door.

Several chairs in the lounge section at the rear of the car were occupied by passengers. The car's porter, Lonnie Clark, was a short, wiry man in his thirties, his face the color of coffee with cream. At the back of the lounge, he leaned over, setting a cup of coffee on one of the tables in front of a small white-haired woman. He tilted his head to one side as the elderly passenger spoke to him, then he nodded and straightened, walking toward Jill.

Jill walked up to the Vista-Dome, where half the chairs were occupied. It was well past seven in the morning now, light enough outside to see the sweep of the eastern plains and the snowy peaks of the Rocky Mountains in the distance to the west. Jill chatted with a few of the passengers, then she turned and went down to the lounge section and retraced her steps, heading forward. Mr. Clark was behind the bar in the buffet now, and Jill stopped.

"How are you this morning, Mr. Clark?" she asked.

"Tolerable, Miss McLeod, tolerable. It's been a good run so far." Mr. Clark's brown eyes twinkled as he smiled at her. His was also a new face, in that she hadn't been on a run with him before. He was based in Chicago, he'd told her yesterday, unlike Frank Nathan, who lived in West Oakland.

Mr. Clark glanced to his left, and Jill turned her head in that direction. A passenger had appeared in the doorway of the buffet. It was Miss Larch, the woman traveling in bedroom C, the berth next to that of Mr. Fontana. Jill had met her late yesterday afternoon while she was making dinner reservations. And she'd seen the passenger again after dinner, having cocktails in the lounge car.

Though she'd boarded the train in Chicago, Miss Larch's voice indicated that she was from somewhere in the South. She had pale porcelain skin and her blond hair, which had been caught up in a French twist the day before, was loose on her shoulders. This morning she wore a crepe dress in a soft shade of green, with a V-neck and elbow-length sleeves. The six-gore skirt set off her figure. Around her slender neck was a thin gold chain.

The young woman paused in the doorway for a moment. Then she stumbled into the buffet and sat down with a thump at one of the tables. She looked up, wincing as though the light hurt her wide blue eyes.

She looks as though she has a hangover, Jill thought, examining the young woman's face with a practiced eye. After two years of traveling on the *California Zephyr*, she knew enough to recognize the signs of overconsumption of alcohol.

Miss Larch pushed an errant strand of hair off her forehead and focused on Mr. Clark, speaking in a deep Southern drawl. "Get me some coffee, boy. I'm just perishing for a cup of coffee."

Mr. Clark's face, which had been open and friendly while he was talking with Jill, got that closed-up look. She had it seen before during her travels aboard the train. The porters and the dining car crew were Negroes. Many times the white passengers were thoughtless, rude, or downright abusive. They called the porters "boy," or "George," the latter appellation after George Pullman, the founder of the company they worked for. Sometimes they called them worse things, using words that Jill had heard before, words that jarred her. She was used to the formality among the crew, where even the porters, cooks and waiters were addressed as "Mister," and it bothered her to hear her coworkers addressed that way.

But she was in a service industry, one where the customer was king—or queen. She figured it was tough on the crew to deal with being called names, but she knew that being a porter was considered an excellent job among the Negro community. Many of the porters owned their own homes in West Oakland, which was the terminus of the route.

The look lasted just a second before Mr. Clark smoothed it away, all politeness as he addressed Miss Larch. "Yes, miss, coffee coming right up." He turned to the counter behind him, reaching for cup, saucer and coffeepot.

"Have a good morning, Mr. Clark," Jill told him as she left the buffet. It was twenty minutes till eight and she had an announcement to make before the train got to Denver.

She retraced her steps through the sleeper cars, collecting another postcard to mail at the Denver station. Then she headed for the dining car, where she reached for the microphone on the train's public address system. She thumbed the key that turned on the mike and began to speak.

"Good morning, this is your Zephyrette, Miss McLeod. I hope you all rested well. As we approach Denver, we get our first glimpse of the towering and irregular profile of the Rockies. Later on this morning we will be right among them."

Chapter Three

THE MILE HIGH CITY—DENVER—loomed in the distance. The Rocky Mountains rose to the west, a dark blue-green. Snow sparkled on the higher peaks. A few white clouds dotted the blue sky. The *California Zephyr* moved through the city, bisecting streets as the engineer blew frequent crossing warnings. The train slowed, entering the Denver & Rio Grande Western rail yard, moving past buildings and freight cars on the sidings.

Jill watched the train's progress from the vestibule of the Silver Scout, the first coach car, where she stood with the car porter and three passengers who were getting off the train in Denver. The train backed into Union Station, positioned so that it would move forward when it departed.

Jill checked her watch. It was 8:20 A.M., and this was an on-time arrival, as the conductor had predicted. The platform was crowded with people. Some of them were there to meet arriving passengers, while others waited to board the train. Others were Red Caps, the railroad station porters who were called that for their red hats. They waited, too, with passengers' baggage to load on the train, ready to take suitcases from passengers getting off the train.

The train stopped and the car porter opened the vestibule doors. Steps unfolded from the floor. Then the porter picked up his metal step box and placed it at the foot of the vestibule steps.

"Welcome to Denver," he said.

Jill stepped down to the platform, followed by the porter, who then reached up to assist a gray-haired woman carrying a carpetbag. Once she was on the platform, a younger woman rushed toward her and enveloped her in a hug. "Aunt Lillie, it's so good to see you. Did you have a nice trip?"

The two women moved off in the direction of the station. Next off the train was a family with a small child. Jill took an overnight case from the mother and told the father where he could collect the rest of the family's baggage.

Up ahead, the baggage car, the Silver Buffalo, was being unloaded, with suitcases piled on a cart for delivery to the station baggage claim, while another cart held suitcases to be loaded aboard.

The yard crew had uncoupled the three Chicago, Burlington & Quincy locomotives as soon as the train had stopped. The engines had pulled forward, routed onto another track. Now, backing slowly into place, came the five Denver & Rio Grande Western diesels that would pull the Silver Lady over those snow-covered peaks in the Rockies. A group of people stood at the far end of the platform, watching the engines being switched out. Among them Jill saw Timothy Shelton and his mother.

Jill turned and walked along the platform, toward Union Station. It was a beautiful Beaux-Arts building constructed of Colorado Yule marble, located at Wynkoop and Seventeenth streets. She quickly walked into the waiting room. It was filled with people, their voices echoing around the high ceiling. All the wooden benches were occupied. Jill took the postcards from her pocket. She checked each of them for stamps and then dropped the cards into a mailbox. At a stand, a radio played while the shoeshine boy polished a man's shoes. The song was called "Night Train," one of her brother Drew's favorites, reminding her of her worry about him. The music segued into a commercial, then Jill recognized the voice of Dinah Washington.

She headed for the door, returning to the platform, where she weaved through the crowd of departing and arriving passengers, Red Caps, and baggage carts. She walked alongside the Silver Crescent, the dome-observation car, and saw the Hamilton family climbing down from the vestibule. On the platform, Mr. Clark, the porter, handed the family's luggage to a waiting Red Cap. Mr.

Hamilton handed a tip to Mr. Clark, then the family walked toward the station, with the Red Cap bringing up the rear.

"Oh, miss. Can you help us find our car?"

Jill turned. The frazzled-looking woman wore a bulky green wool coat and carried a large purse slung over her left arm. She carried a small suitcase, and held several train tickets. A small wool hat perched on her curly brown hair. Standing next to her, bundled into a warm coat and carrying a large suitcase, was a boy of about thirteen. A girl who looked to be nine or ten wore a wool jacket and carried a train case. Her hair was curly as well, what Jill could see of it beneath her knitted cap. Waiting a few steps behind her mother was a teenage girl, perhaps sixteen years old. She had dark brown hair worn in a short flip, the ends brushing the collar of her red-and-green plaid coat. Her eyes were dark and her lips pulled down in a bored, sulky expression. Then her face brightened as she saw a young man in a Marine Corps uniform standing nearby.

Jill looked at the tickets the woman held, passage for four people from Denver to Winnemucca, Nevada. "That's the Silver Maple, the sixteen-section sleeper. It's the third car up. I can show you the way."

But the woman was already moving off. "C'mon, kids. Don't drop that case, Patty. And keep up with the suitcase, Robby."

"Why didn't we check the suitcases?" the boy asked.

"Because we get to Winnemucca at four o'clock in the morning. Aunt Darlene will be waiting and I just want to grab our stuff and go."

"I'm hungry," the boy said. "Can we get breakfast on the train?"

"Me, too," the girl echoed.

"You had breakfast at home." His mother looked exasperated as she shook her head and sighed. "Oh, I suppose we can get something in the coffee shop." She handed him the smaller suitcase. "Now get going. Third car. Get the porter to help you with the bags." The boy grumbled under his breath as he added the second suitcase to his burden. He and his younger sister headed up the platform.

The oldest girl hung back, smiling at the Marine, who lit a cigarette and grinned at her. "Lois!" Her mother snapped. "Quit dawdling and get a move on."

The girl stamped her foot. "Oh, for God's sake, Mother. Quit yelling at me."

The woman rounded on her daughter, herding her like a sheepdog after a recalcitrant ewe. "Don't swear. I've told you a million times to watch your language." She skewered the Marine with a look and he ducked his head, moving farther down the platform. "And don't think I didn't see you flirting with that guy."

Lois gave a gusty, put-upon sigh and allowed herself to be herded.

Jill watched them go, suppressing a smile, then she turned to assist another passenger. The dark-haired man's wool coat was buttoned up against the cold and he wore gloves, carrying the family's tickets in his left hand. His wife was bundled into a coat, a hat covering her blond curls. She carried a small bag and held the hand of a little girl, who was about four. The child's red-and-blue knitted cap matched the mittens she wore. The girl smiled shyly at Jill.

The husband showed the tickets to Jill. "We're traveling coach."

Jill glanced at the tickets, seeing that the family was traveling from Denver to Grand Junction. "Yes, you'll be riding in the second chair car. It's called the Silver Mustang. It's this way. Follow me."

She led the way forward, walking alongside the sleeper cars. She passed Mr. and Mrs. Mays, who had just left the Silver Falls. They walked arm-in-arm toward the station, accompanied by a Red Cap who carried the luggage they'd had in their bedroom. Jill knew that as soon as they'd departed, the porter had quickly cleaned the room, getting ready for the passengers who had booked the space from Denver.

A chef in a white jacket was visible at a small window in the kitchen section of the dining car. Once the train was on its way, and breakfast service was over, the dining car crew would take a break before preparing for lunch service.

She accompanied the new passengers to their car and watched as they climbed into the vestibule. Then she turned as she heard someone call her name.

"Miss McLeod, nice to see you again."

"Good to see you, too, Mr. Wilson." Jill had traveled with Homer Wilson on several runs. He was a thin man with a long nose who wore a pair of round wire-rimmed glasses. His conductor's badge showed the D&RGW insignia—a snowcapped mountain peak. It read MAIN LINE THROUGH THE ROCKIES, the words surrounding the RIO GRANDE. Mr. Wilson would be in charge of the train until it reached Grand Junction, Colorado, then he'd hand off his duties to another D&RGW conductor who would be aboard until Salt Lake City.

Now Mr. Wilson excused himself and walked down the platform toward the front of the train. The engines had been switched out and passengers who'd gotten off the train to watch the procedure began returning to their cars.

An older woman wearing a dark gray wool coat and hat stood near the steps leading to the Silver Falls, with a brown leather train case and a carpetbag at her feet. She had silver hair, worn in a short no-nonsense style, swept away from her face.

"I'm the Zephyrette, Miss McLeod," Jill said. "May I help you?"

"Thank you. I'm Mrs. Warrick, and I'm traveling on this car. I do have these two bags." She indicated the train case and carpetbag. Frank Nathan jumped down from the vestibule and picked up the bags.

"I'll go ahead and put these in your berth, ma'am," the porter said. "Which room?"

"Bedroom D."

The porter nodded and carried the bags up to the vestibule, disappearing into the train car.

Mrs. Warrick turned to Jill. "I'll stay on the platform a bit longer. I'm waiting for my nephew. He's checking my suitcase."

"Where are you going?" Jill asked.

"Sacramento. I'm looking forward to the journey. I always enjoy traveling on the *California Zephyr*."

"Welcome aboard. I hope you enjoy the trip. Let me know if there's anything I can help you with."

"I will." Mrs. Warrick glanced over Jill's shoulder. "Ah, there he is now."

A man in a business suit, about thirty-five, hurried toward them, a luggage check in his hand. "You're all set, Aunt Geneva. Bag's checked to Sacramento."

"Thank you, Simon." The woman tucked the luggage check into the black purse she carried. "I wish you could come to California with me."

"So do I, but I can't get away from work just now. Give my regards to the family."

"I will." The woman gave him a quick kiss on the cheek. He waved and headed down the platform, in the direction of the station.

Frank Nathan had reappeared in the vestibule. He came down the steps and offered his arm to help Mrs. Warrick up the steps and onto the train. "Now, if you'll follow me, ma'am, I'll get you settled into your berth."

As Mr. Nathan escorted Mrs. Warrick into the car, Jill turned. A man and a woman walked toward her. He was tall and lean, wearing a cowboy hat and boots, with a tan jacket worn over his dark brown trousers. He carried a brown leather suitcase in his right hand. With him was a plump, gray-haired woman who was a full head shorter than he was. She wore a beige wool coat and carried a small red train case in her left hand. Looped around her forearm was a cloth bag that looked as though it had been made of quilt patches. Her right hand was tucked in the crook of his left arm.

"Is this the Silver Falls?" she asked, stopping a few feet from Jill.

"Yes, it is," Jill said. "I'm the Zephyrette, Miss McLeod. How may I help you?"

The woman smiled. "I'm Trudy Oliver and this is my husband, Henry. We're traveling on this car. Henry, show Miss McLeod the tickets."

The man didn't speak. He set down the suitcase and pushed back his hat. His hair was thinning and he had the leathery tanned skin of one who'd spent much of his life outdoors. He took the tickets from the inner pocket of his jacket. Jill saw that the Olivers would be occupying bedroom E, the berth which had just been vacated by Mr. and Mrs. Mays.

"The porter is assisting another passenger. He'll be right back to help you board and show you to your berth." As Jill spoke, Frank Nathan appeared in the vestibule. "Here he is now. Mr. Nathan, the Olivers are traveling in bedroom E."

"Right this way, sir," the porter said as he stepped down from the vestibule. "I'll take that suitcase, and the train case."

Mr. Oliver handed over the suitcase without a word, while Mrs. Oliver thanked the porter and gave him her train case. Once they had boarded the train, Jill walked forward. As she approached the chair cars, she saw the conductor walking toward her.

"All aboard!" Mr. Wilson's voice boomed out over the chatter of the people on the platform as he called out the imminent departure of the train. This caused a flurry of activity as the remaining passengers on the platform boarded their cars, assisted by the porters.

"Now boarding, the *California Zephyr*. Destination San Francisco, with stops in Glenwood Springs, Grand Junction, Helper, Provo, Salt Lake City..."

Jill climbed into the vestibule of the Silver Scout, watching as the car porter reached for the metal step he'd placed below the car's steps. He set it inside the vestibule and operated the lever that retracted the car's steps. Then he closed and locked the vestibule door. The train's whistle blew and the *California Zephyr* moved slowly out of the Denver station, heading across the South Platte River.

The train picked up speed as it headed out of the city. Jill walked up to the Silver Scout's Vista-Dome. She always enjoyed this view of the city's outskirts as the train left Denver. The *CZ* passed through the small town of Arvada, climbing now, gaining elevation as it moved from the high plains into the foothills of the Rockies.

She stopped to talk with Timothy Shelton and his mother, listening as the little boy told her about watching the engines back at the station. He bubbled over with excitement, bouncing in his seat. "It was fun! Wait till I tell Grandpa. Those engines are so big."

"This is a lot of train to pull over the mountains," Jill said. "In addition to the five locomotives, we have eleven other cars. There's the baggage car…" She numbered the cars on her fingers, giving the little boy the names. Then she pointed out the window. "We just passed a place called Rocky Siding. Now we're starting up the Big Ten. It's an S-curve. That means it looks like a big S. The train uses it to gain elevation. You see, we're turning south now, and then we'll turn east again. Then the tracks loop south and west."

"Why is it called Big Ten?" The question came from a man in the seat across the aisle.

"I've been told it's due to a ten-degree radius of curve," Jill said. "When the railroad originally built these tracks, the curves weren't supposed to exceed ten degrees. That's five hundred seventy-three feet, according to the brakeman who told me the story. I think some of the curves have been changed over the years, as they've upgraded the railbed."

"The wind's really blowing hard," Mrs. Shelton said, looking out the windows of the Vista-Dome. The train was traveling along the curve. The terrain consisted of rolling, treeless hills, punctuated here and there with tall grass and bushes, now buffeted by the wind.

Jill nodded. "The wind always blows really hard along the foothills of the Front Range, and especially here at the Big Ten." Jill pointed back down the slope. "Now you can see how Denver is spread out. And you can see the dome-observation car at the back of the train."

Timothy jumped up from his seat, craning for a better look. "We won't be able to see it when we get into the mountains."

Jill nodded. "That's right. Soon we'll cross over a bridge at Coal Creek Canyon. Then we go into the first tunnel. There are over thirty of them." Most of the tunnels had been constructed in 1904, she knew, and several had been upgraded in recent years. Some were short, just under two hundred feet long, while most were longer, five or six hundred feet, with several over a thousand feet long.

As the train went over the bridge and headed uphill, Jill excused herself and went downstairs. She walked back through the train. The *CZ* entered the first tunnel, and the cars darkened, lightening again as the train exited. As she went through the next chair car, Jill saw several new faces, passengers who had boarded in Denver. She went through the Silver Chalet. The tables in the coffee shop had emptied out, as many of the passengers claimed seats in the Vista-Dome, so they could watch the Rocky Mountain scenery.

Miss Larch was here, sitting alone at a table. In front of her was a cup of coffee and a plate containing a piece of toast. But she ignored the food, staring instead out the window.

The view out the window was to the north. The bare foothills had given way to steep slopes covered with dark green pines. On the ground were vestiges of the last snowstorm, white mounds under the trees, and out in the open, melting in the pale spring sunshine. Here and there were bare rock faces and high cliffs.

The train was nearing a small community called El Dorado Springs. Jill had visited the resort there, which had a swimming pool, dance hall, hotel and cabins. Lately it had been in the news because El Dorado Springs had been where the new president Dwight Eisenhower and his first lady Mamie had honeymooned after their wedding in 1916. The president liked to fish in the Fraser River, which was farther along the train's route.

"Good morning, Miss Larch," Jill said.

The young woman looked up, startled out of her reverie. Then she smiled. "It's Miss McLeod, the Zephyrette. Will you join me?"

"Yes, I will." Jill pulled out the chair opposite Miss Larch and sat down.

Mr. Peterson, the waiter who worked in the Silver Chalet, entered the coffee shop, carrying a coffeepot. He came over to the table. "Would you like some coffee, Miss McLeod?"

"Yes, thank you, Mr. Peterson."

The waiter poured coffee into the cup already on the table. "More coffee, miss?" he asked Miss Larch. She shook her head, a curious expression on her face as the waiter left the coffee shop. With her right hand, she reached for the thin gold chain around her neck, rubbing it with her fingers.

"You called him 'Mister,' him and that porter back in my

sleeper car," Miss Larch said. "He's a… Well, he's colored. Where I come from, we don't call a colored man 'Mister.'"

"He's my coworker." Jill stirred cream into her coffee and took a sip. "Here aboard the *California Zephyr*, we always use 'Mister and Miss' when speaking to our coworkers. It's considered professional, and the polite thing to do."

"I see," Miss Larch said, though the expression on her face was quizzical. She was still toying with the gold chain around her neck. When she moved her hand she pulled the end of the chain from her V-necked bodice and Jill saw that the chain held a ring, a gold band with a large diamond.

That looks a lot like an engagement ring, Jill thought, remembering her own ring, the one she'd put away after her fiancé's death. I wonder if there's a story about why the ring is hanging from a chain instead of around Miss Larch's finger.

"It's a different world, isn't it?" Miss Larch said. "Outside of Mississippi."

"Yes, it is," Jill said. "So you're from Mississippi."

Miss Larch nodded. "Jackson. That's the state capital. Have you ever been to the South?"

"No, I haven't. I've spent most of my life in the western part of the United States."

"Where are you from?" Miss Larch asked.

Jill sipped her coffee, then answered the question. "I was born in Colorado, in Denver, and I grew up here. After the war, my family moved to California. So I'm a Californian now."

"You have a lot of colored people in California?"

"Negroes? Yes. Many of them worked in the shipyards in Richmond during the war. And they work for the railroad, too. The Pullman porters have worked for the railroads since the nineteenth century."

"I see," the other woman said, almost to herself. "Where I live, in Mississippi, the colored people…the Negroes work in the fields, mostly. Or doing housekeeping."

"It's different in other places," Jill said.

"I expect it is. I should get out more. See the big wide world." Miss Larch shrugged. "I'm going to San Francisco. I expect I'll go to Chinatown and see Chinese people."

"We have a Chinatown in Oakland, too," Jill said. "And of course, the people who live there are Americans, too. They've been in the United States a long time. In fact, Chinese laborers helped build the transcontinental railroad."

"Of course," Miss Larch said. "I look forward to sampling some Chinese food, something I've never tried. Is it good?"

"Oh, yes, I enjoy it very much. There's nothing like a bowl of hot and sour soup on a cold day."

"What is hot and sour soup?"

"It's delicious. It's chicken broth and it has bamboo shoots, mushrooms, and vinegar. That's why it has the sour taste. And I really like chow fun. That's a dish made with wide noodles and beef, with lots of onions and bean sprouts."

"Miss McLeod?" Ezra Mack, the porter from the Silver Maple, had appeared in the coffee shop. "Got a need for your first-aid kit."

Jill got to her feet, then glanced at Miss Larch. "Will you excuse me?"

"Certainly. We'll talk more later. I have lots of questions about San Francisco."

Jill followed Mr. Mack back through the Silver Chalet. They stopped at her compartment and she stepped inside and hoisted the first aid kit from the overhead rack. "What happened?"

"A youngster skylarking in the seats. Got his hand caught in between and scraped off some skin."

Jill shut the door and they made their way back through the dining car, where breakfast service was just finishing up. They headed through the sleepers. When they reached the Silver Maple, Jill found the harried-looking woman who'd boarded the train in Denver holding a damp cloth to her son's left hand while her younger daughter looked on. The older daughter was nowhere to be seen.

"Here's Miss McLeod with the first-aid kit," Mr. Mack said.

"Let me see," Jill said.

"Hold up your hand, Robby," the mother said, removing the cloth. The boy held out his palm. An area about three inches long and an inch wide had been scraped raw and bloody.

"I'm sure that hurts," Jill said, taking a seat next to the boy.

Robby shrugged. "Not too bad."

"That's not what you said before," his younger sister said. "You yelled and said a bad word."

Her mother silenced her with a look.

"Well, this will hurt a bit, too." Jill opened the first-aid kit and took out her supplies. The boy winced, though he tried to mask it, as she cleaned the area with an antiseptic. Then Jill applied Merthiolate, a topical antibiotic, and covered the area with a bandage. "There, you should be fine now."

"Thanks," Robby said.

His mother sighed. "Thank you very much. I really appreciate it. Now, you kids quit horsing around. I don't want any more bandages before we get to Winnemucca."

Jill returned the first-aid kit to her quarters in the Silver Chalet, then she retraced her steps through the dining car to the Silver Quail, the six-five sleeper. The windows darkened as the train went through another tunnel. Just as the train emerged, Mrs. Tyree, the woman traveling in bedroom K, came out of her berth, carrying a book. "I'm going up to the Vista-Dome," Mrs. Tyree said. "I'll probably just look at the scenery but I always take a book just in case."

"I'll bet you watch the scenery, too."

Mrs. Tyree laughed and walked forward, while Jill turned to head toward the rear of the car. Mr. Backus, the porter, stepped out of bedroom E, carrying towels draped over his arm.

"We have new passengers," he said. "A Miss Carolla here in bedroom E, but she's gone up to the Vista-Dome. There are two women in compartment I. And a man in bedroom C."

"Thanks."

Jill knocked on the door of compartment I. It was opened by a stocky, middle-aged woman in a tailored white blouse and black skirt, her strong, square-featured face topped by short gray hair. On the bench seat was a young woman, probably in her late twenties, her brown hair caught back in a ponytail. She wore a navy blue skirt and matching cardigan over a yellow silk blouse with a flowered print. On her lap was a leather case, the top open to reveal a camera and accessories. Next to her, books and magazines were stacked on the seat, to be read during the journey. The periodical on the top was the latest edition of *Look* magazine, its cover shot showing Lucille Ball, Desi Arnaz and their two young children.

"Good morning, I'm Miss McLeod, the Zephyrette."

"I'm Doctor Ranleigh," the older woman said. "This is my niece, Rachel Ranleigh."

"Welcome aboard the *California Zephyr*," Jill said. "That looks like a nice camera."

Miss Ranleigh smiled, ponytail swinging as she nodded. "It is. My trusty Leica. I'm an amateur photographer."

"Aspiring photojournalist," her aunt said.

"Are you a professor, Doctor Ranleigh?" Jill asked.

"I'm a physician at Saint Joseph Hospital in Denver," the doctor said. "It's a teaching hospital, so from time to time I am a professor."

"Oh, I'm familiar with Saint Joseph," Jill said. "My father is a doctor, too. He's a general practitioner. He was at Saint Luke's in Denver before the war. Then he joined the Navy. His name is Amos McLeod."

"McLeod, McLeod..." Dr. Ranleigh looked thoughtful. "I believe I've met him, at some conference or another. Not surprising, since both hospitals are just a few blocks apart. Does your father still practice in Denver?"

Jill shook her head. Her mother and the three McLeod children had lived with Jill's grandmother during the war when Dr. Amos McLeod was away, serving in the Navy. The McLeods had moved to California in 1945, when the doctor was transferred to the Naval Medical Center in Oakland. After the war, he left the Navy and set up his practice in Alameda. "We live in California now. We moved there after the war."

"I volunteered myself, right after Pearl Harbor," the doctor said, "I worked at Fitzsimmons Army Hospital out in Aurora. Before that, I'm sure I must have met your father at some point. His name sounds familiar."

Rachel Ranleigh snapped her camera case shut and set it on the floor. "Aunt Ella knows everyone. Even Doc Susie."

"Really?" Now Jill was impressed. For several years now, she had been interested in Doctor Susan Anderson, better known to Coloradans as Doc Susie. She had first read about the doctor during the war, in an article in *Pic* magazine. And just a couple of years ago, the *Rocky Mountain News* had printed a story about Doc Susie. Jill's grandmother had sent her the clipping. A graduate of the University of Michigan at a time when women doctors were unusual, Doc Susie had been practicing medicine as the only physician in the small town of Fraser, Colorado since 1907.

"Doctor Anderson is in her eighties now," Dr. Ranleigh said. "She's still working, even at that age. I see her from time to time when she gets to Denver. She was, and is, such an inspiration to me. When I was in medical school, there weren't many women in my class. And even now, the profession is still dominated by men. Some of my male colleagues aren't what I'd call welcoming, even though I've been practicing medicine for years."

"I can imagine," Jill said. "We go through Fraser, but it's not one of the *California Zephyr*'s regular stops."

"I know," the doctor said. "When I go to Fraser I usually drive. Rachel and I are going to San Francisco. I'm attending a conference and Rachel wants to see the sights."

"I'm sure there will be lots of wonderful things for me to photograph," Rachel added.

"There certainly are. San Francisco will keep you occupied, but if you have the time, go to Oakland and Berkeley, or up to Marin County," Jill said. "I can give you some suggestions later. For now, welcome aboard, and enjoy your trip. And please let me know if you need anything. I'll be coming through the train this afternoon to take dinner reservations."

Jill walked to bedroom C and knocked. The man who opened the door was tall, with bulky shoulders and a broad chest, dressed casually in slacks and a shirt. He was in his late sixties, with a ruddy face and a head of gray hair.

She stared at him, open-mouthed. Then she found her voice. "Uncle Sean!"

Chapter Four

S EAN CLEARY CHUCKLED. "Well, if it isn't little Jill. I knew you were working on the railroad. Sure didn't expect to see you this trip."

"Where are you headed?" Jill asked.

"Nevada. I'm going to see Teresa, Fred and the grandkids. They moved to Winnemucca a few months back. Fred got a job in some dolomite mining outfit near there, in Humboldt County."

"I know. I had a letter from Teresa," Jill said. "She sent me their new address. She and Fred have lived in a lot of places since they got married."

Jill usually got the family news from Grandma Cleary in Denver, and from her mother, who was Sean Cleary's younger sister. Her cousin Teresa, who was four years older than Jill, had married Fred, her high school sweetheart, in 1946, as soon as he'd returned from his wartime service in the army. Fred worked in the mining industry and in the time they'd been married, the family had moved several times, from Colorado to Wyoming, then to Utah and now Nevada.

"I know Teresa had a little girl last year. So how many grandkids do you have now?"

"Four. Two boys and two girls. The youngest is about ten months now. I got some pictures right here."

Her uncle reached for his wallet and opened it, proudly showing off several photos of his daughter, son-in-law and the grandchildren.

"What a pretty baby. She looks a lot like Aunt Hazel."

Her uncle grinned, looking fondly at the picture of his youngest grandchild. "She sure does. Just look at that smile. She's a little sweetheart, just like Hazel."

Aunt Hazel had been Uncle Sean's sweetheart, ever since they'd met in high school such a long time ago. They married in 1917, a month before Sean sailed for France with the American Expeditionary Force led by General "Black Jack" Pershing. Jill knew from family stories that her uncle had fought at the Battle of the Marne and been wounded in October 1918 during the Meuse–Argonne offensive. Like many men she knew who'd fought in wars, he never talked about it.

Her aunt was gone, though. Sean and Hazel had been married forty years when Hazel died of cancer, in October of 1947.

"Mom says you're retired now," Jill said.

He nodded. "I turned in my badge last November. It's time for younger men than me to go after the bad guys."

Sean Cleary had been a Denver police officer for nearly thirty years, first a uniformed patrolman, then a plainclothes detective. He was married to the job, Aunt Hazel used to say, only half joking.

"It's certainly good to see you, Uncle Sean. Let's have dinner and catch up. I'll be going through the cars later this afternoon to make dinner reservations."

"Sure thing. Right now I'm going to find a cup of coffee." He headed forward, toward the dining car and the buffet-lounge car.

Jill walked back to the next car, the Silver Falls. Frank Nathan was walking toward her, with a batch of fresh towels over his left arm. "The Olivers are all settled into bedroom E, and so is Mrs. Warrick in bedroom D. There's a man who got on in Denver, traveling in bedroom A. He went back to the observation car. He asked me if there was a card game onboard. I suspect he means poker, not bridge." The porter maintained a poker face as he spoke. "I told him to check with Lonnie Clark, the porter back in the Silver Crescent. I heard from him that a few of the passengers were playing in the drawing room yesterday afternoon. Maybe he can get into that game if they play again today."

Jill nodded. It was common for passengers to get together to play cards during the journey, in the train's lounges or the coffee shop as well as their own bedrooms. Whether the game was bridge or poker, any money that changed hands was their business, not that of the railroads or the onboard train crew. The railroads would be more concerned, she thought, by the rumors that Jill had heard that there were sometimes clandestine poker games among the crew late at night, up in the baggage car.

As to the passengers, Jill knew who had been playing poker. The game was in the drawing room occupied by Mr. Fontana. As she went through the train the previous afternoon, making dinner reservations, she'd gone into the drawing room, where Mr. Fontana, Mr. Geddes and two other male passengers were grouped around a table, cards and money in front of them.

Now Mr. Nathan tapped on the door of bedroom C, called, "Porter," and waited for a response from the occupant. When he'd entered the bedroom, Jill went to bedroom E and knocked. Mrs. Oliver opened the door.

"Welcome aboard the *California Zephyr*," Jill said.

The woman smiled. "Hello. How nice of you to stop by. Henry, it's Miss McLeod."

Mr. Oliver was in the seat near the window, his long legs stretched out in front of him. He finally spoke, in a deep rumbling voice. "Morning."

"Where are you headed?" Jill asked.

"We're going to Oroville, California," Mrs. Oliver said, "to see our new grandbaby. A little girl, born just a month ago."

"Congratulations," Jill told her. "A new baby in the family is always cause for celebration."

"It certainly is." Mrs. Oliver sat down in the chair near the door and reached into the patchwork cloth bag she'd brought, now at her feet. She pulled out a ball of fine pink wool and a crochet hook. On closer examination, Jill saw, attached to the crochet hook, the beginnings of a tiny sweater. Mrs. Oliver set to work, her crochet hook flying as she worked with the soft yarn. "This is our third grandchild. I'm glad we were able to get away. Before things get busy at home."

"Always something to do on a farm," her husband said.

"Where is your farm?" Jill asked.

"Near the Front Range, out west of Arvada," Mrs. Oliver said.

"The tracks are south of us, but of course we had to go to Union Station to board the train."

"Let me know if there's anything I can do to make your journey more pleasant," Jill told them. She left bedroom E, shutting the door behind her. Then she stepped over to bedroom D and knocked. Mrs. Warrick called, "Come in." When she opened the door, Geneva Warrick was seated near the window, a book on her lap, and more books visible in the open carpetbag she'd brought with her.

"So you're traveling to Sacramento," Jill said.

"Yes. One of my nieces is getting married this coming weekend. I'm looking forward to seeing all the family."

"We'll be in Sacramento around twelve-thirty tomorrow afternoon. So relax and enjoy the ride. It looks to me like you have plenty to read."

Mrs. Warrick laughed. "I have an absolute horror of running out of something to read while I'm traveling. So I always bring plenty of books."

Jill looked at the title of the book Mrs. Warrick held. It was a biography of William Jackson Palmer, the founder of the Denver & Rio Grande Western Railroad. "That's appropriate reading, since this stretch of the _California Zephyr_ is operated by the Denver and Rio Grande. You must be interested in history."

The older woman nodded. "Yes, it is germane for this trip, and I am very much interested in history. I was a professor of history for many years at Colorado Women's College. I retired a year ago."

"I majored in history at the University of California in Berkeley," Jill told her. "When I graduated a few years ago, I planned to teach."

Mrs. Warrick tilted her head to one side and studied Jill. "Yet you're riding the rails instead. An interesting choice."

"One that suits me for the time being," Jill said.

"I suspect there's a story behind that," Mrs. Warrick said.

"There is, but I won't go into that now. I've been riding the rails for two years now, so I've become interested in railroad history."

"There's a lot of it in this state. My focus is Colorado history," Mrs. Warrick added. "I have a Colorado notable in my family tree—John Long Routt, who was the first governor of Colorado."

"Also the seventh." Jill remembered her Colorado history lessons from school. "I grew up in Colorado, so I'm interested in the state's history as well. What I like about Governor Routt is that he supported women's suffrage."

"Indeed he did. He was a very strong supporter. He escorted Susan B. Anthony when she toured the state, and when women were first able to vote in Colorado, back in 1893, his wife Eliza was the first woman in the state to register to vote."

"There are a lot of interesting women in Colorado history," Jill said. "Margaret Brown, for example."

Mrs. Margaret Tobin Brown, wife of Leadville silver millionaire John Brown, had survived the *Titanic* disaster, earning the title "Unsinkable."

"I'm fortunate to have met Mrs. Brown back in the twenties," Mrs. Warrick said. "She was a remarkable woman."

"I've read a lot about her. Some of it's a bit fantastic, though. It's hard to know what to believe."

Mrs. Warrick shook her head. "Much of what's written about her is made up out of whole cloth, bearing no relation to the truth. She never called herself 'Molly.' It was always Margaret. Separating fact from fiction is always difficult. It's the same situation with the Tabors."

"Also an interesting story," Jill said. Elizabeth McCourt, widely known as Baby Doe, had been the second wife of silver miner Horace Tabor, who also made his fortune in Leadville. Tabor had divorced his first wife, Augusta, to marry the much younger Baby Doe. He had served a brief term as a United States senator, but he'd lost his fortune during the silver panic of 1893. Eventually Baby Doe returned to Leadville, where she died in 1935, frozen to death in a cabin at Tabor's old Matchless Mine.

"Strong women," Mrs. Warrick said. "Mrs. Brown and Augusta Tabor, certainly. I don't know how strong Baby Doe was. Though she must have been, to stay up at that mine until she died. I'm also privileged to have met another strong woman, Doc Susie. She comes to Denver from time to time. Still practicing medicine at her age."

"I was just talking about Doc Susie with another passenger," Jill said. "She knows the doctor. Well, they're both doctors. This passenger's name is Doctor Ranleigh."

Mrs. Warrick's face lit up with a wide smile. "Do you mean to tell me Ella Ranleigh is on this train?"

"Why, yes, do you know her?"

"I certainly do. What a pleasant surprise."

"Her niece Rachel is traveling with her. They're going to San Francisco. You'll find them in the next car, the Silver Quail, in compartment I."

"It's been a while since I've seen her. We'll have a good long visit."

"It's been nice talking with you. I'll leave you to your book, then."

Jill left Mrs. Warrick's bedroom and continued walking back through the train. The CZ went through a tunnel, then another as Jill made her way back to the Silver Crescent. There were seven tunnels on this stretch. After the seventh, the CZ entered El Dorado Canyon and Jill climbed up to the Vista-Dome on the dome-observation car. Every seat was taken by passengers craning their necks as they looked at the scenery. The high plains where Denver and the other Front Range cities were located were no longer visible and the train was now traveling high into the canyon. Another tunnel came up, number eight, and then Jill saw a path leading down a hillside. According to Jill's grandmother on her father's side of the family, years ago there had been a hotel here, called the Crags, and Grandmother McLeod had stayed there. But the hotel was no more. It had burned down years ago.

Another tunnel was coming up. Jill started down the stairs leading from the Vista-Dome to the lounge of the dome-observation car. She turned and went down two more steps to the lounge below the Vista-Dome, where the porter, Lonnie Clark, was pouring coffee for a passenger.

The man at the counter was tall and blond, a good-looking man in his thirties wearing slacks and a long-sleeved shirt. He paid the porter and reached for the cup. Then he glanced to his right and did a double-take.

"Jill? Well, I'll be damned."

Chapter Five

THE CONSENSUS IN THE FAMILY was that Douglas Cleary was a black sheep who had broken his parents' hearts. No one had seen him since that chilly October day back in 1947, the day of Aunt Hazel's funeral.

Jill didn't know what went on in Uncle Sean's head, or heart—or in Doug's, for that matter. But she knew that many of the stories making the rounds of the extended Cleary family were embellished, or simply false. Doug wasn't entirely incommunicado. He kept in touch with his younger sister Teresa, through the occasional letter or phone call. But his sister was the only person in the family who heard from him.

Uncle Sean and his only son had a terrible argument that day. Jill saw the confrontation from a distance, not able to hear what had been said. But the body language had been clear. Sean and Doug faced off in the backyard, away from the relatives and friends who'd come back to the Clearys' house in Denver after her aunt's funeral and interment at Fort Logan National Cemetery. Both men leaned toward each other, exchanging heated words, and at one point Doug raised his hand, clenched into a fist.

Before anything could happen, Jill's father had come between the two men. Whatever Amos McLeod said had defused the situation, but not by much. Sean turned and went back into the house. Doug stalked off, out of the backyard to the street, where he climbed into the Ford he'd been driving. Once he drove off, no one saw him again.

"So you're a Zephyrette." Doug smiled, lines crinkling the

skin in his tanned face, around his deep blue eyes. "Nice uniform. You're all grown up, kid." He waved to a vacant table. "Join me for some coffee?"

"Of course." Jill nodded at Mr. Clark and he poured another cup of coffee. She doctored it with cream, then joined Doug at the table. They sat down facing each other as the train entered yet another tunnel.

"I'd forgotten how many tunnels there are on this route," Doug said.

The train came out of the tunnel, into daylight again, the sun glistening on patches of snow. Jill glanced at the scene outside the windows with a practiced eye. "We're in South Boulder Canyon now. Still more tunnels to come. It's good to see you after all this time. Where have you been? And where are you headed?"

"I've been skiing at Winter Park," he said. "This train doesn't stop in Fraser, so I had to go back down to Denver to catch it. As for where I'm going, the answer is Portola, California."

"That's not a very big town," Jill said. "And there are no ski areas nearby, not that I'm aware of."

"I'll be visiting a friend." He sipped his coffee and didn't elaborate.

"What have you been doing all these years? Skiing?" She hoped her cousin would open up a bit. She and Doug had never been that close, no doubt because of the difference in their ages. He was born in the autumn of 1919, after his father's return from the first war, and Jill was born in the spring of 1927. So Doug was thirty-three and would be thirty-four in September. Jill had just turned twenty-six. Seven and a half years separated them. Doug had graduated from the University of Colorado in 1941, while she was a freshman at Denver's East High School. The age difference didn't matter now that they were both adults, but when she was a child, Doug was already in his teens, seeming so much older.

"Skiing, yes." The train plunged into another tunnel, a short one this time. "I spent some time in Europe. They have great skiing in the Alps. I worked as a ski instructor, too. When I got back from Switzerland, I stayed in New England for a while, working at a couple of ski resorts in Vermont."

Doug had always been an avid skier, and he was good at it. He'd hit the slopes every chance he got while he was in high school and college, at Loveland, Winter Park or Howelsen Hill near Steamboat Springs. When the National Ski Patrol was founded in 1938, Doug joined the Rocky Mountain Branch.

Then came Pearl Harbor, some six months after Doug's graduation from the university. After the start of the new year, he joined the Army and volunteered for the Tenth Mountain Division. Troops were trained for winter survival and skiing at Camp Hale, which was built in 1942, located in a region of abundant snow north of Tennessee Pass, some 9,300 feet above sea level near the old mining town of Leadville.

After two years of training, the Division had been ordered to Italy early in 1945, spearheading the U.S. Army's advance into northern Italy. There Doug and his fellow troops faced the Gothic Line, also known as the Green Line, Germany's supposedly impregnable chain of defense. The line was made up of fortifications—machine guns, bunkers, artillery posts—built along the rugged peaks of the northern Apennine Mountains. In February of that year, the Tenth scaled a cliff at a place called Riva Ridge, attacking German positions. After four days of Axis counterattacks and heavy fighting, the division had prevailed, helping Allied forces move northward. Later that spring, with tough combat in rugged terrain, the Tenth breached the Gothic Line and captured the Po River Valley, which helped liberate the northern part of Italy.

As a result, the Tenth Mountain Division had the highest casualty rate of any U.S. division in the Mediterranean. Nearly a thousand of the ski troopers were killed, and four thousand had been wounded.

Including Doug Cleary.

Her cousin raised the coffee cup to his lips. A scar was visible on the wrist of his right hand, just below the cuff of his blue shirt. The legacy of shrapnel and barbed wire, the scar snaked all the way up his arm to his shoulder, where an inch or so showed above the shirt's collar, on the right side of his neck.

Just as Uncle Sean never talked about his experiences in World

War I, Doug never talked about World War II. After mustering out of the Army, he disappeared, evidently roaming the country, according to Aunt Hazel and Teresa.

"It's the war," Aunt Hazel said. Jill had heard her say it more than once.

Uncle Sean's opinion was harsher. Jill remembered her uncle's mouth turned down in a frown as he shook his head, and she could hear his voice, saying, "I came home from the first war and got a job. I had a family to support. No, Doug is just using the war as an excuse to be a ski bum. I don't know what's going to become of that boy. Nothing good, I imagine."

Jill banished the voices and images from the past and focused on the present. The train entered another tunnel. When they exited at the other end, a passenger at a nearby table asked, "Where are we now, Miss McLeod?"

Jill looked out the window. "We're getting close to Pinecliffe." She pointed at a structure built on the opposite side of the canyon wall. "That's a mining flume, for transporting water. It was built by the Pactolus Hydraulic Mining Company. The company used the water for hydraulic mining, which causes a lot of damage to the land. Later the flume was used to move logs to a sawmill down in the valley."

"You're very knowledgeable," Doug said.

"I've read a lot about mining in the Old West, and railroading, too. Even geography. I get lots of questions from passengers, and I have to be able to answer them." Jill nodded as Mr. Clark asked her if she wanted more coffee. He poured, then replenished Doug's cup.

Three tunnels later, the CZ reached the tiny village of Pinecliffe. Nearby was Pactolus Lake, which had been used for ice production and ice skating.

"We used to go there in the winter." Jill sipped her coffee, looking out at the pine trees and the snow-covered ground. "I tried very hard to be Sonja Henie but I never was much good at ice skating. I kept falling down. It was the same whenever I tried skiing. I once told Mom my idea of a winter sport is a rousing game of Scrabble in front of a roaring fire."

Doug laughed. "It's never too late. We must be getting close to Rollinsville. I have fond memories of that town, from my younger days."

Jill consulted her watch. It was just after ten. The *California Zephyr* had left Denver at 8:40 A.M. Rollinsville, a small mountain town, was about an hour and a half from Denver. The *CZ* didn't stop there, though she did recall that there had been a big accident back in 1935, on this route, near Moffat Tunnel just up the mountain. A train consist of coal cars had coasted down the rails, gaining speed, despite the efforts of a steam locomotive crew to outrun the cars. The whole train had piled up at the curve in Rollinsville, with thirty-two out of thirty-nine cars destroyed.

"Why do you have good memories of Rollinsville?" she asked. "As towns go, there's not much to it."

He grinned. "Oh, that town was wide open in the twenties and thirties. Did you know it was the distilling center of Colorado back in the Prohibition days?"

"No, I didn't." She smiled back. "I was young and led a sheltered life. Besides, you weren't old enough to drink during Prohibition."

Now Doug laughed. "True. I wasn't. But when did age, or Prohibition, stop anyone from getting a drink? I spent my share of time in Rollinsville. It was still quite a place in the thirties, when I was in college. We used to drive up there and listen to music at the Stage Stop. And there was the gambling."

Yes, there was the gambling. Doug liked to play poker. He'd done so ever since he'd learned how at the friendly family games around a dining room table, at the home of this or that uncle, where betting a quarter made a player a big spender. Jill, too, had learned to play the game. Her father figured there was nothing wrong with an informal game of poker between friends and relatives on a Saturday night. Her mother didn't approve of her older daughter gambling, but Jill enjoyed the games. She limited her bets and it was a big day if she won a couple of dollars.

But Doug gambled a lot. That was another source of friction between father and son. Uncle Sean had once called Doug a wastrel.

"Gambling," Jill said. "So it was you."

"What do you mean?" Doug asked.

"Mr. Nathan, the porter on the Silver Falls, told me that a new passenger who boarded in Denver asked him whether there was a card game aboard the train."

"Yes, that was me. The porter in my car told me to ask the porter here in the observation car. So I did." Doug glanced over Jill's shoulder, toward the counter where Mr. Clark was polishing glasses. "He said there was a game yesterday in the drawing room, and there will be again today, around two o'clock. I told him I want in. I like to gamble and I'm good at it. That's how I paid a lot of my expenses in college, including all that skiing I did."

Jill nodded. "Mr. Fontana is the passenger traveling in the drawing room. He and his business associate, Mr. Geddes, were playing poker yesterday. I'm sure they'll be happy to have another player."

"They might not be happy after I'm done with them," Doug said, with a touch of bravado. "Fontana, did you say?"

Jill nodded. "Victor Fontana. He's from Chicago. Do you know him?"

Doug tilted his head to one side. "I've heard the name, but I don't recall where, or in what context. I don't think I've ever met him." Now he shrugged. "Oh, well. Maybe it will come to me. You say he's from Chicago. That's a big city, as you and I both know."

"Yes, it is. I've explored it during my layovers." The train had left Rollinsville and was approaching another small town, this one called Tolland. Jill took a last sip of coffee and pushed away her cup. "I need to go up to the Vista-Dome. We're getting close to the Moffat Tunnel and passengers always have questions about that."

"I'll go with you," Doug said.

They stood and left the lounge, heading up the steps to the rear lounge on the dome-observation car. Jill paused.

"I should warn you that your father is on the train. He's going to Nevada to see Teresa."

Doug stopped and stepped to one side as an older woman

came down the stairs from the Vista-Dome. His expression had been open and easygoing, and now it was guarded. "Where on the train? Coach, or the sleepers?"

"He's in a bedroom on the Silver Quail. That's the car ahead of yours. I just thought you'd like to know."

"Forewarned is forearmed," he said.

Armed for what, Jill wondered.

Chapter Six

U P IN THE VISTA-DOME, there was only one passenger seat available, on the aisle near the back. The window seat was occupied by Miss Larch, who had turned to look at the scenery outside. The sun caught the highlights in her blond hair, falling loosely on the shoulders of her green dress. As Jill walked up the aisle, Miss Larch shifted on the seat and glanced up, smoothing back a strand of hair with her left hand. "Hello, Miss McLeod."

"Are you enjoying the view?" Jill asked.

"I certainly am." A smile lightened Miss Larch's face. "I've had my face pressed to the window since we started climbing into these mountains. I had no idea this part of the country was so beautiful."

Doug leaned closer to Jill, whispering in her ear. "Introduce us."

Jill took a step forward, so that she was even with the row ahead of Miss Larch. Then she turned and faced her cousin. A slow smile spread across Doug's face as he looked down at the young woman in the green dress. "Miss Larch, this is Mr. Douglas Cleary. Mr. Cleary, this is Miss Pamela Larch."

Miss Larch returned Doug's smile and held out her small, slender hand. "I am pleased to meet you, Mr. Cleary."

He took her hand in his. "The pleasure is all mine, Miss Larch. Is this seat taken?"

"Oh, no," she said, her smile widening. "By all means, please sit down. Where are you going, Mr. Cleary?"

Jill watched, bemused, as Doug settled into the seat and

inclined his head toward Miss Larch. "I'm going to Portola, California. It's a small town in the Sierra Nevada mountains."

"Do you live there?" she asked.

"I'll be visiting a friend. And you, Miss Larch? Where are you headed?"

"I'm planning to explore San Francisco." Miss Larch settled back into her seat. "As you may have guessed, I'm from the South. Jackson, Mississippi."

"Yes, I did guess that, hearing your accent," Doug said. "You'll enjoy San Francisco. It's quite a town."

Pamela Larch glanced up at Jill. "Oh, yes, I've been hearing all about it, from some of the other passengers as well as our Zephyrette."

"How long will be you be staying in San Francisco?" Doug asked.

"I don't really know. I thought I'd look up a college friend who lives there now. I suppose I can stay with her until she kicks me out." A flicker of something passed over Miss Larch's face, then she brightened and addressed Jill. "Now, Miss McLeod, I heard someone say we are going to travel under the Continental Divide."

"Yes, we are," Jill said as the train crossed South Boulder Creek. The Continental Divide was visible now as the train curved on its approach to the tunnel. The bare tops of the mountains, towering far above the tree line, were covered with snow, as they were year round. "In a few minutes, we'll be approaching the East Portal of the Moffat Tunnel. It's named for David Moffat, the president of the Denver, Northwestern and Pacific Railroad. He was the one who first proposed building the tunnel, which actually takes us through the Continental Divide."

"This is my first time in Colorado," Miss Larch said, with a deprecating little smile. "And I've never been anywhere near the Continental Divide. Just what exactly is it?"

Jill launched into the explanation she'd made many times, as other passengers turned to listen. "The Continental Divide separates watersheds. It extends from the Bering Strait, which is up by Alaska, all the way to the Strait of Magellen, which is near Tierra del Fuego, at the southern tip of South America. East of the divide, the creeks and rivers ultimately drain to the Atlantic Ocean, including the Gulf of Mexico and the Caribbean. For example, the South Platte River, which we crossed when we left Denver, joins the North Platte in Nebraska. It becomes the Platte, and joins the Missouri, which flows into the Mississippi. West of the divide, the rivers drain to the Pacific Ocean. Soon we'll be traveling along the Colorado River, for over two hundred miles, and that river drains into the Pacific."

Two of the children she'd seen board the train in Denver, Robby and his younger sister Patty, were in seats across the aisle. The boy asked, "How did the trains get over the divide before they built the tunnel?"

"Over Rollins Pass," Jill said, "on a route the railroaders called 'Over the Hill.' That route was about thirty miles long and it took two and a half hours to get over that stretch—when the weather was good. There were lots of switchbacks and it's a steep grade. It was really dangerous to keep the line open in the winter. As you can imagine, there's a lot of snow up here in the winter months, and avalanches were always a concern. So the route was impassable for about two months out of the year. Trains would get stranded up there because of the weather."

"When did they build the tunnel?" a woman asked.

"Construction started in 1923 and finished late in 1927. It opened for rail traffic early in 1928. Unfortunately, David Moffat died in 1911, so he wasn't able to see his dream become reality."

"How far above sea level are we?" Miss Larch asked.

"The East Portal, where we will enter the tunnel, is 9,197 feet." As the passengers exclaimed, Jill added, pointing at the mountains, "Contrast that with the 'Over the Hill' route, that crosses the Continental Divide at 11,600 feet. James Peak, that mountain over there, is 13,250 feet. The other end of the tunnel, the West Portal, is slightly lower than the east side, just over nine thousand feet."

Now other passengers peppered Jill with questions. "How long is the tunnel? And how long does it take to go through it?"

"The tunnel is over six miles long and it takes the train about fifteen minutes to go through," Jill said. "That's a long time to be inside. So we suggest that passengers not move between cars while we're in the tunnel. There are lots of diesel fumes, despite the ventilation fans."

Now the East Portal of the Moffat Tunnel loomed ahead as the *California Zephyr* moved toward it. A few moments later, the train plunged into the tunnel, where the darkness outside was illuminated here and there with lightbulbs. Jill and the passengers talked as the *CZ* burrowed through the darkness. When the train exited the West Portal, the snow-covered slopes of Winter Park Ski Resort were visible on the south side of the train. Passengers pointed at the skiers, tiny figures speeding down the runs, and the lifts that carried them to the top of the mountains surrounding the resort. At this elevation, the ski season usually lasted through late April, and it looked like there was plenty of snow on the ground today.

"We're coming into Winter Park," Jill said. "The town started as a construction camp during the building of the tunnel." She glanced back at Doug, whose head was bent toward Miss Larch. "People who like winter sports began coming to the area in the nineteen-thirties. Once the tunnel opened, people could take the train up from Denver, ski for the day, then take the train back." Jill saw Doug smiling. "You used to do that, didn't you, Mr. Cleary?"

"Took the train, or drove," he said, "when I was in high school and college. They didn't have a lift until 1935. It was just a rope tow. The resort opened in 1940." Doug turned to the woman beside him. "Have you ever skied, Miss Larch?"

"Ski?" Miss Larch laughed. "Oh, my land, no. I'm from Mississippi, remember. The only other time I've seen snow was when I was a child visiting some relatives up in Wisconsin. I was very young but I do recall building a snowman. But I've never seen snow in this quantity, until now. You're a skier, Mr. Cleary?"

Doug nodded. "Indeed, I am. I was just up here at Winter Park a few days ago. You should try it. I'm sure you could learn."

Miss Larch looked doubtful. "Do you think so?"

"I certainly do," he said. "I've worked as a ski instructor, teaching all sorts of people—men, women, young, old. I could teach you."

"Could you?" Miss Larch's voice took on a teasing tone. She certainly seemed smitten with Doug, Jill thought. And he was working his charm on her. Look at him, leaning a bit closer as he responded to her question.

Well, she'd leave them to it.

The train moved past the ski slopes, heading for the small town of Fraser, the same town where Doc Susie lived and practiced medicine. She told the passengers a bit about the pioneering woman physician who had a medical degree from the University of Michigan.

"She came to Colorado in 1907," Jill said, "because she'd been diagnosed with tuberculosis. The dry climate here is supposed to help people recover. Doc Susie treated the people in this area, including the workers who built the tunnel. And she's still here in Fraser, practicing medicine."

She answered a number of questions about Doc Susie as the train went through Fraser, and she pointed out the two-story log cabin where Dr. Anderson still lived, located just a short distance from the tracks.

After Fraser, the train went through a small town called Tabernash and entered Fraser Canyon, which was seven miles long. This was President Eisenhower's favorite fishing spot. The Fraser River, cold and clear, was reputed to have large rainbow trout, though the best places to fish were supposedly kept secret by the locals. From here, it was about thirteen miles to the town of Granby, where the train would follow the river into town and the passengers would catch their first glimpse of the Colorado River. The train would follow that river for another 238 miles, all the way through western Colorado and into eastern Utah.

As the train began its journey through the remote canyon, Jill walked down the stairs to the lounge at the rear of the dome-observation car, where all the seats were filled with passengers. She saw Miss Margate in one seat, talking with the older woman seated next to her. Jill turned to her right and took the two steps that led to the car's buffet. Three men stood by the counter. One was Mr. Clark, the porter, and the other two were Mr. Fontana and his traveling companion, Mr. Geddes. Mr. Fontana evidently wanted something, but the porter was shaking his head.

"May I be of assistance, Mr. Fontana?" Jill asked.

He turned to her, dismissing the porter with a scowl. "Yes, you can. This porter doesn't seem to want to do it. Those two bedrooms, A and B..." He jerked his thumb toward the front of the car. "They're empty. I saw those people get off the train in Denver. I want Mr. Geddes here to move into one of those bedrooms. We're on a business trip and we'd like to be in the same car."

"Bedrooms A and B are reserved." Mr. Clark looked at Jill for support. "We've got four people getting on the train in Glenwood Springs, going all the way to Sacramento."

Jill nodded and turned to Mr. Fontana, her voice polite but firm. "I'm sorry we can't accommodate your request, Mr. Fontana. Since the bedrooms are reserved, we can't make any changes."

Mr. Fontana frowned. He opened his mouth, grumbling, ready to argue.

But Jill preempted him. "You're welcome to discuss this with the conductor, but I'm sure he'll tell you the same thing Mr. Clark and I have."

Mr. Geddes nudged Mr. Fontana. "Leave it, Vic. It's not a problem. Come on, let's go back to your room."

His companion grumbled under his breath but didn't push the issue farther. The two men walked away, heading forward, presumably to Mr. Fontana's drawing room. The Chicago businessman appeared to be a man who was used to getting his own way.

When they'd gone, Mr. Clark sighed. "Thanks, Miss McLeod. He just wouldn't take 'no' for an answer. And he's the kind of man who can create a lot of problems."

"Do you think he'll complain?" Jill asked. "I'm sure the conductor will back you up. You can't move someone to a berth if that accommodation is already reserved."

"That's true," the porter said. "But, well, you know, there are some folks who don't like it when they don't get their own way. And Mr. Fontana, he seems to be that sort. I've heard..." He stopped, compressing his lips in a tight line. His expression looked guarded, as though he realized he'd said too much.

"You've heard what? Do you know something about Mr. Fontana? I suppose you may have heard of him, since you're both from Chicago."

Now the porter's expression looked guarded, as though he realized he'd said too much. "I guess you could say I know who he is. Know him by reputation."

How intriguing, Jill thought. "What kind of reputation? He's a businessman. A liquor distributor. That's what he told me when I first met him."

Mr. Clark took his time answering. "Liquor distributor. Yes, that's what they call it now. Back when I was growing up in Chicago, we called those fellows bootleggers."

"Are you saying he was a bootlegger, back during Prohibition?" Jill asked, intrigued. She had no clear memories of Prohibition. She had been born seven years after the Volstead Act went into effect in 1920. When Prohibition was repealed in December 1933, she was six years old, more concerned with the approach of Christmas than the headlines and photographs in the newspaper, showing people celebrating the return of legal liquor.

The porter shrugged. "Can't say for certain. Just heard stories, that's all. When Prohibition went away, those bootleggers from the bad old days, they went legit. They were still moving liquor around, and selling it. Only difference was, the booze was legal. Some of them got into other businesses, like gambling, the policy game."

"Policy game?"

Mr. Clark smiled. "Numbers racket. I bet you never heard of playing the numbers, a nice, well-brought-up young lady like you."

"I have heard of the numbers," she said. "My uncle was a police detective in Denver. I read about those schemes in a newspaper article, and he explained it to me."

Playing the numbers was illegal. It was a lottery, her uncle had told her, where bettors—suckers, he called them—would pick three numbers, trying to match numbers that would be randomly picked the following day.

"So you're saying Mr. Fontana might be involved in criminal activities, now or sometime in the past."

The memory of the Kefauver hearings a couple of years ago was in Jill's mind. Senator Estes Kefauver of Tennessee had convened a Senate special committee to look at organized crime in interstate commerce, and the hearings had been televised, drawing a wide audience, Jill included.

Mr. Clark shook his head. "I'm not saying any such thing. Might be, might not. And it might not be healthy to talk about such things. I'm sure Mr. Fontana is a legitimate businessman—now. But if what I hear on the grapevine back in Chicago is correct, he's got a past. And the past has a way of coming back to bite people on the... Well, you know what I mean."

"Yes, I do," Jill said with a chuckle. "The derriere."

A passenger at a table in the buffet waved at the porter and he excused himself, walking over to see what the woman wanted.

Playing the numbers, Jill thought, and poker. If what Mr. Clark said was true, Mr. Fontana had more than a passing acquaintance with gambling.

She left the Silver Crescent and walked through the transcontinental sleeper. When she entered the sixteen-section sleeper she saw the frazzled-looking mother who'd boarded the train in Denver stretched out in a seat, napping. Her purse had fallen to the floor and Jill bent down to retrieve it. The woman wakened with a start.

"You dropped your purse," Jill said.

"What? Oh, thanks. Miss McLeod, isn't it? Thanks again for taking care of Robby's hand."

"You're welcome. Please let me know if there's anything else I can do to help during your trip."

"I'm Milly Demarest," the woman said, running a hand through her disarrayed hair. "Sleep, that's what I need. Those kids are driving me crazy." She looked at the empty seats where her children had left their coats and hats. "I don't suppose you've seen them."

"Robby and Patty are up in the Vista-Dome above the observation car," Jill said, pointing a finger back over her shoulder. "I haven't seen Lois."

"Looking for trouble, that one," Mrs. Demarest said with a frown. "Sixteen going on forty. She thinks she's Ava Gardner."

"I'll keep an eye out for her," Jill said. She headed forward, moving from the Silver Maple to the Silver Falls. The train was nearing the town of Granby, not a scheduled stop, but the first place on the CZ's route where the train would join the Colorado River.

As Jill walked along the passageway on the Silver Falls, Frank Nathan stepped out of bedroom C, carrying some towels. From inside the bedroom, Jill heard someone humming a familiar tune. Then the hum turned into a song, a woman's rich alto voice, caressing the words of the ballad from the thirties, "That Old Feeling." The melody and lyrics were familiar. The song had been sung in a movie Jill had seen last year, *With a Song in My Heart*, with Susan Hayward playing songstress Jane Froman.

Jill stopped and looked inside bedroom C. Miss Grant was seated, a book on her lap, but she wasn't reading. Instead she looked out the window and sang, half to herself.

"You have a lovely voice."

Miss Grant looked up, startled. "What? Oh, thank you. I didn't realize I was singing. I'm enjoying the scenery. What's our next stop?"

"Glenwood Springs, at one fifty-three. But we have a lot to see before we get there. I'm headed to the dining car, where I'll make an announcement about some of the scenery you'll see."

Chapter Seven ————————

JILL CONTINUED THROUGH the Silver Falls and into the Silver Quail. Her steps slowed. She had told Doug that his father was on the *California Zephyr*. It was only fair to tell Uncle Sean that his son was on the train. She tapped on the door to bedroom C, but there was no answer. Her uncle hadn't been up in the dome-observation car. Perhaps he was in the buffet lounge car.

She turned away from the door and saw Rachel Ranleigh emerging from compartment I. "Oh, hello, Miss McLeod. I'm going back to the dome-observation car to look at the scenery."

"There's lots to see," Jill told her.

"I've been admiring the mountains from our compartment, but I want to take advantage of the three-hundred-sixty view up in the dome, particularly as we go through the canyons."

After Miss Ranleigh headed back toward the observation car, Jill continued her walk forward. In the dining car, the crew had finished cleaning up after breakfast and some of the waiters were taking a break, drinking coffee at a table as they passed around a newspaper. Soon they'd get ready for luncheon service, which would start around eleven-thirty.

Jill walked to the public address system and picked up the microphone. This westbound announcement was one of the longest she would make. She took a deep breath and keyed the mike.

"This is your Zephyrette, Miss McLeod. We are approaching Granby, Colorado, the gateway to Grand Lake and Rocky Mountain National Park. Grand Lake is the highest yacht anchorage in the world and sportsmen from everywhere compete each year for the Sir Thomas Lipton Trophy.

"Granby is in the heart of Middle Park, a vast mountain bowl which received the name from the early trappers and explorers. Middle Park was a famous wintering place for those hardy fellows of the early days and is now famous as a resort area. The region is threaded by excellent fishing streams and contains many resorts and dude ranches within its hundreds of square miles.

"From Granby to the Utah state line our railroad follows the easy water-level grade of the Colorado River. Some of the most spectacular scenery in the world will be crowded into these two hundred thirty-eight miles. The Gore, Red and Glenwood Canyons are spectacular chasms cut by the Colorado River during many centuries. In the lower Gore Canyon our train will be fifteen hundred feet below the canyon rim. Watch for the Pagodas, chiseled by the elements in the likeness of Buddhist temples, when we are in the Red Canyon. The beauty of the Glenwood Canyon is well known and served as the inspiration for the Vista-Dome cars with which our train is equipped.

"Industry will join our passing parade at Rifle, Colorado. This small community has become known around the world because of the vast shale oil deposits found near it. The government has set up an experimental plant here to determine the best means of extracting the oil from the rock.

"As our journey continues today, you'll want to watch for Colorado's great peach-producing center in the Palisade–Grand Junction area; the bleak, yet beautiful Utah desert; Green River, Utah, at an elevation of four thousand and eighty feet, the lowest point on the entire Rio Grande system; Soldier Summit in the Wasatch Mountains, the highest Rio Grande elevation in Utah; Salt Lake Valley, where the Mormon pioneers made 'the desert blossom as the rose'; the Geneva Steel Plant and the coal and coke producing areas of Utah. All these attractions are outlined in your 'Vista-Dome Views' booklet, and I hope you will make good use of it."

She replaced the mike and walked along the passage between the tables, saying hello to the waiters at the table. In the Silver

Chalet she made a brief stop in her quarters. Then she went to the lounge in the middle of the car. She didn't see Uncle Sean there, so she climbed the stairs to the Vista-Dome.

She spotted her uncle in a seat near the back. As she sat down next to him, he looked over at her and grinned. "I never get tired of looking at these mountains. They're beautiful. God's country, that's what my old man used to call it."

"Yes, they are. We have beautiful mountains in California, too."

"Not as high as the Rockies," he said. "Say, I get a kick out of you making those announcements. You got all that stuff memorized?"

"After two years as a Zephyrette, I should hope so. It's one of our standard announcements. We have a script to work from." Jill paused, uncertain how to begin. She might as well just say it. "Listen, Uncle Sean. I just found out that Doug is on the train."

Uncle Sean frowned. He didn't say anything at first. Then he asked, "What car is he in?"

"The Silver Falls," Jill said. "That's the sleeper car behind yours. But he's back in the dome-observation car now. I told him you are on the train, so I figured I'd better tell you."

Her uncle took her hand. "I appreciate that. Where is he going?"

"Portola. It's a little town in California, a few stops past Winnemucca. So you'll be getting off the train before he does."

"Well, it can't be helped," he said. "I expect we'll run into each other sometime during the next twenty-four hours."

"Uncle Sean, I wish I knew why you and Doug —"

"There's a lot of water under that bridge. And I'd rather not talk about it right now." He gave her hand a squeeze. "I appreciate your telling me that he's on the train."

Jill nodded. What had happened between Sean and Doug? Why were they estranged? She wished she knew.

Was there anything she could do to effect a reconciliation? She doubted it. Uncle Sean didn't want to discuss the rift, and Doug probably felt the same way. It was best for her to stay out of the situation. Whatever had pushed father and son apart, they needed to figure out for themselves how to mend the breach.

The *California Zephyr* rumbled out of the canyon, following the Fraser River into Granby. After the train left the town behind, the Fraser merged with another river flowing from the north— the Colorado River. It originated in Grand Lake, the largest and deepest body of water in Colorado, some fourteen miles north of Granby. There was a town there, also called Grand Lake. Some of her McLeod relatives had a cabin there, and Jill had visited the lake over the years, during the summers.

When Jill stood to leave, she saw Miss Brandon in the first row, in the window seat on the left. The Englishwoman had a pair of binoculars in her hands. As Jill reached the front of the car, Miss Brandon raised the binoculars to her eyes and focused on something in the distance. Jill looked in the same direction. A bald eagle perched on the top branch of a dead tree a few yards from the track, its white-feathered head and yellow hooked beak clearly visible above its blackish-brown body.

Jill pointed out the raptor to other passengers, listening to them exclaim as they caught sight of the eagle. As they watched, the eagle spread its wings and took off from the tree, yellow talons tucked into its body. The eagle gained elevation, heading toward the top of a ridge.

"Oh, capital! A bald eagle, your national bird. It's the first one I've seen this trip." Miss Brandon reached into her handbag and took out a small leather-bound notebook. She opened it, plucked a pen from an interior holder, and made a notation in the book. She glanced up at Jill. "So this is the Colorado River?"

"Yes. We'll be following the river for over two hundred miles. I hope we'll see lots of bald eagles. They're fish eaters, so they congregate near rivers and lakes."

"I've been reading my bird book," Miss Brandon said. "I picked it up at a shop in New York City. It's by a man named Roger Tory Peterson."

"I've seen that one," Jill said. "One of my aunts in Denver likes bird watching."

"What's that up ahead? It looks like a little town." Miss

Brandon pointed at the steam rising from pools near the river and the tracks.

"That's Hot Sulphur Springs." Jill explained that the area had been a resort for a long time. "The Ute Indians used to come here years ago. Then a spa opened in the eighteen-sixties, but it wasn't a success, probably because this area is so remote. Then the land was bought by William Byers, who owned the *Rocky Mountain News*, one of the Denver newspapers. The railroad came through here in nineteen-five, so that brought more people to the springs."

"Hot water, how lovely," Miss Brandon said. "Makes me think of a nice cup of tea. I believe I'll go in search of one. Will you join me, Miss McLeod?"

"Certainly. Though I believe I'll have coffee."

Jill led the way down the stairs to the lower level of the Silver Chalet. As she passed the lounge she saw Florian Rapace, the French graduate student, at a table. He was with Lois Demarest. The girl certainly looked older than sixteen. Now that she'd removed her plaid coat, the teenager showed off a lush, ripe body, the tops of her full breasts visible above her tight, scoop-necked red sweater. Her pouty lips sported bright red lipstick. The gray wool skirt she wore was cinched at her waist with a wide black belt. Now she shifted in the chair, crossing her legs and hiking up the skirt to show them off.

The French graduate student smiled and took out a pack of cigarettes, offering one to the girl. Lois reached for the pack. Then she glanced up and saw Jill looking at her. She straightened in her seat, looking defiant, then she shook her head, refusing the cigarette.

Better keep an eye on that one, Jill told herself.

She paused and spoke to Mr. Peterson, the waiter, who was in the car's small kitchen preparing a sandwich. "The girl in the red sweater, the one with the Frenchman. She's only sixteen."

"Looks older," he said. "Trying to be, anyway. Thanks for the warning. Don't worry, I won't serve her any liquor. And the Frenchman, he's being a gentleman."

"I know he is. But there may be some men on the train who aren't."

In the coffee shop, the young couple Jill had escorted to the Silver Mustang were seated at one of the tables. The two adults were drinking coffee, their chairs close together and their heads tilted toward one another as they talked. The little girl used both hands to raise a glass of milk. On the table was a half-eaten piece of apple pie topped with ice cream and three forks.

The mother was pregnant, her abdomen rounding the front of her flowered maternity smock. Her husband raised his coffee cup with his left hand, dark brown hair visible on his forearm. His right forearm and hand were hairless. Jill realized that the man had a prosthesis. She looked at him more closely and saw a jagged scar on the right side of his face.

Jill took a seat at the next table and Miss Brandon sat down next to her. Mr. Peterson had come in from the lounge, bearing a sandwich that he served to a man sitting at another table. Then he moved to Jill's table.

"What can I get you ladies?" he asked.

"Coffee for me, please," Jill said. "With cream."

Miss Brandon looked up at him. "I should like a cup of tea, young man. The water should be very hot. Sugar, of course. And I'd like milk rather than cream."

"Certainly, ma'am." Mr. Peterson left the coffee shop, heading back to the kitchen.

The young woman at the next table leaned forward, addressing Miss Brandon. "Are you from England?"

Miss Brandon smiled at her. "I am. And you too, from the sound of it. Though I believe you must have been living here in the States for a few years."

The younger woman returned the smile, pushing a blond curl away from her face. "I'm Rose Halleck. This is my husband, Kevin, and our daughter, Polly. I was born in Devonshire, near Exeter."

"Hello," Mr. Halleck said. His smile was tentative, as though he was aware of strangers' reaction to his injuries.

"Edith Brandon," the older woman said. "Born and raised in Hampshire." Mr. Peterson returned with their order. As Jill stirred cream in her coffee, Miss Brandon checked the temperature of the water in the teapot, nodding with approval. "Good fellow. I can see you've had English people on the train."

The waiter nodded. "We have, ma'am. Many times."

Miss Brandon poured milk in her cup, then added tea and sugar. She took a sip and nodded again. "Ah, just what I needed."

Jill looked over at Mrs. Halleck. "Are you a war bride?"

The young woman took her husband's hand. "Yes, I am. I was a Land Girl in Devon during the war."

Jill set down her coffee cup, curious. "What's a Land Girl? I'm not familiar with that term."

"Women's Land Army," Mrs. Halleck said. "We worked out in the country, in the fields, planting and harvesting, all during the war. It was to free up men to fight."

"Vital to food production during the war," Miss Brandon added. "I was a Wren myself, in the Women's Royal Naval Service. A Second Officer by the time I was demobbed. I spent much of the war in Portsmouth and London."

"I was working near the south coast," Mrs. Halleck said. "I met Kev in 'forty-four, right before the invasion."

Polly was wriggling on her chair. Now her father leaned over and spoke to her. "Sit still and finish the pie, Polly Wolly Doodle."

The little girl scooped up a small piece of pie, nibbled at the apples and crust, then set down the fork. She reached out, her small hand stroking the fingers of her father's prosthesis as she announced, "My daddy's got a fake arm."

"Yes, my dear, I see that." Miss Brandon smiled at the little girl. She glanced at Mr. Halleck, her expression more serious. "Were you injured during the invasion?"

He shook his head. "No, ma'am. I made it through D-Day all right, and several months after that. But my number came up during the Battle of the Bulge."

"He got a Purple Heart." Mrs. Halleck squeezed her husband's good hand. "And a Silver Star. We got married in 'forty-five, when he got out of hospital, right before V-E Day."

Miss Brandon nodded. "We owe you chaps a great deal, all you young men, those who came back and those who didn't. Thank you for your service."

Kevin Halleck reddened, and the scar on his cheek stood out. "Just did my job."

"When did you come to the United States?" Jill asked.

"January of 'forty-six," Mrs. Halleck said. "I traveled on the *Queen Mary*. That was a treat. My goodness, I'd never been on such a great big ship. I was a bit seasick during the crossing, though."

"Oh my, yes," Miss Brandon said. "The North Atlantic can be rough during the winter. I took passage on the *Queen Mary* in the winter of 'thirty-seven and again in the summer of 'thirty-eight. There was quite a difference in the weather on those crossings. And I took the ship over this trip. I spent a few days in New York before taking the train cross-country. The ship was still in war service when you came over."

"Same ship I was on going over in 'forty-three," her husband added. "The Grey Ghost, they called it. Sure wasn't fancy like it was in those days before the war. They had us packed onto that ship like we were sardines. I was sleeping in a cot on one of the decks, and they had some of the guys in hammocks in the swimming pool. It was drained, of course." He shook his head at the memory. "And seasick! Oh, my. The way that ship rolled, I was sick as a dog. You see, I was born and raised here in Colorado. Until I shipped out for England, I'd never been on anything bigger than a rowboat."

"Your Colorado is very beautiful," Miss Brandon said. "I so enjoy looking at the scenery. Where do you live now? And where are you bound on your train journey?"

"We live in Denver," Kevin Halleck said. "We're heading for the Western Slope. That's what we Coloradans call the west side of the Rockies. We're going to visit my aunt and uncle. They have a farm near Grand Junction. We should get in there before four o'clock."

"At three forty-seven," Jill said, finishing her coffee.

"And I get to see the cows," Polly said. "I wish we lived on a farm."

Mrs. Halleck shook her head and laughed. "Oh, not me, sweetie. I had enough of farming during the war. Finish that last bit of pie, and we'll go up to the dome in our car and look at all the pretty mountains."

Polly picked up her fork again and conveyed the last of the

apple pie to her mouth, chewing. She washed down the pie with the rest of her milk, leaving a smear of white around her lips. Mrs. Halleck wiped the little girl's mouth with a napkin as Mr. Halleck fished his wallet from his pocket and paid the check, handing the money to Mr. Peterson, who had come to check on the passengers in the coffee shop.

"No change," he said. "Come on, Polly Wolly Doodle. Let's go."

The little girl waved at Jill and Miss Brandon, then followed her parents as they left the buffet-lounge car. "Pretty child," Miss Brandon said. "A great many of our English girls married American servicemen. Talking about the war reminds me of something you'll find interesting. I met Agatha Christie back then."

Jill's eyes widened. "Did you? How wonderful. Please tell me about it."

"She volunteered during both wars," Miss Brandon said. "In the first one, she joined the VAD, you know, the Voluntary Aid Detachment, and worked at a hospital in Torquay, which is where she was born and later had a house. After the VAD, she qualified as an apothecaries' assistant and worked in a dispensary. A pharmacy is what you call that here in the States. During the second war, she volunteered again and worked at the dispensary in University College Hospital in London."

"That must be how she found out so much about poisons," Jill said. "She uses them often in her books."

"I expect so. That's when I met her. I was collecting a prescription at that very dispensary. It was a treat, I must say." Miss Brandon took a sip from her cup. "The tea was most refreshing. I believe I'll go back up to the dome."

"Yes, you should." Jill looked out the window. "We're heading into several beautiful canyons. If you'll excuse me, I should make my rounds."

"Lovely talking with you," Miss Brandon said as both women left the coffee shop. "I'm sure we'll be fast friends by the end of the journey."

Chapter Eight

THE *CALIFORNIA ZEPHYR* slowed as it moved through Byers Canyon. Jill climbed the stairs to the Vista-Dome of the Silver Scout, the first chair car. Lunch service had started and several seats had been vacated by passengers who had gone down to the dining car. Jill moved to one of the empty seats near the front and sat down, looking over the top of the baggage car to the engines ahead. The Colorado River, ice edging its banks, was to her left, on the south side of the tracks, and beyond that, sedimentary rock rose in cliffs. Looming to the north, on her right, were the steep granite walls of the gorge.

The seats across the aisle were taken by a young couple in their twenties, holding hands as they looked at the scenery. The woman beckoned to Jill. Her voice had an accent that said she was from somewhere back East. "We're not moving very fast. Is it because of the canyon?"

Jill nodded. "Yes. The train goes slower because of the terrain, which is very rugged. And it's also for safety reasons. There are some really tight curves through here."

"Do you get rockslides in these canyons?" the man asked.

"Yes, we do. In winter and spring. The rocks freeze and thaw, and they become loose and fall onto the tracks. Usually the rocks are small," Jill added in a reassuring voice. "Mostly pebble-sized, or perhaps as big as a grapefruit."

As if to illustrate, a handful of golfball-sized rocks tumbled down the slope just to the right of the tracks. The young couple looked impressed at the timing of the rock fall.

"Nothing to worry about," Jill told them. "Those rocks are really small." Large rocks on the rails were dangerous, of course, and could lead to derailments. But that didn't happen very often.

Though it was early April, winter lingered here at the higher elevations. Snow was visible on the ground and in places high above the train, on the canyon wall, tucked in the crevices and ledges. As Jill looked out the window, a few snowflakes descended from the sky. Was the wind blowing snow down from the ledges above, or was it actually snowing? Snowing, Jill decided. The flakes, lazy at first, were coming down faster. Springtime in the Rockies, she thought.

The train passed a small waterfall that was now a sheet of ice. Then it moved around a curve and headed out of Byers Canyon, into a wide meadow covered with snow. "This area is called Middle Park," Jill told the passengers across from her. "Park is a term for valley. Here in Colorado we have three big mountain valleys, North Park, Middle Park, and South Park."

The train went through a small town called Troublesome that wasn't really a town any more. Next was a larger town, Kremmling, but the *California Zephyr* didn't stop here.

"We'll be entering Gore Canyon next," Jill said. "To my mind, it's one of the most beautiful canyons on the whole route. And since there are no roads around here, the train is the only way to see the canyon—unless you want to hike in."

The Silver Lady moved into upper Gore Canyon. The passengers in the Vista-Dome leaned toward the windows, craning to see, exclaiming over the beauty on the other side of the glass windows with their three-hundred-sixty-degree view. The Colorado River was visible on the left side of the train, in places just a few feet below the rail bed. The river's banks were rimed with ice and snow. In the center of the river, water ran dark blue and gray, punctuated here and there by whitewater as it coursed over rocks. On both sides, the canyon walls rose a thousand feet.

Beautiful and remote, Jill thought. She looked down at the water, still cold and covered with ice in places, though it was April. It had been colder still last December. The events of that night were never far from her mind. She had been on an eastbound run of the *California Zephyr*, due into Denver on Christmas Eve. A passenger had been murdered and she herself had discovered the body.

Then, as the train made its way through this very canyon, rocks fell from the steep canyon walls, one of them landing on the Vista-Dome in the first chair car, breaking the glass. Another boulder, the size of a grand piano, had landed on the tracks in front of the train. The engineer had put on the brakes, barely stopping the *CZ* in time. The train's brakeman had climbed a telegraph pole to tap into the line and a track crew had been dispatched to blow up the boulder so the smaller pieces could be pushed off the tracks. In the meantime, Jill and several passengers had treated other passengers, most with minor injuries.

Jill shook herself, dispelling her mood. She left the Vista-Dome and went downstairs, walking back through the train. The conductor's office was at the rear of the second chair car, the Silver Mustang. It was a compartment on the right side, with a bench seat and a desk. Jill stopped to say hello to the conductor, Homer Wilson, who was talking with the brakeman, a man named Eddie Brown. Both men were nursing cups of coffee.

"A pleasant trip so far," Jill told them.

"Good, I like to hear that." Mr. Wilson took a sip of coffee. "There's nothing unusual in the train orders. It's snowing now, but not very hard. And they've had snow in Glenwood Springs."

After chatting for a few minutes, Jill decided it was time for lunch. She headed back through the third chair car and into the Silver Chalet, where all the tables at the coffee shop were taken with passengers who had ordered lunch from the limited menu. She made her way past the lounge and her own quarters and entered the dining car, walking to the steward's counter.

Mr. Taylor looked up. "Are you ready for lunch, Miss McLeod? Take this table."

The table for four was near the public address system. It was as yet unoccupied. Jill took the window seat. She poured herself a glass of water from the pitcher on the table and examined the lunch menu. The entrées included lamb chops, sautéed fish and cube steak. None of these appealed to her, but the sandwich plate did. It was $2.90 and included soup or a fruit cup, a hot roast beef sandwich with brown gravy, whipped potatoes, and a choice of dessert.

She waved at one of the waiters. "What's the soup today, Mr. Scoggins?"

"Navy bean," he said. "It's really good, Miss McLeod. Had a cup of it myself."

"Oh, good. Thanks for the recommendation."

"And we've got that floating island dessert you like so much."

"I do love floating island. I'll save room for that." Jill reached for the heavy silver stand holding the menus and meal checks. She marked her choices, selecting the soup to go with her sandwich. Then she handed the check to Mr. Scoggins.

Miss Margate, looking like a bright exotic bird in her cranberry-colored dress, strode into the dining car, coming from the direction of the sleeper cars. She paused at the steward's counter, and Mr. Taylor pointed her to the table where Jill sat. Miss Margate pulled out the chair next to Jill and sat down, smiling. "Good afternoon, Miss McLeod. My goodness, I'm hungry. There's something about train travel that makes me want to eat."

"The food in the dining car is quite good," Jill said.

"Yes, it is." Miss Margate opened the luncheon menu. "Oh, lamb chops. I'll have that." She reached for a menu check. Then she looked up as another sleeper car passenger joined them. It was Miss Grant. She took the chair opposite Jill.

Miss Margate gave her a cheery smile. "Hi, I'm Avis Margate. I'm San Francisco bound. How about you? Where are you going?"

Miss Grant looked at her dining companions over the top of her harlequin glasses. She seemed reluctant to respond. Then she said, "Cora Grant. I'm going to San Francisco, too." She reached for a menu, looked it over, then filled out a menu check.

Now the steward seated a fourth person at their table, an elderly woman in a black dress with white cuffs and collar, who took the chair next to Miss Grant. The woman looked her dining companions over and then spoke to Jill in a reedy voice. "Good afternoon. I'm Mrs. Higbee. You're the Zephyrette."

"Yes, Jill McLeod. And this is Miss Margate and Miss Grant. They're both traveling in the sleeper cars."

"I'm in the coach section," Mrs. Higbee said. "I've been visiting relatives in Denver. Now I'm going home. I live near Provo, Utah."

"I'm heading for San Francisco," Avis Margate said. "So is Miss Grant."

"I visited San Francisco once." Mrs. Higbee sniffed loudly, as though she had detected a bad odor. "I didn't care for it at all. Such a big, noisy place. And all those different people, if you know what I mean. Chinese, Mexicans and colored people. And who knows what else. I am just not a city person. Give me a small town any day. I like to know who my neighbors are."

Miss Grant didn't say anything. The librarian seemed economical with her words, but Mrs. Higbee more than made up for it. She talked nonstop while she looked at the menu. She finally chose a chilled fruit salad and a tuna fish sandwich, and marked her menu check, handing it to the waiter.

Mrs. Higbee turned to Jill. "Now I'm curious about something. And I'm just going to butt right in and say it."

Uh-oh, Jill thought.

"Why aren't you married?" Mrs. Higbee continued. "In my day, a girl your age would have a husband and several children. You seem like a nice young woman. You should be married and raising a family, not riding around on a train, working and encountering all sorts of riffraff."

Jill smiled politely and framed an answer. She'd certainly heard the question before, but not as boldfaced and up-front as Mrs. Higbee had posed it.

Miss Margate laughed. "Marriage isn't all it's cracked up to be."

Mrs. Higbee looked shocked. Miss Grant allowed herself a grim little smile, as though she agreed with the sentiment.

Jill spoke up, giving the answer she'd given so many times over the past two years. "Working on the *California Zephyr* is a wonderful way to see the country. And it's a great way to meet all sorts of people."

Nice people, too, most of them. Overwhelmingly so, in spite of the occasional bad apple. She suspected Mrs. Higbee's definition of riffraff included anyone who wasn't from her small town and small social circle.

"Well, I'm not sure I'd want to spend a great deal of time with some of the people I've encountered on the train," Mrs. Higbee said. "Foreigners! These days, with the Communists everywhere, you just can't be too careful. And people who sit in the lounge and drink all the time, all during the trip."

"I do like a drink now and then. I am partial to a good Scotch." Miss Margate had a wicked look on her face, as though she might signal the waiter and ask him to bring her an alcoholic beverage.

Mrs. Higbee sniffed again. "Utah is dry, of course."

"Of course," Miss Margate echoed. She stifled a smile.

The waiter brought their food. Thank goodness, Jill thought. She picked up her spoon and dipped it into her soup. Delicious.

Miss Grant cut into her luncheon steak, focusing on her meal as Mrs. Higbee peppered Jill with questions. The elderly woman was equally curious about Miss Margate's visit to San Francisco. Then Mrs. Higbee leaned forward over her plate of fish and addressed Miss Grant. "Where do you live? And what do you do?"

Miss Grant looked at her, eyes narrowed behind her glasses, as though she was deciding whether to answer. "I'm a librarian," she said finally. "From Aurora, outside of Chicago."

"Oh, I know Aurora," Miss Margate said. "We lived there when I was growing up. Then we moved to Naperville. I live in Winnetka now. So you're a librarian. Do you work in the old Carnegie library on...? Now, what street is that on? I don't remember."

Miss Grant had been looking past Jill, out the window. Now she looked nonplussed, as though at a loss for words. "The main library?"

"Benton Street, I remember now," Miss Margate said.

Mrs. Higbee gave Miss Grant a hard look. "I should think you'd know the address of the library where you work." When Miss Grant didn't answer, Mrs. Higbee began to hold forth on libraries. She was of the opinion that certain books that she disapproved of should be removed from the shelves. Miss Grant was having none of it. She ignored Mrs. Higbee's remarks and concentrated on her lunch, methodically cutting her steak. Jill and Miss Margate made small talk, steering the conversation away from Mrs. Higbee's various dislikes.

The dining car was filling up now. The steward seated Doug

Cleary and Pamela Larch at the table on the opposite side of the aisle, where an older couple was already eating their lunch. Doug introduced himself and Miss Larch to their dining companions, then both took menus and studied them. Doug glanced up and smiled at Jill, then he returned his attention to the young woman next to him.

Jill heard Vic Fontana's booming voice above the chatter of the dining car. He and Mr. Geddes took seats at a table in the middle of the car. Mr. Fontana caught Jill's eye and smiled, then he turned his gaze on Avis Margate and his smile broadened. Miss Margate looked away, suddenly interested in her lamb chops.

Mrs. Higbee, ever alert, turned slightly in her seat to look back toward the two men. "Who are those dark, foreign-looking men?"

"Mr. Fontana and Mr. Geddes," Jill said. "They're business associates, traveling in the sleeper cars."

Mrs. Higbee gave Miss Margate a pointed look. "Do you know them? That short one acts as though he knows you."

Miss Margate took her time answering, her fork poised over her plate. "I believe I saw them last night in the lounge."

"Hmm. Fontana. Sounds Italian," Mrs. Higbee said, a sour look on her face. "And Geddes. Who knows what kind of name that is. It might even be Jewish."

Miss Grant, at the window seat across from Jill, had turned her head to one side, peering out the window. Now she raised her hand and tapped the glass. "I thought I saw something move out there. An animal."

"It could be a deer." Jill looked out the window. Now that the *California Zephyr* had left the upper section of Gore Canyon, the landscape near the tracks and the Colorado River was open, with thickets of brush. But she didn't see anything moving, other than the train. "Sometimes I've even seen bighorn sheep along this stretch."

Mrs. Higbee launched into a story about her son's recent hunting trip in the Utah mountains, then she finished her lunch and paid her check. When she'd left the dining car, Miss Margate rolled her eyes. "Thank God she's gone. What an annoying woman. I just hate people like that. You handled her nosiness very well, I must say."

"We get all kinds on the train," Jill said.

"How diplomatic of you to say so." Miss Margate smiled.

On the other side of the table, Miss Grant frowned, and her voice was full of venom when she spoke. "She's an old busybody. The world would be a better place if people minded their own business." With that, she reached for her meal receipt and pulled a wallet from her purse. She paid her tab and departed.

"My goodness," Avis Margate said. "That old biddy certainly touched Miss Grant's nerves."

It did seem that the old woman had said something to annoy Miss Grant, Jill thought. She wondered whether it was a particular remark, or simply Mrs. Higbee's numerous questions.

Now the waiter appeared and cleared the two vacated places at the table, setting that side with fresh place settings for two more passengers. "I'll bring your desserts right away," he said. He left and returned a moment later with floating island and a slice of apple pie for Miss Margate.

"I shouldn't have anything, after that enormous lunch," Miss Margate said. "But I have a hard time resisting pie, in any way, shape or form."

Jill dipped a spoon into her dish and savored her first bite. She looked out the window. The train had already passed through the tiny collection of houses known as Radium and another outpost known as Yarmony, which was named, like a nearby mountain, for a Ute Indian chief.

"I can't imagine anyone living here," Miss Margate said as she cut into her pie. "To someone from the Chicago area, it looks like the back of beyond."

"Ranchers and miners," Jill said. "We're approaching State Bridge. It's an old lodge and stagecoach stop. Teddy Roosevelt stayed there while he was president. And it used to be a speakeasy during Prohibition."

"Good Lord, how could anyone get to the place?" Miss Margate asked.

"I believe the remote location was part of its appeal as a speakeasy," Jill said. "It's not easy to get here, which means that the place was so out of the way that the bootleggers didn't have to worry about interference from the sheriff's office. Whichever sheriff's office that would be. At this point, I think we might be in Eagle County, but I'm not sure."

"Hi, Miss McLeod."

Jill looked up and saw Timothy Shelton standing at her table. His mother stood behind him. "Hello, Timothy."

"We're going to have some lunch," the boy said. "I'm really hungry."

"After that enormous breakfast you ate?" His mother laughed.

"That was ages ago," Timothy protested. "I'm hungry now. Can we sit with you?"

"Of course," the dining car steward said, coming up behind them.

Timothy sat down across from Jill. "I'm Betsy Shelton," his mother said, "and this is my son, Timothy."

"We're from Lincoln, Nebraska," the boy added. "How about you?"

"Avis Margate." She favored the little boy with a wide smile. "I live in a town called Winnetka. That's near Chicago, which is a great big city by Lake Michigan. That's where the train started its trip."

"We live by a creek," Timothy said. "And when we go to Omaha I see the Missouri River. That's a pretty big river."

"I know," Miss Margate said. "We crossed it last night."

Mrs. Shelton took a menu from the stand and looked it over. "What would you like to eat, son? I'm going to have a ham and cheese sandwich. Does that appeal to you?" He shook his head. "No? They have chicken salad. You like that."

The little boy nodded. "I'll have chicken salad. Is that your dessert, Miss McLeod? What is it?"

"I'm having floating island," Jill told him.

The boy's eyes widened. "I've never heard of it."

"It's like a pudding, with meringue—that's cooked and sweetened egg whites—floating in a dish of custard. It's very tasty."

"I'd like to try it," Timothy said. "But I was thinking about a chocolate sundae, too. I really like chocolate sundaes."

"I'll order the floating island, and you order the sundae. That way we can taste both of them." Mrs. Shelton marked the menu check and handed it to the waiter.

The boy leaned forward in his chair. "Hey, the train is stopping."

Jill checked her watch and then glanced out the window. It was half past twelve and the *CZ* was on schedule. "We're coming into a little town called Bond. This is a short crew change stop where we get a new engineer and fireman. After that we're going into the Dotsero cutoff."

As the train made its brief stop, Jill explained the history of the cutoff, which connected the Moffat Route and the Denver & Rio Grande Western route. "That long tunnel we went through earlier is called the Moffat Tunnel, and it's named after a man called David Moffat. He had a railroad called the Denver, Northwestern and Pacific, and the name was changed to the Denver and Salt Lake. But the tracks never actually made it all the way to Salt Lake City. In fact, it never got out of Colorado. Mr. Moffat's railroad ended in the town of Craig. But since we left Denver, we've been traveling on what's called the Moffat Route."

"You really know a lot of railroad lore," Avis Margate said, finishing her pie as the waiter brought the Sheltons' sandwiches. The train was moving again.

"I have to," Jill said. "I get so many questions. Anyway, it's only thirty-five miles from Mr. Moffat's tracks to the Denver and Rio Grande tracks, so in the nineteen-thirties they built the cutoff to connect the two. At the northern end of the cutoff is Orestod, and at the southern end is Dotsero, which is Orestod spelled backward."

Timothy had been nibbling on his chicken salad sandwich, rapt as Jill talked about railroads. Now he asked, "What happened to Mr. Moffat's railroad?"

"It's now part of the Denver and Rio Grande," Jill told him. "Soon we'll be going through Red Canyon, and then we'll get into Glenwood Canyon."

"And when we get to Glenwood, we'll see the hot springs on the other side of the river," Timothy finished.

"One of these days I'll have to plan a visit to Glenwood

Springs," Miss Margate said. "From what I've heard, it sounds marvelous, soaking in a hot pool."

Mrs. Shelton nodded. "It's lovely. I recommend it."

The train plunged into darkness as it entered the Yarmony tunnel, over six hundred feet long. As it came back out into the sunshine, Jill said, "We're coming into McCoy now. It was a stagecoach stop before the railroad came through here. Look for the big water wheel on the south side of the tracks."

"I see it," Timothy cried, craning his head. "It has icicles on it."

Miss Margate looked out at the giant water wheel. Then she picked up her luncheon check and looked it over. "It's been fun talking with you, Timothy. Now, I'm so full I do believe I'm going back to my car and take a nap."

"You don't want to miss the scenery in the canyon," the boy told her. "It's spec..." He looked at his mother. "How do you say that?"

"Spectacular," Betsy Shelton said.

"In that case, maybe I'll go up to the Vista-Dome," Miss Margate said. "But I could very well doze off." She put a few bills on top of the check and stood up, heading back toward the sleeper cars.

Jill pushed back her chair and stood. "I should go, too. It's time for me to do another walk through the train. I'll see you later, Timothy."

She stepped away from the table and looked around the dining car. Miss Brandon sat at a table for four, along with Mrs. Warrick, Dr. Ranleigh and her niece Rachel. Jill heard enough of their lunchtime conversation to discern that they were engaged in a lively discussion about history, in Colorado as well as England.

Uncle Sean entered the dining car, coming from the front of the train. He stopped at the steward's counter, waiting to be seated. Then he saw his son.

Doug Cleary and Pamela Larch had finished lunch and were getting ready to leave. As they stood, he turned and saw his father standing next to the counter. Seconds stretched as they looked at each other. But neither man said anything.

Sean followed the steward to a vacant place at a table already occupied by Mr. Poindexter and Mrs. Tyree. He greeted his dining companions and sat down. Doug looked down at Miss Larch and took her arm. They walked down the aisle, heading back toward the sleeper cars. Sean watched them go. Then he pulled a menu from the stand and opened it.

Mr. and Mrs. Oliver entered the dining car. As they passed his table, Sean looked up. He tilted his head and narrowed his eyes, studying Mr. Oliver, as though he recognized him. Then he shook his head and went back to perusing the menu.

Jill left the dining car and made a short stop in her compartment in the Silver Chalet. Then she continued walking forward, checking the lounge and the coffee shop. As she entered the third chair car, the train plunged into the thousand-foot-long Sweetwater tunnel. Once the train exited the tunnel, she climbed the stairs to the Vista-Dome. The *CZ* headed into the Dotsero Cutoff, crossing several bridges on its route. Snow covered the ground on both sides of the river. In Red Canyon, the cliffs above the tracks glowed a dark brick red against the snow visible in the ledges and crevices, with dark green pines clinging to the slopes. Jill pointed out a seep in the canyon walls, frozen during the winter, now trickling as the ice melted to form a waterfall.

"There's an old volcano just east of Dotsero." Jill said to the passengers. "I've read that it's the last active volcano in the state of Colorado. But don't worry. It hasn't erupted in several thousand years. I understand that the crater is mined for red rock."

As the train came out of Red Canyon, it passed near the small town of Eagle, where the Eagle River joined the Colorado. Now the train turned in a more westerly direction, preparing to enter Glenwood Canyon. And Jill had another announcement to make. She left the Vista-Dome, her seat quickly taken by a passenger eager to look at the scenery. She headed downstairs and retraced her steps to the dining car.

Chapter Nine

JILL WALKED DOWN THE passageway alongside the kitchen. Uncle Sean was still at his table in the dining car, lingering over coffee and a piece of apple pie, and talking with Mr. Poindexter. She smiled at him, then she turned to the public address system across from the steward's counter. Picking up the mike, she pressed the key and began to speak.

"We are now entering the Glenwood Canyon of the Colorado River. The canyon's great beauty inspired the creation of the Vista-Dome car. It was here that Mr. C. R. Osborn, Vice President of the General Motors Corporation, first conceived the Vista-Dome idea. In commemoration of that event, a stone monument has been constructed across the river near the highway about midway through the canyon. The monument supports a stainless steel scale model of a *California Zephyr* Vista-Dome car. If you watch carefully, you may see the monument as we pass the station of Grizzly.

"Glenwood Springs, at the western end of Glenwood Canyon, is the railroad gateway to the famous Glenwood Springs–Aspen winter and summer recreational area."

She replaced the mike and started through the dining car, just as Uncle Sean got up from the table. "Guess I'd better get a seat in the Vista-Dome," he said.

"Same here," she said. They walked together through the car to the Silver Chalet, where he climbed the stairs to the dome above the lounge. Jill continued walking forward. In the second chair car, the Silver Mustang, she climbed to the Vista-Dome.

Timmy Shelton and his mother were seated in the front. Across the aisle were Mr. and Mrs. Halleck and their daughter, Polly.

Jill found a seat in the middle of the car and was promptly greeted with questions from the passengers, about the canyon and the river. "The rocks you are seeing are Paleozoic limestone, sandstone and shale," she said. "Further into the canyon are some Precambrian granites. Those are pink in color. There are lots of caves near the town of Glenwood Springs, and that's because of the limestone."

"Are there hot springs in town?"

"Oh, yes. As we approach the town you'll see steam rising from the Glenwood Hot Springs, which is across the river from the station, near the Colorado Hotel. There's another site at the edge of town, called the Yampah Vapor Caves. I've read that they were originally used by the Ute Indians, and that Yampah means Big Medicine. The whole area is honeycombed with springs. Now, just over there is a sheep ranch, called the Bair Ranch."

She pointed at the buildings scattered across a meadow, and chatted with passengers as the train headed toward two short tunnels near Shoshone Dam, which had been built in the early part of the century. So had the Shoshone Power Plant, which was two miles downstream of the dam. At times during the summer and fall, the river downstream from the dam was down to a trickle, as the water was diverted into the power plant tunnel. But now, in early spring, the river was running higher with snowmelt, ice still visible along the banks on either side.

"Glenwood Canyon was the inspiration for the *California Zephyr*'s Vista-Domes," Jill continued. "And there's plenty of railroad history. There were lots of silver and gold mines in the area, so three different railroads were competing to get to Glenwood Springs. The Denver and Rio Grande Western won that competition. It took years to build the tracks. The route was completed in 1887. As we go into the canyon, you will see how narrow it is in places. The company used dynamite to blow up rock and create a shelf for the railbed. At that time it was narrow gauge, with the rails three feet apart. In 1890, the route was switched to standard gauge, which means the rails are forty inches apart. There are three tunnels. The first one is near Hanging Lake, which is a beautiful lake high on the rim of the canyon. After that, there are two short tunnels near Shoshone Dam, which was built in 1905. The last tunnel, before we get to Glenwood Springs, is Jackson tunnel. Keep an eye out for the eastbound *California Zephyr*. The eastbound and westbound trains will pass each other near Grizzly Creek."

Jill saw movement on the far side of the river. She leaned forward, focusing her attention on the bank several feet above the water. Sometimes deer and elk were visible from the train. But this was a real treat. A bighorn sheep, a ram with an impressive set of curved horns, stood on a bluff overlooking the river.

"Timmy, Polly. Look, it's a bighorn sheep. Over there." Jill directed the passengers' attention to the majestic animal, standing still as a statue on the other side of the river. Passengers craned their heads for a view. The ram obligingly posed for a moment more, then turned and disappeared from view.

An excited Timmy Shelton wanted to know more about Rocky Mountain bighorn sheep. Jill told him what she knew about the hardy creatures that lived in the rugged mountain terrain. The males battled each other by charging and clashing those curved horns, and the sounds of their battles could echo for miles.

A whistle blew in the distance, once, twice. Train number 18, the eastbound *California Zephyr*, was approaching. In a blur of movement, sunlight flashing off the shiny cars, the westbound and eastbound trains passed each other on the parallel tracks. Then the other train was gone, heading around a curve.

Soon the *CZ* entered Jackson tunnel, which was over thirteen hundred feet long. As soon as the train emerged from the tunnel, Jill left the Vista-Dome and headed downstairs, walking back through the train. She made a brief stop in her own quarters, then continued back through the sleeper cars.

In the Silver Falls, Frank Nathan was outside the door of bedroom A, carrying an armful of towels. He knocked and Doug answered the door.

As Doug took the towels from the porter, he glanced at Jill

and said, "Hi, cuz." He looked at the porter and said, "Did you know Miss McLeod is my cousin?"

Mr. Nathan inclined his head. "No, sir, I didn't. She hasn't mentioned it." The porter stepped back from the door and continued down the passageway.

"You don't mind my telling him that, do you?" Doug had removed his tie and opened the collar of his shirt. His sleeves were rolled up, showing the scar that ran the length of his right arm. There was a damp patch on his collar, as though he'd just washed his face.

"No, not at all." Jill's voice took on a teasing note. "I'm surprised you're here, instead of with Miss Larch."

Doug grinned. "Thanks for introducing me to her. I would have introduced myself, of course, but having the Zephyrette do it just puts the stamp of approval on things."

"She seems nice."

"She's beautiful." The look on Doug's face softened. "And very sweet. I enjoyed talking with her. She went back to the observation car after lunch. She plans to take a nap, or look at the scenery while I play poker with Mr. Fontana. The game starts at two o'clock, in his drawing room. There will be several of us playing." Doug rolled down his sleeves and fastened his cuffs. "I'm sure I've heard Fontana's name before. Wish I could remember where."

"I wish…" Jill paused and took a deep breath. She waited as the porter walked by, carrying some towels over his arm.

"What?" Doug asked.

She blurted it out. "I wish I knew why you and your father don't get along."

Doug didn't say anything. Instead he draped his tie around his neck, his fingers quickly tying a knot.

"I'm sorry," Jill said. "It's none of my business."

He sighed. "It's a lot of things. And it's complicated."

"I figured it must be. Complicated, I mean. When my family was living in Denver, before the war, it didn't seem that you and your dad were fighting all the time."

He shrugged, tightening the knot on the tie. "You were just

a kid then. And you weren't living in that house. You didn't see everything that was going on. I butted heads with Dad all through junior high and high school."

"I guess you're right," Jill said. "I didn't know that."

Doug's smile was bitter. "It was always hard being the cop's kid. It's a lot like being the preacher's kid. I was held to a higher standard, all the time. I had to toe the line, be perfect, never get in trouble. Believe me, that got old. I felt like I could never be myself around Dad. Mom was different. We always got along. But things at home were always tense. I was glad when I went to college at Boulder. I needed to get away. Even when I was at the university, I couldn't please the old man. He didn't like my gambling and going skiing all the time. But hey, the gambling helped pay for the skiing, and college. It's a hell of a lot more fun than some of the jobs I had, that's for sure. I like to gamble and I'm good at it."

"I thought when you went off to the Army, you and your dad would make it up."

Doug's mouth tightened. "We didn't. And I don't like to talk about the war."

Jill glanced at the scar visible below her cousin's cuff. "But you got a Purple Heart and a Bronze Star. Your sister told me that. She said you were a hero."

He shook his head and checked his appearance in the mirror. "Not me, cuz. The guys who didn't come back from Riva Ridge and the Po Valley, they were the heroes."

Doug reached for his jacket and put it on. Then he picked up a slim leather wallet, opened it and checked the contents, his fingers fanning a sheaf of greenbacks in an assortment of denominations. He was carrying a lot of cash. He closed the wallet and tucked it into the jacket's inside pocket.

He smiled again, putting on his cocky face. "C'mon, enough of this serious talk. Walk with me back to the observation car so the game can begin. I'm feeling lucky today."

They stepped into the corridor and came face-to-face with Miss Grant, who had just rounded the corner from the passageway leading to the roomettes. "Good afternoon." Doug ratcheted up his considerable charm, smiling at the older woman. Then he tilted his head to one side. "Pardon me, you look familiar. Have we met before? I'm Douglas Cleary."

Miss Grant stared at Jill and Doug, her expression startled behind the large harlequin glasses. She didn't say anything at first. Then she shook her head and pulled her oversized handbag close to her, as though using it as a shield. "No, we haven't met. I don't know you."

"My mistake." Doug nodded politely, then stepped aside and let Miss Grant pass. He watched as she walked forward, in the direction of the lounge car. Then he and Jill walked the other way. When they went around the corner, they stopped again. Frank Nathan had just opened the door of the soiled linen locker, blocking their way. The porter smiled politely and deposited several towels in the locker. Then he shut the door and stepped past Doug and Jill, heading forward toward the bedrooms.

"I notice she didn't introduce herself," Doug said. "But you know her name. What is it?"

"Miss Cora Grant. She's traveling in one of the bedrooms just down the corridor from you."

Doug thought for a moment. "Grant. Cora Grant. I have seen her before, I'm sure of it. Now, where was it?" He snapped his fingers. "Chicago, that's it. It was the fall of nineteen forty-one, right before the war started. I spent a week in Chicago with a college pal. We went to a nightclub and restaurant downtown, several times. The food was good, and so was the show. What was it called?" He frowned slightly as he searched his memory. Then his face brightened. "The Bell Tower. That's it. That's where I saw her, at the Bell Tower."

"She was a customer there?" Jill asked.

"Nope. A singer. The headliner, in fact."

"Miss Grant?" Jill shook her head in disbelief. "A singer? She says she's a librarian, from Aurora, Illinois."

"Maybe she's a librarian now, but when I saw her in Chicago, she was dolled up in a slinky red dress, cut down to here." Doug pointed at the middle of his chest. "And her skirt was slit on both sides. She was showing a lot of leg, singing and dancing some red-hot number." He smiled at the memory. "She had a good voice, too. Reminded me a little bit of Jo Stafford."

"A singer." Jill's face turned thoughtful. "As a matter of fact, Miss Grant does have a good voice. Earlier today I heard her singing in her bedroom. I complimented her, and she just clammed up. But Doug, I can't image it's the same woman. You must be mistaken."

Jill had trouble reconciling the image Doug painted, of Miss Grant in a red dress, singing and dancing and showing off her legs. How could that be the woman on the train, middle-aged, wearing dowdy clothes and glasses that hid her face? On the other hand, now that she thought about it, Miss Grant didn't look like any of the librarians Jill knew. It was as though the woman had costumed herself to look like the stereotype of a librarian. What if this was an act, intended as a disguise? But why would Miss Grant do that?

"It's her, all right," Doug said. "She called herself Belle La Tour. Which is French, or close enough, for bell tower. A stage name, of course, what with the name of the nightclub. There was a chorus line, too, eight good-looking, long-legged gals called the Belles. The band was called the Bellringers. Like I said, they were good. The saxophone player was smokin'."

"That's a long time ago, Doug. Twelve years. Are you sure she's the woman you saw at the nightclub?"

He nodded. "Yeah, I'm sure. I've got a good eye for faces. Besides, I got to see her up close. She showed up at the bar after the first set. My buddy and I bought her a drink. She sat at our table for a while, until some guy objected. Her boyfriend, I figured. Then she went backstage."

"Describe her."

"Tall, about five ten, with blond hair and big brown eyes. I'd say she was in her late twenties then."

Jill looked back in the direction Miss Grant had gone. "So she'd be forty now, or maybe in her early forties. Miss Grant looks likes she's about forty-five or so. She's tall and she has brown eyes. And brown hair, though it could be dyed. It's certainly easy enough for a woman to color her hair. But it's a stretch to think she's the same woman, just because she resembles that singer you saw more than a decade ago. I'm guessing the woman in the nightclub didn't have a scar on her face."

"No, she didn't."

They began walking again, down the passageway between the roomettes. "When I was having lunch with Miss Grant and a couple of other passengers," Jill said, "Miss Grant said she worked in the library in Aurora. One of the other women asked her whether she worked in the building on Benton Street. Miss Grant acted flustered, as though she didn't know the location of the building. Surely if she is a librarian she would. If she isn't, why would she pretend to be a librarian?"

"She has something to hide," Doug said. "She wouldn't be the first to reinvent herself."

"Or maybe she's hiding from someone," Jill said, more and more intrigued. "Someone on the train. But we can't be sure that Miss Grant and Belle La Tour are the same person."

"Even if I say they are?" Doug's tone was teasing.

"I need a second opinion," Jill said. "Mr. Clark, the porter in the dome-observation car, he's from Chicago. I'll ask him if he's ever heard of Belle La Tour, or a nightclub called the Bell Tower."

"Are you always this inquisitive?" Doug asked.

"I shouldn't even be discussing another passenger with you," she said. "But yes, I am inquisitive. Especially if something appears to be out of the ordinary. And if I have a feeling it's important."

She did have the feeling, though she wasn't sure why.

They entered the vestibule of the sixteen-section sleeper and made their way through the car, where the man who had been playing solitaire earlier that day flagged down Jill, asking a question about dinner in the dining car. Doug waved and continued walking. Jill assured the passenger that she'd soon be taking reservations, then she headed back to the next car, the transcontinental sleeper.

As she walked down the passageway, a bedroom door opened and Mr. Fontana stepped out. Then he turned, standing in the doorway of the room. He was talking with his usual booming voice, and Jill could hear every word he was saying. He sounded angry, and his fist struck an impatient tattoo against the wall.

"Dammit, Art, you're acting like an old woman. It's late in the game to be having second thoughts."

Mr. Geddes, his New York accent flavoring his words, spoke from inside the bedroom, his voice raised, with an edge. "So I'm cautious. I didn't get where I am today by taking crazy risks. We're supposed to be partners, Vic. Equal. But you're always calling the shots, telling me what to do."

Fontana snapped back, angry at being challenged. "You wait a goddamn minute —"

"No, you wait, let me have my say," Geddes interrupted. "You say you want me in on this deal. Well, that means I get a say. I go into a deal, I've got my eyes open and all the details. Makes sense to look before I leap. This guy in San Francisco, Charley Holt, I don't know him from a hole in the ground. How well do you know him?"

"Charley and I go back a long time," Fontana growled. "We did business during the war, before he went out to California. And we made a pile of money." His tone turned wheedling. "There's such a thing as being too cautious, Art. I'm telling you, this liquor deal is worth millions. All we have to do when we get to San Francisco is sign on the dotted line. What I don't need is for you to get cold feet when we're this close to signing off on the deal."

Art Geddes spoke again, his voice lowered now, so that Jill couldn't hear what he was saying.

Mr. Fontana waved his arm. "Get a grip. You worry too much." He turned in the doorway, a scowl on his face. Then he saw Jill and pasted on a broad smile. "Afternoon, Miss McLeod. We must be getting close to Glenwood Springs."

"Yes, Mr. Fontana. We'll be at the station soon."

"Glenwood's a great town," Mr. Fontana said. "I've stayed at the Hotel Colorado several times. Sure did enjoy soaking in the hot springs. It's been a while, though." He glanced at his watch, then threw words over his shoulder. "Get a move on, Art. Poker game starts at two. And I'm feeling lucky."

With a jaunty salute, he walked toward the rear of the train.

Jill followed Mr. Fontana back to the Silver Crescent. He went into his drawing room and she went upstairs to the Vista-Dome. She took a vacant seat and was joined a few minutes later by Uncle Sean.

"Did you have a good lunch?"

"Sure did. I'll probably be taking a nap soon, but I wanted to get a look at Glenwood. Your aunt Hazel and I went there a time or two, stayed in the Hotel Colorado."

The train headed into the outskirts of the picturesque town of Glenwood Springs. On the north side of the Colorado River was the Glenwood Hot Springs resort, with its huge swimming pool. Jill had vacationed at the resort with her family several times over the years. The smaller pool was kept at a temperature of about 104 degrees, while the large pool was somewhat cooler, around 90 degrees. On this early April day, steam rose from both pools.

On the hill above the pools was the impressive brick and sandstone bulk of the Hotel Colorado. Modeled after the Villa de Medici in Italy, the hotel was the first in the area to be lit by electricity. When the hotel had opened, it featured a courtyard fountain spraying skyward some 180 feet, and a spa and swimming pool with medicinal hot springs. During the war it had been a naval hospital.

Jill pointed out the hotel to the nearby passengers. "The Hotel Colorado has had lots of famous visitors. President Theodore Roosevelt stayed there, and so did President William Taft. The movie actor Tom Mix was here in Glenwood Springs during the nineteen-twenties when he was filming a movie."

"I saw that one," Sean said. "*The Great K&A Train Robbery.* Back in nineteen twenty-six, it was. Capone used to stay there, at the Hotel Colorado."

"Really? Al Capone? I didn't know that."

Her uncle nodded. "Yeah. Capone and some of the other Chicago gangsters. The Verain brothers, and a guy they called Diamond Jack Alterie."

The whistle blew as the *California Zephyr* approached the Glenwood Springs station. The station had been built in 1904, its architecture matching the design of the Hotel Colorado and the building in front of the hot springs resort. Jill excused herself and went downstairs, heading for the vestibule of the Silver Crescent, where the porter waited.

The train came to a stop at the station. The platform had been cleared of snow, and people were waiting to board, or to meet arriving passengers. Jill felt the chill in the air as the porter unlocked the door, lowered the stairs, and stepped down to the platform.

Jill looked out and smiled as she saw four familiar faces. "Why, it's the Carsons."

Chapter Ten

"MISS McLEOD!" AUDREY CARSON exclaimed, returning Jill's smile. "You're our Zephyrette? What a coincidence." The Carsons were from Sacramento. Stanley Carson was a tall man with dark hair who used a cane and walked with a limp, the result of a wartime injury. Mrs. Carson was a pleasant, down-to-earth woman whose blond hair just touched the shoulders of her gray wool jacket. They had two children, a girl and a boy. Twelve-year-old Gail was an avid reader and no doubt had brought a stack of books to read during the journey. The boy, Ricky, was seven and he loved trains. The Carsons traveled frequently on the *California Zephyr*, visiting relatives in Chicago. Jill had traveled with them several times in the past. During an earlier trip, Jill had learned that Mr. Carson was an attorney, and that Mrs. Carson had volunteered with the Red Cross during the war.

Lonnie Clark stepped down to the platform and took train cases from Mrs. Carson and the two children. He set them on the floor of the vestibule and offered his arm to Mrs. Carson as she went up the steps. "You're in the first two bedrooms, ma'am."

"Do I have to share a bedroom with her?" Ricky complained, sticking his hands in the pockets of his plaid jacket. "She stays up late reading."

Gail fiddled with the end of her blond ponytail. "He talks in his sleep."

Their father fixed them with a stern look. "We will discuss the sleeping arrangements later."

When all four of the Carsons had climbed into the vestibule,

Mr. Clark reached for his step box, then raised the stairs. The conductor called, "All aboard." The porter shut and locked the door. The train whistle blew and the *California Zephyr* began to move, leaving Glenwood Springs right on schedule.

Jill followed the Carsons to their accommodations. After setting down their cases, the porter departed. "It's lovely to see you again," she said.

"Nice to see you, too." Mr. Carson set his cane in the corner and helped his wife remove her jacket. He had a leather camera case slung around his neck. He took it off and set it on a nearby seat. Then he removed his topcoat and hung it up. "Every time we come through Glenwood Springs on the train, we see the hot springs and the Hotel Colorado, and they look so inviting, and we say, we really need to come for a visit."

"So we did," Mrs. Carson added. "And we had a lovely time."

"Did you do any fishing, Mr. Carson?" Jill asked. The train was now passing over the Roaring Fork River, which emptied into the Colorado River. Farther upstream were the Fryingpan and the Crystal Rivers, both tributaries of the Roaring Fork. Jill had heard that the rivers provided good fishing.

"Yes, I did. Very good fishing," he said. "I caught several trout."

"And they get bigger every time he tells the story," Audrey Carson added, with a teasing smile. "They were quite tasty, I must say. The chef at the hotel prepared them for us."

"And you stayed at the Hotel Colorado?" Jill asked.

"Oh, yes, it was wonderful," Mrs. Carson said.

"It's haunted," Gail said. "Did you know that?"

Jill nodded. "I have heard rumors to that effect. Do you suppose it's Theodore Roosevelt? He used to stay at the hotel."

Gail shook her head. "No, it's a girl. One of the maids told me that she saw the ghost and she says it's a girl in old-fashioned clothes playing with a ball. She saw the girl in the hallway on the second floor when she was cleaning."

"I wish I'd seen the ghost," Ricky added.

Their father smiled. "I heard stories, too. One was about the elevator moving from floor to floor with no passengers inside.

That could be explained away as an electrical malfunction, I suppose. But ghost stories are so much more fun. The bellman told me that sometimes the staff smells perfume in the dining room, and hears dishes being moved around."

"Stan, you are just as bad as the children are." Audrey Carson shook her head, looking exasperated. "Ghost stories, for heaven's sake. A lot of rubbish, if you ask me."

Jill smiled. "Well, there is a story about a ghost on one of the *California Zephyr* cars."

"Oh, tell us," Gail said, as Ricky joined in. "Please, we want to hear the story."

"Now, Miss McLeod, don't get them started," Mrs. Carson said. "They'll be pestering you the whole trip."

"Maybe I'll tell you the story later," Jill said. "I have some things to do now. I'll let you get settled into your rooms."

The *California Zephyr* picked up speed as it moved out of Glenwood Canyon, the landscape opening up as the train traveled west along the Colorado River. Jill walked through the dining car, where the waiters were cleaning up after lunch service. The CZ was approaching the old coal mining town of New Castle. On the south side of the river was a scarred, rocky outcropping officially named Roderick Ridge, but the locals called it Burning Mountain.

This was all that remained of the Vulcan Mine, which had a dark history. In 1896, a methane gas explosion in the coal mine killed forty-nine miners. Just two months after that, the mine caught on fire. Unable to extinguish the blaze in the coal seam, the owners abandoned the mine. Then another company took over the mine in 1910, hoping to unearth the rich coal reserves and seal off the vein that was still burning. Another explosion occurred in 1913, this time caused by coal dust, killing thirty-seven miners. After two more explosions and three more deaths, the coal seam fire continued to burn. People in town refused to go near the mine. The owners sealed the Vulcan Mine, signaling the end of the coal mining industry in the area.

The fire still burned, forty years later, making its presence known on the surface of the land. It was visible because plants didn't grow there, where the earth was too hot. During the winter, heat from the fire melted the snow and sometimes sent smoke and steam into the air. Today, in fact, as Jill looked out the window, she saw steam rising from the rocky scar on the mountain.

New Castle disappeared from sight as the train sped by. The *California Zephyr* was due at the next stop, Grand Junction, in less than two hours. Jill walked past the steward's counter and up the passageway alongside the kitchen, leaving the dining car and going through to the buffet-lounge car. She opened the door to her roomette and retrieved her reservation binder. Then she headed back through the sleeper cars to the dome-observation car.

In the Silver Crescent, she made her way past the bedrooms and the buffet to the lounge at the back of the car. All the chairs were full. Miss Grant was in a chair near the rounded back of the car. She was reading one of the Denver newspapers that had been brought aboard the train during the stop that morning. Nearby sat Henry and Trudy Oliver. Mrs. Oliver was crocheting, her hook moving rapidly through the soft pink yarn. Her husband drank coffee and gazed out at the mountains.

"Good afternoon," Jill said. "I'm making dinner reservations for tonight. We have seatings at six, seven, and eight." Sometimes when the train was full, there was a nine o'clock seating, but that wasn't the case this trip.

Miss Grant turned a page in the newspaper. Then she looked up over the rims of her harlequin glasses, her face closed and unwelcoming. Jill wondered if it had something to do with the earlier encounter in the sleeper car, where Doug had insisted he'd seen Miss Grant before.

"Seven o'clock," she said, her voice chilly.

The reservation cards were in Jill's binder, different colors for different times. She filled out a white card for the seven o'clock seating, marking it with the notation "17/2." This indicated the train number 17, for the westbound train. The number 2 indicated that this was the second day of the journey.

Miss Grant took the card, with a quick "Thank you." She opened her large handbag and tucked the card inside, then removed a metal vanity case, a rectangle, about three by five inches.

Because the case had a handle, it could be used as an evening purse. The front of the case was decorated with rhinestones in a diamond pattern. Jill's mother had a case that looked very much like this one, without the rhinestones. Miss Grant opened the case and Jill saw the built-in compartments for powder and lip rouge. There was also a tiny comb and a clip which could hold cigarettes or a few greenbacks. Miss Grant checked her face in the little mirror, and then snapped it shut and put it back in her purse.

Jill turned to the Olivers. "We'll take a six o'clock reservation," Mrs. Oliver said. "Henry and I really don't like to eat too late in the evening." Her husband nodded in agreement. "That goes with being a farmer, and a farmer's wife. We start and end our days early."

Jill pulled two red cards from her binder and filled them out, handing them to Mrs. Oliver. She moved to the next group, making reservations for the passengers in the lounge, handing out cards. As she worked, she noted the numbers and the times in her binder. This way she could keep track of the seatings and hold back space for the coach passengers.

Once she'd finished in the lounge, she climbed the stairs to the Vista-Dome and began working her way through the passengers there. Toward the front of the dome, she saw the Demarest family, the four of them spread out on two seats. Ten-year-old Patty was talking with Gail and Ricky Carson, who sat in the seat directly in front of her. Older sister Lois was next to her, slouched down on her backbone, looking bored. Across from them, Robby was in the window seat, while his mother sat on the aisle.

"I'm making dinner reservations," Jill told Mrs. Demarest. "We have the Chef's Early Dinner at five, which is for families traveling with children, and then we have seatings at six, seven, and eight."

"I could eat dinner at five," Robby said.

Mrs. Demarest made a face. "You could eat any time, all the time, son of mine." She looked up at Jill. "Five o'clock is way too early for my taste. Six would be better. I want to get these kids to bed early, since we get into Winnemucca about four in the morning."

Jill nodded and filled out four red reservation cards. She moved through the Vista-Dome, making reservations, then went downstairs. There were several passengers seated in the dome-observation car's buffet. Mr. Clark was behind the counter, pouring drinks.

"Would you like to make dinner reservations for the dining car?" Jill asked Mrs. Baines and Miss Larkin, who were seated at the table nearest the entrance, playing another game of gin rummy. Mrs. Baines was shuffling the cards while Miss Larkin tallied up the score.

"I'd rather eat later." Mrs. Baines set down the cards, inviting Miss Larkin to cut them. "How about you?"

Miss Larkin nodded. "Yes, I think eight. Tell me, Miss McLeod, will they have the Rocky Mountain trout on the menu?"

"They usually do," Jill said. "I will check with the dining car steward and let you know."

She filled out two blue cards and handed one to each woman. Mrs. Baines began dealing the hand for their gin game. Jill moved on to other passengers, making more reservations. After leaving the buffet, she walked a short distance up the passageway to bedroom D, the drawing room occupied by Mr. Fontana. As she knocked on the door, she heard men's voices, then a loud guffaw. The door opened and Mr. Geddes peered out at her, a frown on his long, sallow face. Behind him, Jill saw Victor Fontana, scowling. "Is that the colored boy?" Fontana called in his booming voice. "Get him in here, damn quick. I need a refill."

Then he saw Jill and smoothed away his scowl, pasting on a smile instead. "Well, it's my favorite Zephyrette. Sorry for my bad language in front of a nice young lady like you. C'mon in, Miss McLeod. What can we do for you?"

Jill stepped into the drawing room, pausing just inside the door. The air was full of smoke from cigarettes and the cigar Mr. Fontana held clamped in his hand. The drawing room was the largest berth on the train but today it was crowded with people and furniture. The two chairs that normally belonged in the room had been augmented by a third chair and a small square table. Mr. Fontana sprawled comfortably on the long bench seat that folded down to make the bed. He'd removed his jacket and loosened his tie. The glass in front of him was empty save for a few ice cubes.

To Mr. Fontana's right was Mr. Haverman, a thin, balding man in a gray suit who was traveling on the transcontinental sleeper. Geddes had vacated the chair on Fontana's left, to answer Jill's knock. The fourth chair, across the table from Fontana, was occupied by Doug. He was shuffling cards, the familiar red rider-back deck with its image of a winged Cupid on a bicycle. Each man had stacks of poker chips—white, red and blue—in front of him. It looked as though Doug had the largest pile.

"I'm making dinner reservations for this evening," Jill said. "Do you know what time you would like to eat?"

Mr. Fontana waved his hand, cigar smoke painting gray streams in the air. "Dinner, huh? We'll eat at seven. That okay with you, Art?" Mr. Geddes nodded. "What about you gents?" he asked, glancing at Doug and Mr. Haverman. "Gonna have dinner in the diner?"

Doug looked up from the cards he was shuffling. "I'll check with you later, Miss McLeod."

Mr. Haverman nodded as he puffed on a cigarette and set it in an ashtray. "Same here, thanks."

"Okay, then. Ante up and deal the cards," Fontana snapped.

Doug finished shuffling and passed the deck to Mr. Haverman on his left. The thin man cut the cards and Doug picked up the deck as each man tossed a white chip into the middle of the table.

"The name of the game is seven-card stud." Doug began to deal the hand, two cards down for each of the four men at the table. At the third round, he dealt the cards face up. "Eight of clubs for Mr. Haverman, jack of hearts for Mr. Fontana, deuce of clubs for Mr. Geddes, and the dealer gets spades, a trey. The jack bets, Mr. Fontana."

"It sure does. Bet five bucks." Fontana tossed a white chip into the pot without glancing at his two hole cards. Geddes followed suit, as did Doug and Haverman.

"Pot's right," Doug said, dealing the fourth round of cards, again face up. This time Mr. Haverman got the nine of diamonds, while Mr. Fontana picked up another heart, a ten. Mr. Geddes got a heart, too, the ace. "And the dealer gets another trey," Doug said as he dealt himself the three of diamonds. "Pair of threes. I think that's worth ten." He tossed a red chip into the pot, then he glanced at his two hole cards.

Jill filled out two white reservation cards for the seven o'clock seating. Doug dealt the fifth round, cards face up. "Seven of spades to Mr. Haverman, possible straight. King of hearts to Mr. Fontana. Three hearts showing, possible flush. Mr. Geddes gets the deuce of diamonds, so that's a pair. And the dealer gets the queen of spades. Pair of threes is still high."

She handed the reservation cards to Mr. Geddes. She should go, but she wanted to see how this hand turned out. The players tossed chips into the middle of the table and Doug dealt the next round, the sixth, and the last card to be face up. "Ace of clubs to Mr. Haverman, no help for the straight. Six of spades to Mr. Fontana, no help for the flush. Deuce of hearts to Mr. Geddes. Queen of diamonds to the dealer. Three deuces bets, Mr. Geddes."

Across the table, Fontana scowled as he consulted his hole cards. Next to him, Geddes, with three of a kind showing on the table, squinted at his own hole cards. Then he picked up a blue chip. "Bet is twenty bucks." He tossed the chip into the pile. The others called the bet.

"Last card down," Doug said. He quickly dealt the seventh round of cards and set the deck on the table. With his right hand he picked up a corner of the card, then placed it down again. He looked up. "Your bet, Mr. Geddes."

The cadaverous-looking man at his right frowned. "Another twenty." He added a blue chip to the pile in the middle of the table.

"Your twenty," Doug said, "and another twenty." Doug put two blue chips in the pile.

"Forty to me," Mr. Haverman said. "Too rich for my blood. Fold." He placed his cards face down on the table and reached for his cigarette.

Victor Fontana grinned, his cigar clamped between his teeth. He counted out four blue chips. "Your forty, and another forty."

Goodness, Jill thought. Mr. Fontana must have gotten his

flush after all. Mr. Geddes didn't look very confident in his three deuces. He slapped his cards face down on the table and said, "Fold."

Doug had two pair, threes and queens, showing on the table but he must have more in his hand. He called Mr. Fontana's bet and raised it another forty. Mr. Fontana glowered at him as he threw more chips into the pot, calling and raising Doug's bet. Then Doug called Mr. Fontana. "Let's see what you've got."

Mr. Fontana turned over his hole cards, revealing a total of five hearts. "Flush, jack high." He grinned, confident that he'd won the hand.

Doug smiled and turned over his cards, revealing a third queen. "Full house, queens over threes." He raked in his winnings. Jill did a quick calculation of the stacks of chips in front of Doug and guessed that he'd won several hundred dollars.

And Mr. Fontana wasn't happy about it. He scowled again, eyes flashing with anger, then he quickly masked it. "Well, you're having a good run today, Cleary." He looked up at Jill. "You like to play poker, Miss McLeod?"

"I do, but strictly nickel-dime-quarter. I think a dollar would be a big bet for me." She smiled. "I've stayed long enough. I need to get busy with these dinner reservations."

She turned to leave as Mr. Haverman, who'd been shuffling the cards, said, "All right, let's play five-card draw. Maybe my luck will change. Everyone ante up."

"Wait a minute, Miss McLeod," Mr. Fontana said. "I almost forgot. Would you mail this for me at the next station?" He reached for his jacket, discarded on the seat next to him. He removed an envelope from the inner pocket and held it out to her. "Do you have stamps?"

"I do." Jill stepped back into the drawing room. Haverman had finished dealing the cards. Jill reached over the poker table, taking the envelope from Mr. Fontana. "I'll mail this as soon as we get to Grand Junction."

"Thanks a lot." He picked up his cards, then waved his hand. "Hey, Art, get that colored boy. I need another drink."

Mr. Geddes followed Jill out of the drawing room to the passageway. He spotted Lonnie Clark at the entrance to the buffet and waved to him. "Hey, Porter. Need more drinks in here."

Mr. Clark walked quickly to the doorway of the drawing room and looked inside. "How can I help you gentlemen?"

"Get me another Scotch, boy," Mr. Fontana called from the drawing room. "And be snappy about it."

Jill looked at the envelope. It had been addressed in large slanting letters, to Mr. Charles Holt in San Francisco. She tucked the envelope into the top of her reservation binder. Then she tapped on the door to bedroom C, Miss Larch's berth. The door opened. Miss Larch stood just inside, holding her tan leather train case. She'd removed the plastic insert that held her makeup and was rummaging around in the case. Then the train lurched. The case slipped from her grasp and fell to the floor, landing on its side with a thunk. The contents tumbled across the floor. A small silk jewelry bag wound up at Jill's feet, along with a lacy brassiere and several pairs of silk panties. A bottle of *L'Air du Temps* perfume rolled into the passageway outside the bedroom. Jill bent down to gather up the undergarments. Then she stopped when she saw what lay in the bottom of the train case.

"What's this?" Miss Grant was walking along the corridor, coming from the lounge at the back of the car. She paused and looked through the open door, a twist of her mouth passing for a smile. "My goodness, is that thing real?"

"Yes, it is." Pamela Larch picked up the case. "It's not loaded."

The small revolver had a short barrel with a legend reading SMITH & WESSON. Just above the wood grip were two superimposed letters, an *S* and a *W*. Tucked into the case next to the gun was a box of cartridges, .38 special. Pamela took the panties from Jill and covered up the gun.

"Do you know how to use it?" Miss Grant asked.

"I certainly do. I learned to shoot when I was growing up." Miss Larch shrugged, giving Jill and Miss Grant a deprecating smile. "My brother gave me that gun. He insists that I carry it with me when I travel. I suspect he thinks that bad things will happen if I don't."

"You can't be too careful," Miss Grant said. She knelt and

picked up the perfume bottle and handed it to Jill. Then she continued on her way.

"I bet she thinks I'm a dangerous woman. I'm not. That's why I don't keep the gun loaded. I just carry it with me. Doesn't make any sense, I suppose. Anything to keep my brother happy. I'm sure you don't see a lot of passengers carrying guns."

"You'd be surprised." Jill handed the perfume bottle to Miss Larch.

"I'm so glad that bottle didn't break. It would really have stunk up the place if it did. I love perfume, but one should use it sparingly, I believe." Miss Larch laughed as she put the bottle into the case. She placed the plastic insert inside and closed the lid.

"I'm making dinner reservations. What time would you like to eat?"

"I had dinner at seven o'clock last night," Miss Larch said. "But, well, I'd like to wait a bit, to see if Mr. Cleary is interested in having dinner with me."

"I understand. I'll check back with you."

"He seems like a very nice man. He told me he's your cousin. Is that true?"

Jill nodded. "His father is my mother's older brother."

"I see. He's older than you are."

"Nearly eight years." Jill turned to leave.

"Miss McLeod, could I talk with you? In private?"

"Certainly." Jill stepped into bedroom C and shut the door.

Miss Larch sat down and smoothed the skirt of her soft green dress. With her other hand, she reached up and rubbed the thin gold chain around her neck. "I like your cousin a lot."

Jill shifted the reservation binder from one arm to another, choosing her words carefully. "You only met Doug this morning. So you don't know him very well."

"I don't know him at all," Pamela Larch said. "I just know that I like him. And I'd like to get to know him better."

"He's getting off the train in Portola tomorrow," Jill said. "That leaves the two of you several hours to get better acquainted."

"Not much time, is it?" Miss Larch gave Jill a wistful smile. "And just to complicate matters, I'm engaged to be married."

Yes, that did complicate things, Jill thought. Miss Larch wasn't wearing an engagement ring, not on her finger, anyway. She didn't look like a radiant bride-to-be. Instead she looked like a woman who wasn't sure she wanted to go through with her planned marriage.

"That puts a different perspective on things."

"My fiancé is a cotton broker. In New Orleans. It'll be fun, living in New Orleans." Miss Larch sounded as though she was trying to convince herself. "It's such a beautiful city. Have you ever been there?"

Jill shook her head. "I'd like to visit New Orleans some time."

"Me, I want to see the Pacific Ocean. That's one reason I'm going to California. I've seen the Gulf of Mexico, of course. We go down to Biloxi all the time. I have an aunt that lives down there. That's where I met Nicky."

"Is Nicky your fiancé?"

Miss Larch shook her head and her fingers toyed with the gold chain at her neck. "No, my fiancé's name is Earl. Why do you ask about Nicky?"

"You mentioned Nicky," Jill said. "You said you met him in Biloxi."

"Did I? Well, Nicky was the man I thought I was going to marry. Then Korea happened."

"I lost my fiancé in Korea, too. He was killed a couple of years ago."

Miss Larch's laugh was brittle. "Oh, Nicky didn't die. He just threw me over. He was in the ROTC at Ole Miss and went into the army after that. He met some sweet young thing when he was in training out in California and he married her instead."

"I'm sorry," Jill said.

Miss Larch shrugged. "I kept telling myself I didn't care. But I do. I loved him." Then she shook herself. "Anyway, he's gone now. Good riddance to bad rubbish. That's what my granny said. He wasn't good enough for me. My family kept shoving eligible men at me. Consolation prizes. Nice men. But they didn't make me feel the way Nicky did."

She sighed. "I went to New Orleans for Mardi Gras. That's

when I met Earl. He's older than me, almost forty. A nice man, very wealthy, from a fine old family. He has a grand house in the Garden District. It was a whirlwind courtship, you know. He asked me to marry him right away. I said yes and we set the date for June. He gave me this lovely ring."

Miss Larch tugged at the chain she wore around her neck and pulled it out of the bodice of her pale green dress. Dangling at the end of the chain was the ring that Jill had seen that morning, a band of gold with a large square-cut diamond. Miss Larch slipped the ring onto the third finger of her left hand. Then she held out her hand. "Isn't it beautiful? A whole carat."

"You don't love him." The words came out of Jill's mouth before she realized she'd said them. "I'm sorry, I didn't mean to say that. It's none of my business."

"Maybe it isn't your business. But you're right." Miss Larch removed the ring from her finger. She held the chain and twirled the ring. Then she tucked the ring and the chain back into her bodice. "I don't love Earl. He deserves someone who does. He's a nice man. But he just doesn't spark me the way Nicky did." She looked up at Jill. "I wonder if anyone else will make me feel that way. I want to get married and settle down. Isn't that what girls our age do?"

"Some people don't," Jill said.

"I guess I could work. Like you do." Miss Larch favored Jill with a lopsided smile. "I must confess, I don't think I'd be any good as a Zephyrette. Maybe there's something else I could do. Besides sit at home in Jackson and stare at the walls. I have a degree in English. Mainly because I didn't know what else to study. Getting married seemed like something to do. When Earl proposed all of a sudden, I just said yes. Why not?"

Now Miss Larch laughed. "I'm supposed to be in Memphis shopping for wedding gowns. I told my mother that's where I was going when I left home. Told her I was going to stay there a few nights, with this girl I went to school with at Ole Miss. Except I didn't get off the train in Memphis. I rode the *City of New Orleans* all the way up to Chicago and I spent the night there. I'd never been to Chicago before. My, it's a big place. Then I bought me a ticket on the *California Zephyr*. I'm going all the way to San Francisco, and after that, I don't know what I'll do. I guess I will get my chance to see the Pacific Ocean."

"I hope you enjoy the ocean. It's beautiful," Jill said. "Now, if you'll excuse me, I have to get back to making reservations."

"Of course," Miss Larch said. "Thank you for listening."

Jill opened the door and stepped out of bedroom C, closing the door behind her. Just then, the door to the drawing room opened and Doug stepped out. She heard Fontana's voice. The man from Chicago sounded angry.

"Seems like a good time to take a break," Doug said.

"Are you ahead?"

He grinned. "I'm doing all right. Won three hands in a row and Fontana's upset. He'd like to accuse me of cheating, but I don't and he knows it. I'm a better poker player than he is and that gets his goat. So I'm letting things cool off. Say, about dinner reservations, I was thinking seven o'clock, but I wanted to ask..." He pointed at bedroom C.

"I suspect the answer will be yes." Jill watched as he knocked on Miss Larch's door. Her cousin was as smitten with Miss Larch as she was with him.

Chapter Eleven —————————————

JILL KNOCKED ON THE DOOR OF bedroom A. Inside, Audrey Carson called, "Who is it?" When Jill replied, Mrs. Carson invited her in.

Mrs. Carson sat near the window, with a book on her lap. It was a copy of *Rebecca* by Daphne du Maurier. She stuck a bookmark between the pages of the novel. "One of my favorites. Every now and then I reread it."

"Mine, too. As for rereading, my mother's the same way with *Gone With the Wind*." Jill stepped into the compartment, binder in hand.

Mr. Carson was in the seat facing the window, his legs stretched out in front of him, his eyes closed. A soft snore rumbled from his mouth. His wife smiled at him and looked up at Jill. "The children are in the Vista-Dome, I'm sure."

"I saw them. I was just up there."

Mrs. Carson glanced at her watch. "We'll eat dinner at six. That's a good time for us."

Jill filled out the cards and handed them to Mrs. Carson. Just then Mr. Carson woke up, with a snort. He sat up in the chair and ran a hand through his dark hair. "Hello. Making dinner reservations, I'll bet."

"Yes, I am."

"We're eating at six," his wife added.

"Good, good. Miss McLeod, who is the man traveling in the drawing room? I saw him earlier in the corridor. I believe I heard him say he's going to San Francisco. And," he said with a smile, "the porter told me he has a poker game going on in his room."

"His name is Victor Fontana," Jill said. "He's a businessman from Chicago. He is going to San Francisco. And yes, there is a poker game in progress. Do you know him?"

Mr. Carson looked thoughtful. "Not really. I have heard the name before. Thanks."

Jill took her leave of the Carsons and stepped out into the corridor. The door of bedroom C opened, and Doug waved at her. "Miss Larch and I will have dinner at seven," he said.

Jill made a note in her reservation binder and filled out the cards. When she handed them to Doug, he gave her a jaunty salute and opened the door to the drawing room. She heard Mr. Fontana's voice. "C'mon, Cleary, it's your deal. Give me the chance to win back the money you took off me this afternoon."

Jill walked forward, encountering Mr. Clark at the front of the car, where his small compartment was located. The porter stood at the open door of the supply locker. He moved aside to let her pass, but she stopped. Something had been on her mind since her earlier conversation with Doug.

"Mr. Clark, can you tell me something about Chicago?"

He smiled. "Sure, be happy to answer anything I can about my Windy City."

"Have you ever heard of a Chicago nightclub called the Bell Tower?"

"I have." The porter closed the door to the supply locker and turned to face her. "The Bell Tower was a fancy club on South Wabash. It was a good place to see a show and have dinner. The club had a band, a lead singer, and a chorus line. My cousin worked there, in the kitchen, before he joined the Army. When he got out of the service, he went back to see if he could get a job, but the place was shut down."

"Do you know anything about a woman who worked at the Bell Tower?" Jill asked. "She called herself Belle La Tour."

"That I do," he said. "She was the lead singer, and a dancer, too. I saw her once, not in the show, but leaving the club. That night I met my cousin at the back door of the Bell Tower, after he got off work. She came outside and said hello. Her lighter wasn't working, so I lit her cigarette. Then this fancy Cadillac coupe pulled up the alley and she got in. My cousin told me she had a fella, the guy that owned the place, and he was connected to the mob, if you know what I mean."

Jill filed that away for future reference. "Would you recognize Belle La Tour if you saw her again?"

The porter thought about this. "I don't know. That was, let's see, nineteen forty-four. That's nine years ago. Why are you asking, Miss McLeod?"

"There's a passenger on the Silver Falls, a Miss Grant. A librarian from Aurora. Dresses like one, too. Plain clothes and big harlequin-framed glasses."

The porter nodded. "I know the lady you mean. Has that scar on her face. She comes back to the lounge in the back of this car, but she keeps to herself. Doesn't talk much to any of the other passengers. She was in the lounge just a while ago. Then she left. What has she got to do with Belle La Tour?"

"One of the other passengers says he thinks Miss Grant *is* Belle La Tour."

Lonnie Clark gave a low whistle. "Belle La Tour didn't look anything like that librarian lady. She was tall and blond. But like I said, that was a long time ago."

"Different hair and different clothes," Jill said. "And the glasses."

"I'll take a closer look at her next time she's in the car," Mr. Clark said. "Maybe I'll recognize her." He shrugged. "Or maybe I won't."

"Thanks," Jill said. "I appreciate your doing that. Let me know what you think."

I don't know why this is important, she told herself as she walked through the vestibule into the transcontinental sleeper. I just have a feeling it is.

Jill went down the row of roomettes, making reservations for the passengers. In bedroom C, Miss Brandon sat looking out the window, her leather-bound book and binoculars in her lap. As Jill stood in the doorway, Miss Brandon raised the binoculars and peered out the window. Just this side of the river, at the top of a bare-branched tree, a large bird perched, its white-feathered head contrasting with the dark brown of the tree trunk.

"Another bald eagle. That's six I've seen today," Miss Brandon said triumphantly, making a notation in her book. "Now, I suspect you want to know what time I'll have dinner. Seven o'clock, just like last night."

———

After making reservations in the rest of the transcontinental sleeper and the sixteen-section sleeper, Jill moved to the next car, the Silver Falls. There she encountered Frank Nathan, just outside his small porter's compartment. He opened his mouth as though to speak, then he stopped, a cautious look on his face.

"Is there something you want, Mr. Nathan?" Jill asked.

"I don't know whether to say anything to you," the porter said. "But it was odd."

That certainly triggered Jill's curiosity. "Go ahead and tell me."

"It was Miss Grant, the one who's traveling in bedroom C. I'm sure she was eavesdropping. It was earlier, when you were talking with your cousin, Mr. Cleary. I was standing by the linen locker when I saw Miss Grant come into the car, coming from the rear of the train. When she went round the corner, that was about the time Mr. Cleary came out of his bedroom and the two of you started walking toward her. Since I was right there, I couldn't help overhearing. Mr. Cleary asked Miss Grant if they'd met before."

"That's right," Jill said. "He thought she looked familiar."

"Well, she said no, and kept walking. But she didn't go far. When I left the linen locker and went round the corner, heading toward the bedroom section, she was there, hovering around the door to bedroom A, like she was listening to you and Mr. Cleary talk. I was about to ask her if I could help her, but she gave me a look, and I just kept going."

Jill considered this. So it was possible Miss Grant had overheard her and Doug speculating about whether the librarian from Aurora was actually a former Chicago nightclub singer named

Belle La Tour. That would explain the cold look Miss Grant had given her while she was making a dinner reservation for the woman back in the dome-observation car.

"I'm sure it was nothing," Jill said now. "Thanks for telling me."

Frank Nathan nodded and headed up the passageway between the roomettes. Jill stood for a moment, lost in thought.

Why would Miss Grant listen to her conversation with Doug? Unless she really was Belle La Tour, the former singer, in disguise as a librarian. If so, Doug's question must have alerted Miss Grant that someone was aware of her past.

Or maybe it's all nonsense and I'm making a mountain out of the proverbial molehill, Jill told herself, shaking her head.

Mrs. Allard, a middle-aged woman traveling in roomette one, appeared at the doorway. "Hello, Miss McLeod. Are you making dinner reservations?"

"I certainly am." Jill smiled and opened the reservation binder. "What time would you like to have dinner?"

Jill worked her way down the row of roomettes. When she came to roomette ten, the berth occupied by the French graduate student, Florian Rapace looked up from the book he was reading. He had requested an eight o'clock seating the previous night, but now he looked at Jill, his face suddenly reserved. "Please, Mademoiselle McLeod, can you tell me what time Mademoiselle Lois will have dinner?"

Should she alert the young Frenchman to the fact that Lois Demarest was only sixteen? But it really wasn't any of her business.

"Miss Demarest and her family have reservations at six o'clock," she said.

"So early?" He frowned. She knew from previous trips that many French passengers were used to eating dinner at a later time. Then he sighed. "All right, I will eat dinner at six."

She filled out a card for him, then moved to the bedroom section of the Silver Falls. Once she finished there, she went into the next car, the Silver Quail. She found Uncle Sean napping in his bedroom. "Just resting my eyes," he said, yawning as he opened the door. He hesitated. "What time will Doug be in the dining room?"

"At seven," Jill said. "He made a reservation for himself, and a friend."

"That girl I saw him with during lunch?"

"Quite possibly."

"He always did have an eye for the ladies," Sean said, with a wry smile. "Well, give me a reservation for six."

She knocked on doors in the rest of the car, finally meeting the passenger in bedroom C who had boarded in Denver. Her name was Miss Carolla, and she was traveling to Stockton, California. When Jill finished in the Silver Quail, she moved on to the Silver Chalet. In the lounge, she found Mrs. Warrick sitting with Dr. Ranleigh and her niece, talking as they sipped coffee. They looked up as she approached, and decided on an early dinner, at six o'clock.

Miss Margate sat alone at a table at the back of the lounge, a drink in front of her. She frowned, intent on reading what was written on the piece of paper she held. Jill recognized the paper, and the envelope on the table, as *California Zephyr* stationery. On the front of the envelope someone had written "Avis Margate." Jill caught a glimpse of what was written on the paper but she couldn't make out any of the words, not that it was any of her business anyway. But the note seemed to have upset the woman who was reading it.

Miss Margate quickly folded the note and tucked it into her handbag. Her face brightened with a smile. "Hi, Miss McLeod. Time for dinner reservations? I'll take a seven o'clock seating."

Jill filled out the card and handed to her. Miss Margate picked up the glass in front of her and downed the rest of her drink. With a wave of her hand, she summoned Mr. Peterson to bring her another. Then she looked down at the envelope poking from the top of her handbag, staring at it as though it were a snake.

Chapter Twelve

THE *CALIFORNIA ZEPHYR* LEFT the narrow confines of DeBeque Canyon and the train sped toward the little town of Palisade, some ten miles east of Grand Junction. The agricultural town was named for the palisades of shale north of town. And it was famous for its fruit orchards, which produced peaches, apples and cherries. In the late 1890s, settlers had used water from the Colorado River to irrigate their crops, aided in 1913 by a dam and a series of irrigation canals built by the Department of Reclamation. In the early years, farmers in the area had produced tons of wine grapes but the onset of Prohibition meant the end of vineyards and more fruit trees. Cold winters and a long growing season with high-altitude sunlight contributed to the area's flavorful fruit.

When Jill finished making dinner reservations for passengers in the chair cars, she had conferred with Mr. Taylor, the dining steward, and returned the binder to her quarters. She put a stamp on Mr. Fontana's letter, then she walked through the train, collecting postcards and letters to mail during the stop in Grand Junction. She tucked these into her pocket and returned to the Silver Mustang, where she climbed the stairs to the Vista-Dome, taking a seat near the front to chat with passengers. Timmy Shelton, with his mother in a nearby seat, pointed out the window at the town as the train rushed past buildings. "That's Palisade. That's where my grandma and grandpa live. They're on their way to Grand Junction right now to meet us at the station."

Polly Halleck, on her father's lap in the seat across the aisle, piped up. "My auntie and uncle will be there, too."

"Indeed they will," Rose Halleck said in her crisp English

accent. "We should go downstairs and gather up our things, so we can get off the train and meet them." She got to her feet and so did her husband.

Jill followed as the Hallecks made their way down the stairs to their seats in the lower level of the Silver Mustang. Timmy Shelton and his mother brought up the rear. Other passengers in the chair car were getting ready to leave the train, taking suitcases and coats from the overhead racks, tucking books, knitting, and decks of cards into bags.

The train began to slow as it entered the outskirts of Grand Junction, the whistle blowing the warning signal at crossings where vehicles waited for the *CZ* to pass. The city, the largest in Western Colorado, was located at the junction of the Gunnison and Colorado Rivers. In fact, the Colorado River had once been known as the Grand River, but the river's name had been changed in the early 1920s. South of the city was the Colorado National Monument, a rugged area with cliffs and canyons. To the north was a formation called the Bookcliffs, shale topped with sandstone.

Grand Junction was a crew change stop, about seven minutes in duration. Homer Wilson, the conductor who'd ridden the train since Denver, would change places with another D&RGW conductor. There would be a new brakeman as well as a new engineer and fireman.

People stood on the platform in front of Grand Junction's yellow brick depot. The *Zephyr* rolled slowly into the station and stopped. In the Silver Mustang, the car attendant quickly opened the door and left the train to assist departing passengers. Timmy Shelton didn't wait for a helping hand. He jumped off the step box and ran to a gray-haired man and woman on the platform. "Grandpa! Grandma!"

The waiting couple swept the little boy into a hug. "You've grown a good six inches since the last time we saw you," the man said.

The woman put her arms around Mrs. Shelton, who'd followed her son off the train. "Betsy, honey, it's so good to have you home for a visit. I wish John was with you."

"He had that business meeting to go to," Mrs. Shelton said. "Maybe all three of us can come back during the summer."

Her father took her suitcase and the family moved off, walking past Mrs. Saxby, who was parceling out luggage to her son and daughter. Nearby, the Hallecks talked with a middle-aged couple as Polly clung to her father's coat. The little girl saw Jill watching her and waved, her fingers wriggling.

Jill waved back and headed toward the station, taking the letters and postcards from her pocket. One of the items slipped from her grasp, falling onto the platform. She reached down and retrieved the envelope Mr. Fontana had given her to mail. She looked at the address written there, noticing the slanting handwriting. Was it her imagination? Or did the writing on this envelope look much like that on the note Miss Margate had been reading in the lounge?

A man asked her a question and she answered, directing him to the Silver Quail. He hurried toward the car. She went into the station and dropped the letters into a mailbox.

The conductor and brakeman who had joined the train at Grand Junction stood near the dining car, looking down the platform as they talked. Both were familiar faces, people Jill knew from previous runs. Otis Perkins, the conductor, was a large man, his shoulders straining the seams of the uniform jacket. Most of his hair was gone and what was left was a silvery gray. He had worked for the Denver & Rio Grande Western for nearly forty years.

"Good to see you again, Miss McLeod," he said in a gruff voice.

"Hello, Mr. Perkins. How are you?"

"Fine, just fine. You know Bob Saylor?" Mr. Perkins pointed at the middle-aged brakeman.

"Yes, we've met."

"Anything I should know about?"

"An uneventful trip," Jill said. "So far."

"Good, let's keep it that way." The conductor pulled out his pocket watch. "Time to go. I'll see you onboard the train."

He walked toward the rear of the train, calling, "All aboard."

The brakeman nodded to Jill and headed in the opposite direction toward the engine.

Jill climbed into the vestibule of the Silver Quail. After the porter locked the door, the whistle blew and the *California Zephyr* moved out of the Grand Junction station.

Half an hour later, the Silver Lady entered Ruby Canyon, where late afternoon sunlight glowed on the red sandstone cliffs. Pinnacles and spires rose above the Colorado River as the train wound its way around curves that hugged the river's course. Sometimes the tracks were right under the cliffs, and other times the canyon broadened, with side canyons visible. Here and there were stands of cottonwood trees.

The twenty-five-mile canyon straddled the Colorado–Utah state line. Once the train emerged from the canyon, it entered a broad valley near the last vestiges of an old railroad town called Westwater. Here the passengers had their last glimpse of the river the tracks had followed for more than two hundred miles. The Colorado River's course led to the south, while the train continued west into the rugged Utah desert. The landscape outside the windows of the *CZ* changed from cliffs to weathered hills and washes, changing colors as the afternoon light faded.

For the trip through Ruby Canyon, Jill had been in the Vista-Dome in the Silver Ranch, the third chair car. Now she took the stairs down to the main level and walked back through the train, making a stop in her quarters. Then she entered the dining car, where several families were eating the Chef's Early Dinner. She stopped at the steward's counter.

"Mr. Taylor, do we have Rocky Mountain trout tonight? Some of the passengers have been asking."

"We certainly do," the dining car steward said. "We took on a supply in Denver."

One of the chefs poked his head out of the busy kitchen. "We have plenty, Miss McLeod. Real tasty, with a butter and lemon sauce. And we have chocolate pie tonight. I know you like chocolate pie."

Jill gave him a rueful smile. "I like any kind of pie. I'll let the passengers know that trout's on the menu."

She headed back through the train, to the lounge in the dome-observation car where she'd seen Mrs. Baines and Miss Larkin, who'd asked about the trout. They weren't in the lounge now, though. She continued walking to the lounge area at the back of the car, where she saw several passengers reading and talking. The two women were there, taking a break from their gin game, so she walked over to tell them that the trout was on the dining car menu. When she'd done so, she nodded to Lonnie Clark, who was making the rounds of the passengers in the rear part of the Silver Crescent, taking orders for beverages.

Miss Grant descended the stairs from the Vista-Dome and sat down in a vacant chair near the writing desk at the front of the lounge. She reached into her oversized handbag, took out a hard-back book and set it on her lap. Then she took out a pack of cigarettes and a lighter, shaking a cigarette from the pack. She lighted the cigarette and took a drag, exhaling smoke. Then she opened the book to the page she had marked with a bookmark.

As he passed Jill, the porter glanced at her, and then at Miss Grant. He approached the seated woman and said, "May I get you a beverage, miss?"

Jill hoped that Miss Grant wouldn't notice the porter's scrutiny. She seemed not to, though. She glanced at him over the top of her glasses and favored him with a tight smile. "Coffee, please."

"Certainly, miss. I have a fresh pot in the lounge."

Jill turned as one of the other passengers asked her a question. When she glanced toward the front of the car, Mr. Clark was delivering the coffee to Miss Grant. He moved on, handing a drink to another passenger. Jill walked forward, heading for the front of the car. She took the steps down to the lounge and turned to the right, waiting near the counter in the buffet. A few moments later, Lonnie Clark returned to the buffet and stepped behind the counter.

"I took a look at Miss Grant, like we talked about," he said in a low voice. "I have to say, I'm not sure that's Belle La Tour. I know I saw her up close that one time, but like I said, it was nine years ago. I'm sorry I can't be more help in that regard."

Jill shrugged. Corroborating Doug's identification with that of Mr. Clark had been a long shot, of course. Doug had seen the woman in 1941 and the porter had seen her a few years later. In either case, that was a long time ago. "That's all right. I've decided the passenger who thinks Miss Grant is Belle La Tour is mistaken. Thanks, I appreciate it."

She stepped away from the counter, leaving the lounge. Just as she walked past the door to the drawing room, it opened and Doug came out. A miasma of cigar smoke followed him, then Vic Fontana appeared at Doug's side. He slapped Doug on the back and laughed, glancing at Jill. He had a friendly grin on his face, but there was an edge to his voice.

"What d'ya think, Miss McLeod? This guy's a heckuva poker player. He took a couple hundred bucks off me today, but he better watch out tomorrow. I plan to win it all back before we get to San Francisco."

Doug's only response was a slight smile.

"I'm glad you gentlemen had an enjoyable afternoon of cards," Jill said. She left them in the doorway and continued forward.

Chapter Thirteen ─────────

JILL LOOKED AROUND THE Silver Banquet and saw the Carsons at a table in the middle of the car. There was Milly Demarest with her three children. Florian Rapace had managed to get a table right across the aisle. Uncle Sean was at the same table, along with Miss Brandon and a woman who was traveling in the first coach car.

"Miss McLeod, please join us for dinner." Mrs. Warrick was at a table near the steward's counter in the Silver Banquet. With her were Dr. Ranleigh and her niece Rachel.

"I'll sit with those passengers," Jill told the steward. She walked down the aisle and pulled out the empty chair next to Mrs. Warrick. Once she'd settled into the seat, she pulled the menu from the stand and opened it.

"We've just ordered," Dr. Ranleigh said. "Geneva and I are having the trout."

"Not me," Rachel said. "I don't care for fish. I'm having the roast sirloin."

"I do like fish, so I'll have the trout." Jill marked her meal check for the boneless Rocky Mountain trout and selected a lettuce and tomato salad and green peas to go with it. "I've been told there's chocolate pie for dessert."

"Oh, good," Rachel said. "I love chocolate anything."

Jill turned her meal check over to the waiter. She looked around and saw Lois Demarest lean across the aisle to speak to Florian. At that moment the Olivers walked by, heading for a table. Once again Uncle Sean looked at Henry Oliver, a narrow-eyed assessment that told Jill he was trying to place the man.

She poured herself a glass of water and spoke to her dining companions. "Are you enjoying the trip?"

"I am indeed," Ella Ranleigh said. "I always enjoy traveling by train." She gestured at the window. Outside, the sun had dipped in the west, painting the rugged landscape of southeast Utah in hues of red and orange. "Just look at that sunset."

"It's been about two hours since we left Grand Junction," Rachel said. "I wonder where we are now."

"I live by the clock," Jill said, checking her watch. "We're about an hour from our next stop. That's Helper, Utah. We'll be in the station at seven-ten."

"Why is it called Helper?" Rachel asked.

"The town is named for the helper locomotives the Denver and Rio Grande Western used to help the westbound trains get up the steep grade to a place called Soldier Summit, which is the other side of the town."

The waiter brought their first courses, salads for Jill and Mrs. Warrick, vegetable soup for the Ranleighs. The doctor raised her spoon to her lips and tasted her soup. "Mmm, this is good. How long have you been a Zephyrette, Miss McLeod?"

"Two years." Jill gave her dining companions an abbreviated history of her tenure on the *California Zephyr*.

"When we talked earlier," Mrs. Warrick said, "you told me you grew up in Colorado."

Jill nodded. "Yes. We lived in the City Park neighborhood in Denver. Then during the war, we lived with my grandmother near Cheesman Park."

"You must have gone to East High School," Rachel said, finishing up her soup. "So did I. Class of 'forty-one. Then I went to the University of Colorado in Boulder."

Jill smiled. "Yes, I did go to East High. I graduated in 'forty-five. But I went to the University of California instead. You see, my father joined the Navy after Pearl Harbor."

"Yes, Pearl Harbor." Dr. Ranleigh glanced at her niece. There was a somber look in Rachel's eyes. Jill suspected that the young woman on the other side of the table had lost someone that day, just as Jill had in Korea.

"Rachel was in school at Boulder and lived on campus," the doctor continued. "Her mother moved in with me while her father—my brother—was overseas. And I started working at Fitzsimmons Army Hospital in nineteen forty-two."

"Dad went to officers' training in 'forty-two," Jill said. "Then he stopped in Denver on leave before going to the West Coast. He was a doctor on a ship. We didn't see him again for three years. At the end of the war he was assigned to the Naval Hospital in Oakland, so we packed up and moved to California."

The war. Interesting to talk about it now, but it was not so distant, really. It had been almost eight years since V-E Day.

How well Jill remembered those days after Pearl Harbor, when the United States had entered the war already raging around the globe. Since Cheesman Park was southeast of downtown and still in the children's school districts, her parents had made the decision to sell the family's much smaller house. Lora McLeod and her children had moved in with Grandma Cleary, for the duration, however long that might be.

During the war, the big rambling house, just a block from the park, was full of people. There was a housing shortage then, and Grandma offered space to a number of relatives who came to Denver to work, some of them at defense industry jobs at Lowry Field and the Rocky Mountain Arsenal. Lora McLeod got a job at Lowry Field, doing secretarial work, while Grandma volunteered at the USO.

Grandma even rented out rooms, to help make ends meet. So Jill had to double up with her sister, Lucy. A walk-in closet was turned into a bedroom for their younger brother Drew. There was always a bed available for the family members, men and woman, who were in uniform, passing through the Mile High City on their way to wherever, even if that meant a cot in a hallway. Queuing for the bathroom was crowded, and time-consuming.

"I was still teaching at Colorado Women's College during the war," Mrs. Warrick said. "My late husband was in the civil service. He traveled quite a bit, working for the Office of Price Administration, at the regional office in Denver."

"Rationing." Rachel rolled her eyes and sighed. She reached

for a roll from the basket on the table and buttered it. "I'm so glad to have real butter. That nasty margarine we had in the dorms was white. It looked like lard. You can't imagine how I hated that stuff."

"Yes, I can," Jill said. "I hated it too."

The Office of Price Administration had been formed before the United States entered the war. Its role was controlling prices and rents. In May 1942 the OPA froze prices and issued ration books. Butter, sugar, milk, coffee, meat—everything was in short supply for civilians, who now had to keep track of their rationing points as well as their money. Favorite recipes had to be rewritten to take into account the restrictions of rationing.

That first spring, Jill, her siblings and several cousins dug up the grass in Grandma's yard, front and back. They planted a huge victory garden, growing enough vegetables to feed the house's occupants. On one side of the backyard was a tree that produced plenty of McIntosh apples, so they didn't let any of the fruit go to waste. On the other side of the lot, they built a chicken coop. Several hens provided precious eggs. Relatives who lived in Boulder County kept bees. During trips to Denver they brought jars of honey, to take the place of hard-to-get sugar.

Those trips from the beekeeping relatives were infrequent. Gas, oil, tires, all of these were rationed. People walked, or carpooled, and the Sunday drives to the mountains Jill remembered from her childhood became just that, memories. Such recreational travel was discouraged. Because of gas rationing, most ordinary citizens got an *A* sticker for their cars, entitling the holder to three or four gallons of gas per week. War workers got *B* stickers, which gave them eight gallons per week. *C* stickers went to doctors, like Dr. Ranleigh, and to ministers, mail carriers and railroad workers, while the truckers who hauled goods from place to place had *T* stickers, giving them an unlimited supply of gas.

The waiter appeared at their table, bringing their entrées. Jill picked up her fork. Thinking about wartime rationing made her even hungrier. The trout that was a favorite on the *California Zephyr* menu looked wonderful and smelled even better. It had been dredged in flour and sautéed, finished with a lemony brown-butter sauce. She cut off a small piece and raised her fork to her lips, savoring her first bite. Delicious.

The conversation turned away from the war to subjects more current—the first months of the Eisenhower presidency and Dag Hammarskjöld, who had just been named Secretary-General of the United Nations.

"The most exciting news for me," Dr. Ranleigh said, "is that announcement by Doctor Jonas Salk a couple of weeks ago. He's developed a vaccine for polio."

"Yes, it's wonderful," Mrs. Warrick said. "I had a cousin who had a severe case when he was a young man. He was confined to an iron lung."

Jill nodded, remembering a high school classmate who'd been stricken with the disease. The girl had recovered, but she walked with a limp.

"That epidemic last year was the worst in a long time," Dr. Ranleigh said. "Nearly sixty thousand cases, and over three thousand deaths."

They talked about the promising vaccine a while longer, then they moved on to lighter topics, such as books and movies. Jill confessed to her passion for Agatha Christie, while Mrs. Warrick preferred historical novels, such as her current book, *The Silver Chalice* by Thomas Costain. Rachel was enjoying a new book, a historical romance called *Désirée*, by an author named Annemarie Selinko. The doctor's reading was usually confined to medical journals, she said, but she was reading *The Uninvited*, by Dorothy Macardle. "I saw the movie years ago," she added, "with Ray Milland and Ruth Hussey. It was good, and I'm enjoying the book."

The Academy Awards had been televised for the first time in March, and *The Greatest Show on Earth* won Best Picture. It was something of an upset, since everyone seemed to think *High Noon* was going to win. At least Gary Cooper won the Best Actor award.

"I liked *The Greatest Show on Earth*," Jill said.

Rachel laughed. "So did I. It was a lot of fun."

"You just like Charlton Heston," her aunt said.

Jill and Rachel agreed on something else, that the chocolate pie was delicious.

Chapter Fourteen

"COME ON, HONEY. Let's have a nightcap."

It was after eight. Jill had just finished an evening walk through the train, returning from the chair cars. She planned to spend some time in her quarters in the Silver Chalet before the train arrived in Provo just after nine.

When she entered the buffet-lounge car, she saw Uncle Sean in the coffee shop, talking with Mr. Poindexter, both of them sipping from cups on the table in front of them. She smiled at the two men and went down the steps to the lounge.

Then Jill turned her head as Victor Fontana's voice boomed out. At first, she thought the invitation to have a drink was directed at Avis Margate, who had just come down the opposite steps, from the rear of the train. Then Jill realized Mr. Fontana was directing his attentions to Pamela Larch, who stood near the counter with Doug.

"No, thank you," Miss Larch said, her voice polite. "I don't care to have a drink this evening."

"Come on, honey. One little nightcap before you turn in for the night." Mr. Fontana took a step toward her. Now Miss Larch backed away from him, crowding closer to Doug

"The lady doesn't want to have a drink with you." Doug's voice was steely as he looked down at the shorter man.

"Who made you her keeper?" Fontana snapped. "You damn cardsharp. I got my eye on you."

He leered as he moved past Doug, leaning toward Miss Larch. "You had a couple of drinks with me last night, honey. And you looked like you were enjoying it. You weren't so particular about who you were keeping company with then." He reached for Miss Larch's arm. She pulled away from him.

"Keep your hands off her." Doug pushed between Mr. Fontana and Miss Larch, his right hand balled into a fist.

Fontana growled, deep in his throat, his face angry. Behind the kitchen counter, Mr. Peterson looked alarmed, and so did the other passengers in the lounge.

"Go find the conductor," Jill told Mr. Peterson. "I just saw him in his office."

The waiter nodded and slipped out of the kitchen, hurrying forward toward the chair cars. Then Jill moved into the lounge. "Gentlemen, please."

"Doug, let's go," Miss Larch said, her voice trembling.

Before she could say anything else, Fontana leaned closer to Doug and Miss Larch and said something in a hiss. Jill couldn't hear what he'd said, but the words had their intended effect on their targets. Miss Larch looked as though she was about to burst into tears. Doug grabbed Fontana's collar with his left hand, balling his right fist again. He shook the shorter man, as though shaking a rag doll. Fontana's head rocked back. He sputtered, rage sparking in his dark eyes. He too clenched his fists. He cocked back his right arm, ready to take a swing at Doug. "You want a fight, cardsharp? Bring it on."

Art Geddes scrambled to his feet, taking a step toward the two men. He put his hands on Fontana's right arm, pulling it back. "Vic, Vic. Drop it."

Suddenly Uncle Sean was there, coming from the coffee shop. He clamped a hand on Doug's arm. "Hey, what's going on? Let's break it up, okay?"

Doug, with a poisonous glare at Fontana, dropped his hand. Pamela Larch seized his arm and tugged at him. In the corridor, Miss Margate stared at Mr. Fontana, her mouth looking as though she'd just tasted something sour. Then she did an about-face and went back up the steps, heading toward the rear of the train.

Geddes loomed in back of Fontana, his hand on his associate's shoulder, pulling him away from the confrontation.

"C'mon, Vic. Let's go back to your room. We'll do our drinking someplace else."

Just then the conductor rounded the corner, his bulk filling the doorway to the lounge. "Is there a problem?" Otis Perkins asked in a rumbling voice, his face stern below his hat with the Denver & Rio Grande insignia.

Uncle Sean smiled at him, steering Doug away as he stepped up to speak to the conductor. "No problem. We've got it solved. Just a misunderstanding, that's all."

"Right, just a misunderstanding. We're leaving." Art Geddes nudged Fontana toward the door. The conductor stepped aside to let them pass.

"I'm just going to have a nightcap with these folks." Sean smiled at Mr. Perkins. Then he beckoned to the waiter, who had accompanied the conductor back to the lounge.

"I'll be right there, sir," Mr. Peterson said.

Sean turned to his son and Miss Larch. "Now, suppose you introduce me to this young lady."

Doug still looked angry, his jaw clenched, his lips compressed in a thin line. But he nodded. He took Miss Larch's hand and followed his father to a table at the back of the lounge.

The potential explosion had been defused, for now. Jill found that she was holding her breath. She released it in a sigh.

"Miss McLeod, tell me what happened," Mr. Perkins said.

Jill stepped into the corridor and gave the conductor a report of the incident. "Miss Larch didn't want to have a drink with Mr. Fontana, and he said something that I didn't hear, although I suspect from her reaction that it was very unpleasant. I also suspect that Mr. Fontana has had too much to drink this evening."

He gave a rumbling laugh. "It happens. At least once every run. Some man gets a snootful and starts forcing his attentions on one of the ladies. Let's hope that's the end of it. I'll brief the new conductor when we get to Salt Lake."

Yes, let's hope, Jill thought. But she wasn't sure. Whatever Fontana had said to Doug must have been about Miss Larch. It must have been terrible, to make her cousin so angry. And Doug would be on the train until the *CZ* got to Portola, another twenty hours or so from now. So would Victor Fontana. During that time, there was potential for another confrontation.

When the conductor had gone, Jill went into the lounge and walked to the table where Mr. Peterson was taking orders. Miss Larch shook her head, indicating she didn't want anything.

"Will you join us, Jill?" her uncle asked.

"Not for a drink," she said, "but I'll chat for a while."

Mr. Peterson moved away, heading back toward the kitchen.

"What happened last night?" Doug asked Miss Larch. "He said he'd bought you a drink. Did he make a pass at you?"

From the troubled look on her face, it was plain that Pamela Larch was reluctant to talk about what had happened on the first night of the westbound run. Then she took a deep breath.

"Well... Yes, to both questions. It was some time after dinner, I'm not sure when. I was sitting by myself in the buffet there in the dome-observation car, just sipping at a bourbon on the rocks and talking with another passenger who was at the table next to me."

She toyed with a strand of her blond hair. "Mr. Fontana was in the buffet, too. He kept looking at me. He wasn't alone, though. He was with that man from New York City, the one with the accent. Mr. Geddes, his name is. After a while, Mr. Geddes left, and so did the woman I'd been talking with. Then Mr. Fontana came over. He sat down at the table next to me, asked what I was drinking, and offered to buy me another drink. Well, one drink led to another. I'm afraid I was a bit worse for wear the next morning."

Jill nodded, remembering how Miss Larch had looked when she came out of her room that morning, coming into the buffet and demanding coffee from the porter.

"He seemed charming at first. Then he began making advances. So I got up and left." Miss Larch looked worried. "I swear, I was just drinking with him to be sociable. I must have given him the wrong impression. It's all my fault."

"It's not your fault," Doug said. "The guy's a jerk. He's angry with me because I'm a better poker player than he is."

"He called you a cardsharp," Jill said. "Earlier today he said you took a couple hundred dollars off him this afternoon."

Doug grinned. "It was closer to a thousand. Fontana shouldn't try to draw to an inside straight."

"Did he accuse you of cheating?" Sean asked.

"After I won that last hand, he implied it."

Sean nodded, rubbing his chin. "Yeah, Fontana's the type. You shouldn't get on his bad side."

"If he can't stand to lose, he shouldn't play poker," Doug said. "As for tonight, if you'd heard what he said. He called her a —"

"Doug, please. It's over, let's forget it." Pamela Larch reached for his hand and smiled. "I must say, it's very gallant of you to come to my rescue."

"Do you know Mr. Fontana?" Jill asked her uncle.

He scowled. "'Mister' Fontana. Calling a guy like that 'mister.' He's a jumped-up hoodlum from Pueblo. He moved to Denver in the late twenties and worked for the Smaldones, running booze and gambling operations, up until he went to Chicago."

The Smaldones were Denver's crime family. Brothers Eugene, Clyde, and Chauncey, along with a host of relatives and associates, were involved in organized crime, from bootlegging during Prohibition to gambling and bookmaking after repeal. Jill knew her uncle had had run-ins with the Smaldones and their organization during his tenure as a Denver police officer, and now it appeared he had encountered Vic Fontana as well.

"Let's talk about something else, please," Miss Larch said as the waiter brought drinks for the two men.

"Sure." Sean raised his glass, an easygoing smile on his face. "Where are you from, Miss Larch? And where are you going?"

She returned his smile. "I am from Jackson, Mississippi, and I'm going to San Francisco. And how about you, Mr. Cleary?"

———

Several passengers got off the train in Provo, Utah, including Mrs. Higbee, the inquisitive and opinionated woman who'd sat with Jill at lunch. The *California Zephyr* pulled out of the station at 9:10 P.M., and the lights of the town gave way to darkness as the train headed for Salt Lake City. Jill walked to the dining car to make her last announcement of the day. She lifted the mike from the public address system and pressed the button.

"Attention, please. Before retiring this evening, please set your watches back one hour, as we pass from the Mountain to the Pacific Time Zone during the night. Good night."

Good night, Jill thought as she replaced the mike, but not quite time for bed. She would stay up until the train left Salt Lake City. The train was due to arrive in the Utah state capital in less than an hour, at 10:05. After twenty minutes in the station, the CZ would depart at 10:25. A number of passengers were leaving the train and no doubt there would be quite a few boarding. The next scheduled stop was Elko, Nevada, just before two in the morning. The time zone change would occur as the train crossed from Utah into Nevada.

Jill walked through the train once more. In the chair cars, many of the passengers had retired for the night, covering themselves with blankets, their heads pillowed by coats. The coffee shop would be open until ten. Several of the tables were occupied by passengers, among them Florian Rapace and Lois Demarest. They were sharing a piece of pie, coffee cups in front of them. Florian laughed. Lois joined in, leaning her head closer to his.

Jill smiled at them and continued through the buffet-lounge car. When she looked into the lounge, Doug and Miss Larch weren't there, and neither was Uncle Sean. Perhaps they'd turned in for the night.

Frank Nathan was at the entrance to the kitchen, talking with Mr. Peterson as the waiter assembled a tray that held a single cup and saucer, a coffeepot, and a creamer and sugar bowl. "Coffee for Mrs. Warrick in bedroom D," the porter said.

Jill smiled. "If I drank coffee this late, it would keep me awake. And I'm looking forward to a good night's sleep."

The porter hefted the tray and carried it back in the direction of the sleeper cars. Jill lingered. "Mr. Peterson, I'm sorry about that unpleasantness earlier this evening."

"With Mr. Fontana?" The waiter frowned. "It's not the first time, I'm afraid."

"Was there another incident last night?" The waiter seemed reluctant to answer. Like other waiters and porters on the train, no doubt he had seen it all and kept his mouth shut most of the time.

"It's just that I heard voices in the corridor outside my door," Jill said. "This was about ten o'clock, the time the lounge would have closed. The voices were those of a man and a woman, and I'm sure the man was Mr. Fontana."

Mr. Peterson nodded. "He likes his liquor. And he fancies himself a ladies' man. As to what happened last night, Miss Margate came into the lounge sometime during the evening. She was sitting with a couple. After awhile Mr. Fontana and Mr. Geddes came in. They had several drinks, then Mr. Geddes left. So did the people Miss Margate had been sitting with. So Mr. Fontana moved over to Miss Margate's table. He bought her a drink."

Just as he had with Pamela Larch earlier that same evening, in the buffet back in the Silver Crescent.

"Then what?" Jill asked.

"A bit later, I saw Mr. Fontana put his hand on Miss Margate's knee," the waiter said. "She pushed it off. Then he did it again. He was being awfully familiar with her. But she seemed to be handling him. Anyway, it was getting on toward closing time and I gave them the last call. I heard Mr. Fontana say it was too early to call off the party. He told her he had a bottle of fine old Scotch back in his room on the Silver Crescent, and why didn't they go back there and break that open."

Mr. Peterson shook his head. "I didn't hear what Miss Margate said, but next thing I know, they got up and left the lounge, heading back toward the rear of the train. I closed the lounge, cleaned up, and went to the dormitory. So I don't know if the lady actually did go back to his room."

"Thanks, Mr. Peterson."

It must have been Mr. Fontana and Miss Margate I heard outside my door that night, Jill thought. The timing is right. She wondered if she should talk with Miss Margate.

She continued walking back through the train. The dining car was closed now, but in the kitchen, the crew was still busy, cleaning and preparing for the next day. Crew members would be back at work in the early hours of the morning, getting ready for breakfast. As Jill headed through the sleeper cars, it looked as though many of the passengers had retired for the night. Thin slivers of light were visible under several doors, while others were dark. In the sixteen-section sleeper, the seats had been converted into curtained-off beds. Jill passed the ladies' room and walked past the berths. At the third set of curtains, the youngest Demarest child, Patty, wearing a pair of red-and-yellow plaid pajamas, peeked at her from the upper berth. Jill waved at her and the child giggled and disappeared from view.

In the dome-observation car, Doug and Miss Larch stood in front of the door to bedroom C. Doug had his arms around her, leaning in for a kiss. Miss Larch returned his kiss, her hands around his neck. Then she stepped back when she saw Jill.

"Pardon me," Jill said. "I didn't mean to startle you."

Miss Larch smiled shyly. Then she took Doug's arm and opened the door to her bedroom. "Let's go inside, just to talk for a bit."

Doug chuckled, with a sidelong glance at Jill. "I'd welcome the privacy."

They went inside and shut the door. Well, well, Jill thought. It certainly looked as though this relationship was heating up fast. That didn't alter the fact that Miss Larch was engaged to someone else, and that Doug was getting off the train in Portola tomorrow morning.

Lonnie Clark was in the buffet kitchen of the dome-observation car, washing glasses. In the buffet itself, Art Geddes sat with Victor Fontana, whose face was still angry as a thundercloud as he drank from the glass in front of him. Miss Larkin and Mrs. Baines sat nearby, chatting and sipping coffee as they played yet another game of gin rummy.

Jill smiled at the porter and then walked up the steps that led to the observation lounge at the end of the car. Avis Margate was in the first seat on the right side of the car, staring into space, as though she were miles away. Should she ask Miss Margate whether she'd been with Mr. Fontana last night? No, it didn't seem to be the right time for such a personal conversation. There were others in the lounge. The fourth seat, angled so that it faced toward the front of the lounge, was occupied by Cora Grant. She had a book on her lap, turning the pages as she smoked a cigarette. Both of the small bench seats that faced the rear of the car were empty.

On the left side of the car, opposite Miss Grant, was Rachel Ranleigh, who was also reading.

All quiet, Jill thought, surveying the lounge. She turned and walked toward the front of the lounge. Miss Grant looked up and to her left. Jill followed the direction of her gaze, seeing Mr. Geddes leave the buffet. He turned to his left and went up the steps, heading forward toward the sleeper cars.

Miss Grant leaned forward and stubbed out her cigarette in a nearby ashtray. Rachel covered her mouth as she yawned. Then she stuck a bookmark into her book and closed it. She stood. "Well, I'm all in. I'm going to bed. Good night, Miss McLeod."

When she'd gone, in the direction of the sleeper cars, Jill retraced her steps to the buffet. The two women were still playing cards. Mr. Fontana sat alone now, his glass in front of him. He looked at his watch, frowning. Then he picked up the glass and downed the rest. When he stood, he seemed unsteady on his feet. Or was it just the motion of the train? He bumped into the table where Mrs. Baines and Miss Larkin were playing cards and muttered something. The two women gave him looks of disapproval. He straightened, as though getting his bearings. "Miss McLeod," he said with a boozy smile. "My favorite Zephyrette." He dropped a heavy hand on Jill's shoulder, pulling her toward him.

Jill stepped to one side and dislodged his hand. "Good night, Mr. Fontana."

"G'night." He weaved past her toward the corridor.

"In his cups," Mrs. Baines said when he'd gone.

"Absolutely awash," Miss Larkin agreed. "The things you must put up with, Miss McLeod." They returned to their game.

Jill turned to Mr. Clark. "Has Mr. Fontana been drinking a lot?"

"Oh, yes. He was already well on his way when he got here. That was about an hour ago." The porter came around the counter and went into the buffet to retrieve the empty glass. Then he stopped and spoke to the card players. "May I get you ladies some more coffee? Or anything else?"

"No, thank you," Miss Larkin said. "We're almost finished with this game. We're going to bed."

Mr. Clark picked up their coffee cups. Then he returned to the kitchen and set the dishes in the sink. He added detergent and turned on the hot water.

"Gin!" Mrs. Baines cried from the buffet. She and Miss Larkin gathered up the cards and got up from the table. Then they left the buffet, agreeing to meet in the dining car at eight o'clock for breakfast.

"Mr. Clark," Jill asked, "did you see something happen between Miss Larch and Mr. Fontana last night?"

He hesitated, washing the dishes and setting them on a dishtowel. Then he nodded and spoke in a lowered voice. "Yes, Miss McLeod, I did. Mr. Fontana was, well, not to put too fine a point on it, he was being a little too familiar with Miss Larch. Ever since she boarded the train in Chicago, he's been looking at her, looking her up and down, like he was in the market and she was something tasty. You know what I mean."

"I certainly do," Jill said. In the two years she'd been working on the *California Zephyr*, she'd had her share of encounters with the wolves, amorous passengers who thought the Zephyrette was fair game. She'd learned early on how to dodge the men who backed her into corners or doorways, and slip away from the ones who tried to pinch her bottom or put their arms around her, as Mr. Fontana had.

"He bought her a couple of drinks," the porter said. "And she got a little tipsy. I guess he figured that entitled him to make a pass. She got up and left, went to her bedroom. Did he try it again today?"

"I'm afraid so, in the lounge of the Silver Chalet. When she said no, he made a nasty remark. I didn't hear it, but I certainly saw her reaction."

"And that young man, Mr. Cleary? The one who's been paying attention to her, he didn't like it."

"Not a bit," Jill said. "He very nearly hit Mr. Fontana. I do hope we've heard the last of any trouble."

Mr. Clark picked up another dishtowel and dried the dishes. "I hope so, too."

"Good night, Mr. Clark."

Jill walked forward through the transcontinental sleeper. As she entered the sixteen-section sleeper, she encountered Mr. Oliver, who was walking the opposite way. She nodded at him and continued forward, until she reached the Silver Chalet. She sat on the bench seat in her compartment, making notes for her trip report. Then she picked up *Funerals are Fatal*.

When the train entered the outskirts of Salt Lake City, Jill put away the book and left her compartment. Mr. Peterson, who'd closed up the coffee shop and lounge, was opening the door to the crew's dormitory. He looked tired, past ready for his bunk inside. "Good night. Sleep well, Mr. Peterson."

"You too, Miss McLeod."

In the vestibule of the Silver Ranch, Jill stood with the car porter and a passenger, an old man holding a small suitcase. The *CZ* slowed, pulling into the Salt Lake City station. As soon as the train stopped, the car porter unlocked the door and flipped the lever that lowered the steps. Once he'd put his step box in place, he reached up to assist the passenger.

A man and a woman waited on the platform. When they saw the old man, they hurried toward him. The woman threw her arms around him, saying, "Grandpa, it's so good to see you. You look wonderful." Her husband took the suitcase and beckoned the old man toward the station entrance.

Next to depart the train was a young man, carrying a small valise in his hand. He waved to another man wearing a University of Utah letter jacket. "Hey, Johnny, over here." The two men then headed for the station, talking a mile a minute.

Once the passengers had left the vestibule, Jill stepped down to the platform. She assisted a passenger who was boarding the Silver Mustang, then she walked toward the front of the train, where Mr. Perkins stood with the new conductor, briefing him on any train orders and the journey so far. Nearby was the new brakeman. The Denver & Rio Grande Western diesels that had pulled the *CZ* from Denver were being uncoupled. Then the engines pulled forward, onto a siding. Three Western Pacific Railroad engines backed into place, ready to pull the train across the Great Salt Desert and the rugged expanse of Nevada, into California and down the Feather River Canyon to California's great Central Valley. Here, too, the crews were changing, with D&RGW personnel handing the Silver Lady over to WP employees.

Otis Perkins waved at Jill, then walked toward the station. The new conductor and brakeman were headed her way. The conductor was a middle-aged man with a wiry build, and she hadn't seen him before. He must be new to the route. The brakeman she recognized, a tall lanky fellow named Carl Mooney.

"Good evening. I'm Jill McLeod." She held out her hand and the conductor shook it.

"Bill Dutton. Pleased to meet you. I just started working on the *Zephyr* a month ago. I've heard your name. You're related to Pat Haggerty, right?"

"Not really. I was engaged to his nephew."

"Oh, yes, the young man who was killed in Korea a couple of years back," the conductor said. "Sorry about your loss."

Jill tamped down the inner twinge she always felt when Steve's death came up. In some ways she would never get over losing him. But she was making every effort to move on.

She put on her brightest smile. "Glad to have you aboard, Mr. Dutton. And it's good to see you again, Mr. Mooney."

"Hope we have a nice, quiet run," the conductor said.

"Amen to that," the brakeman added.

As soon as the engines had been switched out, the conductor made his way down the platform with his familiar cry of "All aboard." Jill climbed into the vestibule of the first chair car, the Silver Scout. The car porter grabbed the step box, then closed and locked the door. The whistle blew and the *California Zephyr* pulled out of the Salt Lake City station.

She glanced out the vestibule window. The train left the lights of the station and the wide city streets, heading for the western edge of the city. The buildings faded into darkness, punctuated at regular intervals by street lamps. The train's route would take the *CZ* along the southern shore of the Great Salt Lake, the vast body of water that gave the city its name. In fact, at a place called Lakepoint, the tracks crossed a small part of the lake. Depending on lake level, which varied throughout the year, the tracks crossed water or mudflats. Had it been daylight, she might have been able to see the elaborate beach pavilion at Saltair, an old beach resort that had been built and rebuilt over the last decades. Generations of bathers had reached Saltair by a railroad from the city.

Jill turned and walked back through the train to the Silver Chalet. In her compartment, she put on her pajamas, brushed her teeth and washed her face. Then she converted the bench seat into her bed and climbed in, tucking the blankets around her. She propped her head with the pillow and reached for her book, reading a few more pages of Hercule Poirot's case.

But sleep tugged at her eyelids. She realized that she'd read the same page twice. Time to call it a night, she told herself. She set the book aside and turned out the light.

Chapter Fifteen

"MISS McLEOD? MISS McLEOD? Wake up, please."
Someone was tapping on her door. Jill shook off sleep and reached for the light switch. She propped herself up on one elbow and looked at her watch. She hadn't been asleep long. It was just after eleven.

She heard it again, a low, insistent voice. "Miss McLeod?"

"I'm coming."

She threw back the blanket, stuck her feet into her slippers, and got out of bed. Reaching for her blue plaid robe, she put it on and tied the belt around her waist, taking a deep, steadying breath.

There was only one reason anyone would wake her in the middle of the night—a crisis of some sort. Perhaps someone was injured. She unlocked and opened the door.

Lonnie Clark, the porter from the Silver Crescent, stood in the corridor, a worried look on his face. "Come quick, Miss McLeod. Bring your first-aid kit."

"Who's hurt? How bad is it?"

"It's Mr. Fontana, in the drawing room. Something's wrong. I think he's ill. Best you see for yourself."

"I'll be right there," she told the porter.

Mr. Clark nodded and turned, heading back to the Silver Crescent. Jill shut and locked her door. *CZ* policy prohibited her from responding to these late night calls in her nightclothes. She quickly shed her pajamas and put on her uniform. Then she pulled the first-aid kit off the luggage rack above her bed and left her compartment.

Usually when she was called upon to give first aid to passengers, it involved something minor, like the scrape on Robby Demarest's hand earlier today. Or motion sickness among the passengers, whether adult or child. But Mr. Clark's demeanor suggested that this was more serious. Jill wouldn't know what she was dealing with until she saw Mr. Fontana for herself.

Jill walked quickly through the train. At this time of night, nearly an hour out of Salt Lake City, most of the passengers were asleep. In the Silver Quail, all was quiet. There were no lights showing under the doors of the berths, and Joe Backus dozed in the porter's seat on the Silver Quail. He didn't wake as she passed him. Back in the Silver Falls, the door to the porter's compartment was closed. She assumed that Frank Nathan was also asleep.

In the sixteen-section sleeper, she encountered Lois Demarest coming out of the women's restroom. The girl wore a silky red nightgown and robe. Bundled in her arms she carried her clothing and her shoes. The teenager smiled and put a finger to her lips, then she tiptoed to one of the berths and slipped behind the curtain.

Jill continued down the aisle. Snores and mutterings came from several of the berths she passed. She went past the men's restroom at the rear of the car and into the next car, the transcontinental sleeper. Finally she entered the Silver Crescent, walking past the porter's compartment and the closed bedroom doors.

The porter waited for her in the passageway outside the drawing room door, a strained look on his dark face. He motioned with his hand and she stepped toward the doorway.

The light was on inside the drawing room. The seat perpendicular to the window had been folded down into a bed. The pillow had tumbled to the floor. Mr. Fontana lay on his right side, his arms in front of him and his shoulders hunched forward. His right leg was drawn up, completely on the bed, while his other leg, the foot encased in a maroon slipper, dangled over the edge. He wore gray silk pajamas under his plush maroon bathrobe. His breathing was slow and irregular, the air rasping as he drew it in and expelled it from his lungs.

"Mr. Fontana?" The man on the bed didn't respond. Jill

turned to the porter. "I don't like the way he's breathing. Do you have any idea what happened? Did he fall?"

Mr. Clark shook his head. "No, I don't know. I didn't see or hear anything. I was up in the Vista-Dome. When I came back down I checked the lounge and the buffet, like I always do before going to bed. Then I headed up the passageway to my own quarters. I saw Mr. Fontana's door was open. It was moving back and forth like it hadn't closed right. I reached for it, going to shut it. The light was on. I looked in, and I saw Mr. Fontana."

The porter stopped and ran a hand over his face. "He was on the bed like that, on his side, in his pajamas and robe. It looked to me like he was taken sick and fell. Or passed out. You saw how he was when he left the buffet tonight. He was drinking a lot. When I found him like this, I called out his name. Then I stepped inside, called his name again. I didn't go all the way over to the bed. I just took a look and saw his face all pale like that. And the way he's breathing, well, I figured I'd better get you."

Jill walked into the drawing room and set the first-aid kit on the floor near the bed where Mr. Fontana lay. His face, usually ruddy, was pale. In this light, it almost looked blue. And when Jill touched his forehead, the skin felt cold. His eyes were closed, but as Jill stood over him, his eyes opened and he stared up at her. His breath rasped and his mouth worked, as though he was trying to say something. Then he moaned.

Could this be alcohol poisoning? Her father had once described the symptoms to her, and Mr. Fontana's symptoms were similar. Or was this something far more serious?

"Mr. Fontana?" Jill reached out and put her hand on his shoulder. He moaned again. Then his arms moved. He rolled back, revealing the front of his robe and the blanket where he'd lain.

Behind her, the porter gasped.

The blanket wasn't supposed to be that color. Jill stared, horrified at what she saw. The maroon color of Mr. Fontana's robe had hidden the dark red stain. Blood, and lots of it, had soaked into the robe's thick plush fabric and stained the gray silk pajamas underneath. The letters *VF* were embroidered in gold on the left breast. A hole had obliterated the leg of the *F*.

Jill straightened. She looked down at the pillow on the floor and saw another hole on the white pillowcase, this one rimmed with black. She had no doubt that the other side of the pillow was stained with blood.

Mr. Fontana had been shot. And the pillow had been used to muffle the sound.

Jill took a deep breath to steady her nerves. She was surprised that her voice didn't shake when she spoke. "Mr. Clark, please get Doctor Ranleigh. She's traveling in compartment I on the Silver Quail. And find the conductor."

The porter nodded and disappeared from view. Jill turned back to Mr. Fontana. A gunshot wound was far beyond the scope of her first-aid training. She touched his temple gently with her index finger. He groaned. His eyes opened, wide and dark, and he stared up at her.

Jill leaned forward. "Mr. Fontana, it's Miss McLeod. I've sent for a doctor. Can you hear me? What happened?"

Something flickered in his eyes and he groaned again. Guttural sounds came from his mouth. But she couldn't understand the words. His eyes closed, but he was still breathing, that awful raspy sound, in counterpoint with the clacking of wheels on rails.

A few minutes later, the door opened and Dr. Ranleigh bustled into the drawing room, wrapped in a plaid flannel robe. She carried her medical bag.

"Thank goodness you're here," Jill said. "This is Mr. Fontana. He's been shot."

"I can see that. It looks like he's lost a lot of blood." Dr. Ranleigh leaned over Mr. Fontana, her fingers opening the robe and the pajama top to reveal Mr. Fontana's chest. Now Jill could see the entry wound, just below the man's heart. "It's bad. This man needs a hospital. Can we get him back to Salt Lake City?"

Before Jill could say anything, Mr. Dutton, the conductor, entered the drawing room, followed by Mr. Winston, the Pullman conductor, and Mr. Clark. "Miss McLeod, the porter says one of the passengers has been injured."

"He's been shot," Dr. Ranleigh said.

Mr. Dutton looked aghast, momentarily at a loss for words.

Then he narrowed his eyes and addressed the middle-aged woman at the bedside. "Who are you?"

"Doctor Ella Ranleigh," she said in a no-nonsense voice.

"She's a passenger from Denver," Jill added. "I sent for her."

Mr. Dutton moved to the bed and stared down at Mr. Fontana. "Good God, what a mess. How bad is it?"

"Very bad," the doctor said. "We've got to get him to a hospital or he won't survive."

On the bed Mr. Fontana moved again and his eyes opened. He grabbed Jill's wrist, twisting it painfully as he tried again to speak. Then he sighed, the air leaving his lungs in a long, gusty exhale.

That was the last sound he made.

Chapter Sixteen

JILL LOOSENED HER HAND from Mr. Fontana's grip. "Too late. He's gone." She stepped away from the bed. Dr. Ranleigh reached for the man's throat and felt for a pulse. The room was silent except for the familiar rhythm of wheels on rails.

Then the doctor nodded. "He's dead."

"Son of a bitch," the conductor said. "Sorry, ladies. What happened? I want the whole story."

Jill raised a hand. "If I might suggest, sir. There are too many people in here. We should go to the lounge at the back of the car, where we won't be heard by the passengers in the other bedrooms. Besides, we need to seal the drawing room and preserve whatever evidence is in here. For the murder investigation."

"Murder investigation." The conductor shook his head and motioned to the others. "Yes, I guess it is. Mr. Winston, you've got the porter's key. Lock that room. We'll go back to the lounge."

The Pullman conductor nodded. They all walked back to the end of the car, which was dimly lit. Mr. Clark turned up the lights.

"Who found him?" Mr. Dutton asked.

"I did, sir," the porter said. "After we left Salt Lake City, I went up to the Vista-Dome. I like to go up there after everyone's gone to sleep, to look at the stars. It was quiet, everybody was in their berths, and there wasn't a soul in the Dome or the lounge. Like I told Miss McLeod, I didn't see anything or hear anything, certainly not a shot."

"What time was this?" Mr. Dutton asked.

"I closed the buffet at ten," Mr. Clark said. "That was right as we were getting into Salt Lake City. There wasn't anyone else in the lounge. I finished cleaning up. I was done by the time we left Salt Lake. We left on time, so that was ten twenty-five. I went upstairs to the Vista-Dome. I like to look at the stars, when it's good and dark and I can pick out the constellations. It took a little while for the train to get far enough out of town. I sat up there for a while, then I came downstairs. But I'm not sure what time it was. Maybe about eleven o'clock."

"And that's when you found him?" Mr. Winston asked.

The porter nodded. "Yes, sir, it is. I was headed toward my own compartment when I saw the door to the drawing room was open a bit, like someone shut it and it hadn't latched. I looked in, and there was Mr. Fontana on the bed, lying on his side. I thought maybe he'd had too much to drink or been taken sick. You see, he was in the buffet earlier, drinking quite a bit. I'd say he was fairly drunk when he left the buffet and went to his room."

Mr. Clark paused and went on. "I looked in on him because the door was open. I called his name and he didn't answer. He was breathing kind of strange. I didn't like the sound of it. I figured he must have been taken sick for sure. So I went looking for Miss McLeod, asked her to bring the first-aid kit. I thought maybe she could help." He stopped and shook his head. "I didn't have any idea the man was shot. I didn't see any blood. Guess that was because he was on his side. That, and the color of his robe."

Jill continued the story. "I went to bed after we left Salt Lake City. It was a few minutes after eleven when Mr. Clark came to my door. I came back to the car as soon as I got dressed. Mr. Fontana was on his right side. I moved closer, to see what was wrong with him. When I touched his shoulder, he rolled onto his back. That's when I saw the blood and realized that he'd been shot. I sent Mr. Clark for the doctor, and you, Mr. Dutton."

The conductor consulted his watch. So did Jill. It was eleven-twenty now. The train was nearly an hour out of Salt Lake City.

"This is a hell of a note," the conductor said. "We're in the middle of the Great Salt Desert and we've got a killer aboard."

"Back in December we had an incident, another murder," Jill said.

Mr. Dutton nodded. "I heard about that. You found the body."

Just like now, Jill thought. Though technically Mr. Clark found this body and Mr. Fontana wasn't dead at the time.

She got back to the situation at hand. "On that trip, we had someone aboard who had been a military police investigator. He took lots of pictures of the crime scene. We need to do that now."

"One of the passengers surely has a camera," the conductor said.

"I'm no photographer," Dr. Ranleigh said, picking up her medical bag. "But my niece is. She has a camera back in our compartment. I'll get her."

Mr. Dutton frowned. "You sure she'll be all right, taking pictures of a body?"

"Of course." The doctor swept past him.

"We have an investigator aboard the train," Jill said. "My uncle is a retired Denver police detective. He's traveling in bedroom C of the Silver Quail."

"Fine. Please get him." The conductor ran a hand over his jaw. "We'll have to make an unscheduled stop in Wendover. That's another hour from here, maybe more. Right now we'll have to stop the train and let the brakeman tap into a telegraph wire to report this to Dispatch."

He turned to the Pullman conductor. "Mr. Winston, when the doctor gets back with her niece and that camera, have them wait until the detective gets here. He can tell them what pictures she should take."

Jill and the conductor walked forward through the sleeper cars. In the Silver Quail, they passed the porter's seat, where Joe Backus was sleeping. He woke up, startled to see them. He spoke to Jill in a whisper. "Miss McLeod, what are you doing up so late? Is there a problem?"

"Yes," Jill said. "In another car."

Mr. Dutton kept walking forward, going in search of the brakeman. Jill stopped at the door to bedroom C. She knocked. No answer. She knocked again. "Uncle Sean? Wake up, please."

The door opened and he peered out, bleary-eyed with sleep. "Jill? What's the matter?"

"We need you in the dome-observation car. There's been a murder."

"What?" He shook himself and the sleepy look disappeared. "Who?"

"Mr. Fontana."

While her uncle was digesting this news, another door opened toward the front of the car. Dr. Ranleigh stepped into the corridor, followed by Rachel, both of them in bathrobes. Rachel carried the camera case.

As they reached Jill, she said in a low voice, "This is Doctor Ranleigh and her niece Rachel, who's a photographer. They're going to take pictures."

"Wait for me before you do that. I'll get dressed and be right there." He closed the door.

Chapter Seventeen ───────

L IVE BY THE SWORD, die by the sword."
Sean Cleary stood in the doorway of the drawing room, his mouth twisted in a bitter smile as he looked at the body on the bed.

"You knew Mr. Fontana?" Dr. Ranleigh asked.

"Our paths crossed, years ago. I even arrested him a time or two."

The doctor and Rachel were in the corridor. Now the doctor said, "Really? I understood that Mr. Fontana was a businessman from Chicago, a liquor distributor."

Sean laughed. "Oh, he distributed liquor, all right. He was a bootlegger."

"Prohibition was repealed nearly twenty years ago," Dr. Ranleigh said. "Even if he was a bootlegger back then, he was a legitimate businessman now."

Sean didn't look convinced. "That depends on how you define legitimate, Doctor. Well, Miss Ranleigh, let's take those pictures."

Jill stepped aside as the others entered the drawing room. Rachel took a quick breath at the sight of the corpse, then she fought down the shock and raised her camera. With Sean's direction, she took the first photo, shutter clicking, flashbulb flooding the drawing room with light.

Jill looked at Mr. Clark and Mr. Winston. "We're in the way here."

In the lounge at the rear of the dome-observation car, the Pullman conductor and the porter conferred in low tones. Jill paced between the chairs, going over things in her mind, moving people around like pieces on a chessboard. When she had come back here to the Silver Crescent, after the train left Provo, she'd found Doug and Miss Larch in the corridor, kissing. Then they'd gone into Miss Larch's bedroom. Mr. Fontana and Mr. Geddes had been in the buffet. Then Geddes left. Then Fontana left the buffet, followed by the two women who'd been playing cards. Back here in the lounge there had been three people—Rachel Ranleigh, Cora Grant, and Avis Margate. Rachel had been the first to leave, carrying the book she'd been reading and saying she was going to bed. Jill had left after that, with both Miss Grant and Miss Margate still here in the lounge. What time had they left? Perhaps Mr. Clark could tell her.

Jill looked up as Rachel, the doctor and Sean joined the others in the lounge. Rachel had finished photographing the scene. Now she removed the roll of film from her camera and handed it to Sean.

"I'll lock the drawing room," Mr. Winston said. The Pullman conductor walked forward, heading for the corridor in front of the bedrooms.

"Where's the conductor?" Sean asked.

"He went forward, to get the brakeman," Jill said. "They'll stop the train and send a message to Dispatch."

Even as Jill said the words, the *California Zephyr* slowed, coming to a gradual stop. It would take a few minutes for the brakeman to climb a telegraph pole next to the tracks and tap into the telegraph wires to send a Morse code message, and a few minutes more to get a response.

Sean looked at Jill. "So the porter found him and came to get you. Start at the beginning and tell me everything."

Jill and Mr. Clark repeated their stories, each of them answering questions from her uncle during the telling. As they were talking, the train started moving again. But Jill noticed that the *California Zephyr* wasn't traveling as fast as it had been before. Was there a problem up the line?

A few minutes later, the conductor arrived, a troubled frown on his face. He held out his hand to Sean. "Bill Dutton, the conductor. You must be the detective."

"Sean Cleary. I retired last year, after thirty years on the Denver police force. My niece and the porter were just telling me how they found the body."

"Cleary," Mr. Dutton said. "Did you have some sort of confrontation with Mr. Fontana in the lounge car earlier this evening? The last conductor told me it was a passenger named Cleary, when he briefed me in Salt Lake City."

"That was my son Douglas," Sean said. "He was upset about something Fontana said to the young lady Doug was with."

"I see," the conductor said. "So you've taken photographs of the scene?"

Sean nodded. "Miss Ranleigh took the pictures. She's given me the roll of film. My niece tells me the train is going to stop in Wendover. We can turn the film over to whoever's going to handle the case."

"The brakeman sent a message to Dispatch," Mr. Dutton said. "And we got a response. The dispatcher is contacting the Tooele County Sheriff's Office. We've been in that county since we started across the Great Salt Desert. But there's a problem. A freight train derailed east of Wendover and there's some damage to the tracks. Dispatch isn't sure how long it's going to take to get that cleaned up. That's why the train is moving so slowly. It will take us longer than expected to get to Wendover."

Jill turned to her uncle. "You said you'd crossed paths with Mr. Fontana in the past, and you'd even arrested him. Can you give us some background?"

Mr. Dutton nodded. "Mr. Fontana has a criminal record? I would like to hear about that."

"Might as well sit down," Sean said. He sat down in one of the lounge chairs, leaning forward as he talked. "Fontana was born in Walsenburg, in southern Colorado. It's coal country. His parents were immigrants from Italy. A lot of Italians that came over to this country around the turn of the century wound up working in the coal mines in that part of the state, places like Walsenburg, Trinidad, Pueblo. And Ludlow, where those people were killed during that coal miners' strike back in nineteen-fourteen."

He paused and ran a hand through his unruly gray hair. "Right after World War One, Fontana went to work for the Pueblo mob. First the Danna brothers, then the Carlinos. Both of those families, and their gangs, were hijacking stills and trucks, and killing each other over their bootlegging operations. The Carlinos won, if you can call it that. They killed off both the Danna brothers."

"Good Lord, what an unpleasant bunch of people," the conductor said.

"Unpleasant doesn't cover it. All through the twenties, Fontana was running hooch and holding up stills in southern Colorado. Then he moved to Denver and joined up with the Joe Roma outfit. After Roma was gunned down in 'thirty-one, a couple of guys named Charlie Blanda and Joe Spinnuzi were in charge. Then the Smaldones took over the Denver crime operation."

"The Smaldones," Dr. Ranleigh said, nodding. "Three brothers, I believe, and various cousins and nephews. I've read about their escapades in the Denver newspapers. One of them was arrested in a gambling raid several years ago."

"More than one. And more than once," Sean said. "Clyde and Eugene Smaldone are the older brothers. They call Clyde 'Flip Flop,' and Eugene's nickname is 'Checkers.' Clarence is about twenty years younger than his brothers. His nickname's 'Chauncey,' and he's just as bad. All three of them have done time, for all sorts of crimes. The Smaldones run gambling operations all over northern Colorado. Liquor is legal now, but that just means the bad guys who used to sell booze and hijack stills moved into other things, like gambling, bookmaking, and loan-sharking. Vic Fontana may have called himself a legitimate businessman these days, but back then he was a hood. With his track record, I wouldn't be surprised if he was involved in illegal operations in Chicago."

"He may have been. At least there were rumors about that." Jill looked at the porter. "Mr. Clark, please tell Mr. Cleary what you told me."

The porter looked reluctant to say anything. But he finally nodded. "I'm from Chicago, and I've heard talk about Mr. Fontana. Heard that he was a bootlegger way back when. And that he was involved in the policy game."

"Numbers racket," Sean said. "Gambling. That's interesting, but not surprising. Once a hood, always a hood."

Mr. Dutton cleared his throat. "Be that as it may, Mr. Fontana is dead now. He's been murdered, and whoever killed him is aboard this train. My train, the one I'm responsible for. Mr. Cleary, I need you to set aside your personal feelings about this man and take a look at this crime. It would help the sheriff's office in Wendover if we could report some progress when we get there."

Uncle Sean met the conductor's gaze before answering. "I'll do what I can." He turned to Dr. Ranleigh. "Doctor, any ideas as to the gun?"

Ella Ranleigh shrugged. "I don't know. I can't be sure. Not until there's an autopsy and the bullet has been extracted. I see one entry wound. Close range, of course. And it looks like the pillow was used to muffle the noise of the shot."

"I would guess that Fontana was carrying a gun," Sean said. "He always did in the past."

"Assuming he was carrying a weapon," the doctor said, "do you think someone else could have gotten it away from him and shot him?"

"Possible. It's also possible someone on the train had a gun and came looking for him. We have to explore all the avenues. And find out whether any of the other passengers is carrying a gun."

Pamela Larch, Jill thought. Miss Larch had a gun, tucked in her train case. And Miss Larch knew how to use it, or so she said. Though she claimed she always left the gun unloaded and simply carried it at her brother's insistence.

Would she have shot Victor Fontana? He had bought her a drink the first night out, and tonight, when he wanted to do the same thing, that had led to the quarrel with Doug, who'd come to Miss Larch's rescue, like a gallant knight. But try as she might, Jill couldn't reconcile the picture of the young woman from Mississippi, who seemed to be quite taken with Doug, shooting Mr. Fontana because of his unwanted attentions.

Who else would have a reason to be angry with Victor

Fontana? Who would be angry enough to kill him? Jill turned the questions over in her mind. Was Fontana's murder the result of something that had happened during the current journey? Or did it have something to do with Fontana himself, something that had happened in the past?

"Anyone could be carrying a gun," the conductor said. "We don't check people's luggage before they board. We just expect the passengers to behave with common sense and not shoot each other."

Mr. Winston, the Pullman conductor, harrumphed. "If you'll excuse my saying so, Mr. Dutton, the porters have seen many passengers behave without a shred of common sense. Of course, usually they don't talk about it."

"I know they don't, and the railroad appreciates their discretion." Mr. Dutton sighed. "Passengers getting drunk and acting like idiots is one thing. Murder is another."

"We should talk with Mr. Geddes," Jill said. "He and Mr. Fontana were business associates. They were on their way to San Francisco. Something about finalizing a business deal. I heard them discussing it."

"Good idea," Mr. Dutton said. "Mr. Winston, would you please get Mr. Geddes?"

"Should I tell him Mr. Fontana's dead?"

"No, leave that to me," Mr. Dutton said. "Just say that there's been an incident and we need to talk with him."

Rachel yawned and looked at her aunt. "We might as well go back to bed."

"I agree." The doctor stifled a yawn of her own and addressed the conductor. "Please wake me before we get into Wendover. I'm sure the sheriff's office will have questions, and I want to be available to answer them."

———

Art Geddes, roused from sleep, looked rumpled. He was dressed in blue pants and a shirt, unbuttoned at the neck. His brown hair was swept back from his long hangdog face, his jaw darkened by the five-o'clock shadow of a persistent beard. He looked around at the people gathered in the Silver Crescent's lounge. His eyes lingered on Sean Cleary before he spoke in his nasal Brooklyn accent. "What's going on? This porter here says the conductor wants to talk to me."

"Yes, I do," Mr. Dutton said. "I'm sorry to tell you this, but Mr. Fontana is dead."

"Dead?" Geddes's expression changed to one of consternation. "What do you mean, he's dead? When did this happen? How?"

"He was shot, sometime this evening," Mr. Dutton said. "We don't know exactly when it happened. The train will stop in Wendover and we'll turn all of this over to the sheriff's office there." The conductor glanced at Sean. "In the meantime, Mr. Cleary has some questions. He's a retired police officer from Denver."

Mr. Geddes snorted derisively, jerking his chin in Sean Cleary's direction. "I know who he is. Vic told me he was a cop. So you got him investigating Vic's murder? That's like the fox guarding the hen house. You better take a good long look at Cleary. I wouldn't be surprised if it was him that shot Vic."

Sean Cleary's face reddened. He got to his feet and took a step toward Geddes. "I didn't kill him. I didn't have anything to do with it."

"Bullshit," Geddes said. "You had it in for him, for years, since back when he was in Colorado."

The conductor raised his hand. "Watch your language. There's a lady present."

"Excuse me, Miss McLeod." Geddes nodded at Jill. "All I'm saying is Cleary and Vic had some history. I don't trust him."

"What sort of history?" Jill asked. Her uncle didn't say anything. "What happened?"

"I don't know all the details," Geddes said. "I just know when Vic saw Cleary was on the train, he said to me, that guy's a Denver cop. He made trouble for Vic before the war and Vic said he'd do it again if he got half a chance."

"You better believe I made trouble for him before the war," Sean snapped. "He was a hoodlum, working for gangsters."

"Says you." Geddes tossed the words back at Sean. "He never got convicted of anything. Never went to jail."

"He should have. He was in it up to his neck, bootlegging, hijacking, gambling. And murder."

"Sounds to me like maybe you got your half a chance, Cleary."

Both men faced off, talking at once. The conductor moved toward them, raising both hands. "Quiet, please. This isn't getting us anywhere. I think we'd better cool things off here."

"I have a question for you, Mr. Winston," Jill said. "Mr. Cleary was in his nightclothes when I went to his berth to get him. What about Mr. Geddes?"

The Pullman conductor nodded. "Yes, Miss McLeod. He was in his pajamas when he answered the door. I waited while he got dressed."

"So it appears both of you were in bed when Mr. Fontana was killed." Jill looked at Sean and Geddes, who glared at each other.

The conductor turned to Geddes. "What was your relationship with Mr. Fontana? How long had you known him?"

"I don't have to answer any of your questions," Geddes snapped. "You, or anybody else."

"Mr. Geddes, please," Jill said. "We're trying to find out what happened to Mr. Fontana, and why. It's possible that whoever killed Mr. Fontana could hurt someone else on the train. I would hate for that to happen. Wouldn't you? We need your help."

He thought about it for a moment. Then he relented. "All right, Miss McLeod. Since it's you that's asking. I don't know what I can tell you. We were business associates. That's how I know him. He was in the liquor business in Chicago. I'm in the liquor business in New York City. I met him in 'forty-seven. We started doing business. Him and me, we're back and forth between New York and Chicago. Nothing illegal." He shot a poisonous look at Sean. "Our dealings were on the up-and-up."

"When did you see him last?" Jill asked. "What time?"

"Tonight. We had a few drinks in the buffet. I don't know what time it was or what time I went to bed. I was tired. Traveling on trains makes me sleepy. I'll tell you something else," Geddes added. "You better talk to that other guy, Cleary's son, the one who's keeping company with the Southern belle. He was plenty steamed at Vic, because Vic was paying attention to the little lady.

The son, he was all wound up to hit Vic, but Cleary grabbed his arm."

Yes, what about Doug? Jill glanced at her uncle, knowing he was thinking the same thing. Instead he asked Geddes a question. "Did Fontana carry a gun? Did he have one with him this trip?"

"I don't know," Geddes said. "I mean, I know he carries a gun sometimes. But I don't have any idea if he brought one along this trip. If he did, I haven't seen it."

"What kind of gun?"

"A thirty-eight special. Just like most of the cops I know," Geddes added, his voice tart.

"Do you carry a gun?"

Geddes scowled at him. "Sometimes. For protection. Also a thirty-eight. But I don't have it with me this trip. Didn't see the need. We were just going to San Francisco on business."

"How did you and your partner get along?" Sean asked.

"He wasn't my partner," Geddes said. "Not exactly. We had a business relationship. We did some deals together. And we got along just fine."

"But you had a disagreement with Mr. Fontana," Jill said.

Geddes's face closed up. "I don't know what you're talking about."

"Perhaps I misunderstood. You and Mr. Fontana were talking about a business deal. It sounded to me as though you were having an argument."

Jill recalled the incident that afternoon, outside Mr. Geddes's bedroom aboard the transcontinental sleeper. The words had been rather heated. Geddes was concerned about the deal with the man in San Francisco. What was his name? Holt, that was it. Fontana had been upset with Geddes getting cold feet, as he put it, telling him that he worried too much. Fontana and Holt had done business before, during the war, he said, and they'd made a lot of money.

Geddes was staring at her. "I didn't know you were such an eavesdropper, Miss McLeod."

"I'm sorry. I didn't mean to listen. But Mr. Fontana was in the corridor while the two of you were talking, and his voice carried."

"So what's this deal?" Sean asked. "And why were you concerned about it?"

"It's a business deal. It's got nothing to do with who killed Vic," Geddes said.

"Maybe it does," Sean said. "If you didn't like the deal, maybe you killed your partner."

Geddes snarled at him. "I know what you're trying to do, Cleary. You think you're going to pin this on me, so as to take the heat off of yourself, or your son? Forget about it!"

"We'll talk to my son, in good time," Sean said.

"Are you done?" Geddes didn't even wait for an answer. "Well, I am. I'll be in my bedroom. Let me know when we get to the next stop." He stalked off.

The conductor sighed. "He has a point. What about your son, Mr. Cleary?"

"I can't believe Doug would have anything to do with this."

"Maybe not. But he did threaten to hit Mr. Fontana earlier this evening, in front of witnesses."

"We should talk with him, Uncle Sean," Jill said.

Sean's mouth thinned into a grim line. "My son and I don't get along very well. I think it would be a good idea if Jill comes with us."

They left the lounge and walked forward. As they passed the drawing room, Jill's eyes were drawn to the door, thinking of Mr. Fontana's body behind it. Did he have a wife? Children? She looked at bedroom C as well. Although Doug had visited Miss Larch in her bedroom earlier in the evening, Jill assumed that he had been enough of a gentleman to return to his own quarters.

Or had he? How well did she know her cousin? That wasn't always the case with men and women traveling on the *California Zephyr*. Things did go on behind the closed doors of the bedrooms in the sleeper cars. Jill had seen enough during her two years as a Zephyrette to know that.

More importantly, if Doug had been in bedroom C when the murder occurred, had he or Miss Larch heard anything? She guessed that the shot that killed Mr. Fontana in the drawing room had been loud enough to be heard in the next compartment.

Maybe not, though. The ever-present clack of the train's wheels on the rails could have muffled the noise. And it was clear that the pillow, with its black-rimmed hole, had been used as a silencer.

Her cousin and Pamela Larch weren't the only potential witnesses, though. Both Miss Grant and Miss Margate had been in the observation lounge when Jill left the Silver Crescent. Given the distance from the bedrooms, they might not have heard anything. But they'd both been sitting in chairs with a view of the corridor. Perhaps they'd seen something, or someone.

Avis Margate had removed her wedding ring before boarding the *California Zephyr* in Chicago. What about that note she had received, written in what Jill was sure was Victor Fontana's handwriting? Whatever was in that note had certainly put a troubled expression on Avis Margate's face.

When they reached the Silver Falls, Frank Nathan was awake. He stood in the doorway of the tiny porter's compartment, speaking to the conductor in a whisper. "Has something happened, sir? I notice you've been back and forth. Then we stopped. Now the train's going slower."

"We've had an incident in one of the other sleepers," the conductor said, his voice also low. "And there's a derailed freight ahead of us. Is Mr. Douglas Cleary in his bedroom?"

"Bedroom A, yes, sir. I made up his bed sometime during the evening. I saw him go in there before I went to bed."

Mr. Dutton nodded and led the way down the corridor between the roomettes, with Sean and Jill close behind him. They went around the corner to the passageway in front of the bedrooms. Coming toward them from the front of the train was Carl Mooney, the brakeman. He beckoned to the conductor.

"Looks like I'll have to leave this to you," Mr. Dutton said. He continued walking forward to join the brakeman, then both men headed toward the front of the train.

Uncle Sean knocked on the door of bedroom A. The door opened. Doug peered out, his blond hair tousled as he belted a robe over his pajamas. He stared out at them. "Jill? Dad? What's going on?"

"May we come in?" Sean asked.

Doug looked perplexed. "Be my guest." He stepped aside to let them into the bedroom, then he shut the door as they crowded in. "The train stopped a while back. When it started moving again, it's going really slow. Is there a problem?"

"A freight train derailment," Jill said. "We must be getting close to the place where it happened. That's probably why the brakeman came looking for the conductor."

"That's interesting," Doug said. "But I don't think that's why the two of you came to see me at this hour. What's going on?"

"Fontana's dead," Sean said. "Somebody shot him."

Jill felt the brakes of the *CZ* begin to engage. There was a jolt. She put her hand on the door jamb to steady herself.

Something slid out from under the bench seat that had been made into Doug's bed. It was a gun with a wooden grip, the light from above glistening on the dark metal surface of the weapon's body and short barrel.

Chapter Eighteen

D OUG'S FACE BLANCHED as the gun skittered across the floor. "I don't know where that came from. I've never seen it before."

"Hell's bells." Uncle Sean stared down at the gun. "Smith and Wesson, a thirty-eight special. Five-round capacity, swing-out cylinder." He pulled a handkerchief from his pocket and covered his hand. Then he knelt, picking up the gun. He carefully swung out the cylinder and looked inside. "No cartridges. But..." He sniffed the barrel. "It's been fired recently."

Doug shook his head. "Not by me. I had nothing to do with Fontana's death."

"I know that and so does Jill," his father said. "But this looks bad. I'll have to tell the conductor. Get dressed and go back to the lounge in the dome-observation car. We'll talk there."

Jill and Sean left bedroom A so Doug could change clothes. As her cousin shut the door, the train slowed again. Jill looked out the window. But she couldn't see anything in the darkness that covered the Great Salt Desert.

Uncle Sean was already walking back to the Silver Crescent. Jill hesitated, looking at the door to bedroom B. Should she wake Miss Margate and ask the questions that had been roiling in her mind? Or was she getting ahead of herself?

She raised her hand. Suddenly the door opened. Avis Margate stood there, wearing a peignoir set of peach-colored silk trimmed with white lace.

"I heard voices," Miss Margate said. "And it seems there are a lot of people walking back and forth. Now the train's moving at a snail's pace. What's happening?"

"A freight train derailed up ahead. So we'll be delayed."

Miss Margate smiled. "Is that why you were going to knock on my door? To tell me about a derailment?"

"No, it isn't," Jill said. "Mr. Fontana is dead."

Various emotions flickered over Miss Margate's face, including relief. "Come in, Miss McLeod. I think we should talk."

Once Jill was inside, Miss Margate shut the door and sat down on the bed she'd just vacated, running her hands through her tousled brunette curls. "You saw the note."

Jill nodded. "I did. I wondered about that, because you seemed so upset. Then I recognized Mr. Fontana's handwriting, because he'd given me a letter to mail. What was in the note?"

Avis Margate's mouth twisted. "He threatened me, the son of a bitch."

"I can guess why," Jill said. "I know you're married. I saw you take off your wedding ring in the Chicago station."

The other woman smiled. "You don't miss a trick, do you? You must see a lot riding the rails."

"Yes, I do. Ordinarily a passenger's private life is none of my business."

"Unless I kill one of the passengers. Is that it?"

Jill wasn't sure she'd have said it that way. But now that the subject was out in the open, she might as well proceed. "I have some questions."

"I'll bet you do." Avis Margate leaned back on the bed and crossed one shapely leg over the other. The peignoir slipped off her shoulders and the V-neck of her nightgown revealed the top of her lush bosom. "Well, ask away."

"How did Mr. Fontana know you were married?"

"Evidently he met me and my husband at some function in Chicago," Avis said. "Not that I recall meeting Fontana. If I'd known that, I would have steered clear of him."

"What happened?"

"Well, there's a story. My husband's an attorney. Socially prominent, respectable, fine old family. He's also boring and he works all the time. So I decided to go visit a friend in San Francisco and kick up my heels. Be single again, for just a little while. What better place to start than on the train? I thought it would safe and anonymous. Nobody knows me, right?" She laughed.

"But I was wrong. The first night out of Chicago, at dinner, I sat at the same table as Fontana and Geddes. We were bantering back and forth. Well, Fontana and I were bantering. Geddes is a cold fish. He couldn't banter if his life depended on it. But Fontana can be charming when he wants to. The little bastard," she added.

"After dinner, I came back here, to my bedroom. Then later I went to the lounge in the buffet car. While I was there, Fontana and Geddes showed up. Geddes left a while later, and so did the people I was talking with. Fontana moved over to my table and bought me a drink. Fontana started taking liberties, so I decided to call it a night and go to bed. He followed me, and grabbed me in the hall. Damned octopus. It felt like he had eight hands. I broke away from him and slapped him, hard. He called me a bitch."

Jill nodded. She'd thought it was Mr. Fontana she'd heard outside her door the previous night. Now that was confirmed, and so was the identity of the other person, Avis Margate.

"I got out of there and came back here to my bedroom. Thank God he didn't follow me. But today I got that damn poisoned pen note from Fontana. He said he was going to tell my husband. And believe me, my husband will be furious." Miss Margate cocked her head to one side and looked at Jill. "So what you want to know, Miss Zephyrette, is whether I would kill Fontana over that."

"The thought crossed my mind," Jill said.

"When I got the note I wanted to wring his damn neck. But that was immediate. I cooled off later. How did Fontana die?"

"He was shot."

"There you go," Avis said. "I don't have a gun. Wouldn't know how to use one, really. Anything else?"

"Tonight, when I did my last walk-through, you, Miss Grant and Miss Ranleigh were in the observation lounge. That was before we got to Salt Lake City at five minutes after ten. Miss Ranleigh left before I did. What time did you leave?"

"Not long after you did. I'm not sure of the time, though. Miss Grant was still there when I left, smoking like a chimney and reading."

"Did you talk with her at all?"

Avis shook her head. "Good Lord, no. Miss Grant is not the most stimulating conversationalist in the world."

"No, she isn't. Did you see or hear anything unusual?"

Miss Margate thought about it. "I saw Mr. Cleary, the younger one, leaving Miss Larch's bedroom. Being a gentleman, I supposed. It wouldn't have surprised me if he'd spent the night with her. He's an attractive man, but he hasn't paid any attention to me, not since he first laid eyes on Miss Larch. That was before I decided to call it a night. I left the observation lounge. Said good night to the porter, he was in the kitchen by the buffet. Oh, yes, I did see that tall man, Mr. Oliver. He and his wife are in bedroom E. He was coming into the observation car just as I was leaving."

Jill nodded. She'd seen Mr. Oliver walking toward the rear of the train when she'd left a few minutes earlier. She needed to talk with him, and Miss Grant.

"Who else did you see?"

"Some man in a bathrobe coming out of the men's room in the sleeper with all the curtains."

"The sixteen-section sleeper," Jill said.

"Yes, that's the one. And when I got to this car, I did see the Frenchman, Florian, that nice-looking graduate student." Miss Margate smiled. "He was doing some serious necking with that girl Lois in his roomette. I'll bet she's fifteen or sixteen, even though she looks older. Serious jailbait. Anyway, I went past them, here to my bedroom. It was late, so I went to bed. I didn't see anyone else. And I didn't hear anything, until I heard you and your uncle next door, talking to Mr. Cleary. By the way, when I saw him earlier in the lounge car, he was ready to deck Fontana."

Avis Margate chuckled. "I would have paid money to see that."

Chapter Nineteen

JILL STEPPED OUT OF Avis Margate's room just as Doug was leaving bedroom A. He'd taken his time getting dressed. Unlike Mr. Geddes, who'd also been roused from sleep, Doug was impeccably turned out in the clothes he'd worn earlier.

"Am I tried and convicted?" he asked, the lightness of his tone belying the seriousness of the question. "Believe me, Jill. I didn't kill the man. Someone planted that gun in my bedroom."

"I believe you," she told him. "But we've got to convince other people. The train is going to stop in Wendover and the conductor will turn the whole mess over to the sheriff's office there. I hope we can get things cleared up before we get there."

"So do I. Let's go." He gave her hand a squeeze. Jill looked at the door to bedroom C, where Cora Grant slept. Then she followed Doug back through the car. As they passed roomette ten, where Florian Rapace was berthed, she paused. Inside the roomette she heard a loud snore. M. Rapace was evidently asleep, and she hoped Lois Demarest wasn't with him.

The train had slowed to a crawl but it still hadn't stopped. They must be getting close to the freight derailment.

When they went through the sixteen-section sleeper, all was quiet. Jill looked at the upper berth where she'd seen Patty Demarest earlier. Was Lois in the lower berth? Had she and Florian seen anything while Lois was back in the Silver Falls?

They reached the Silver Crescent and walked back to the observation lounge. Doug glanced at his father. Then, looking relaxed and unruffled, he faced the conductor. "I'm Douglas Cleary. You want to ask me some questions?"

"Bill Dutton, conductor with the Western Pacific Railroad. We're trying to get to the bottom of this mess. I joined the train in Salt Lake City. Before the Denver and Rio Grande Western conductor left, he briefed me, and said you'd been involved in an altercation with Mr. Fontana. Could you tell me about that?"

"It was after dinner, after eight, I think. Miss Larch and I went to the lounge in the buffet car, for a drink."

"Miss Larch is a passenger? A friend of yours?"

Doug nodded. "Yes, to both questions. She's traveling in a bedroom here in the observation car. Anyway, Mr. Fontana was there in the lounge, with Mr. Geddes. It was obvious he'd been drinking, quite a bit. He was upset with me because we'd been playing poker in his drawing room earlier in the afternoon and I won several hands. Then he insisted that Miss Larch have a drink with him. She wasn't interested. He wouldn't take 'no' for an answer. I told him to back off and leave her alone. Then he said something insulting."

"What did he say?" Mr. Dutton asked.

"I hesitate to repeat such a crude remark in front of Miss McLeod." Doug glanced at Jill. "Miss Larch was understandably offended, and visibly upset. I took offense as well. I would have hit Mr. Fontana if my father hadn't stopped me. At that point, Mr. Fontana and his friend left the lounge."

"Did you see Mr. Fontana later in the evening?" Mr. Dutton asked.

"No, I didn't. Miss Larch and I had a drink with my father in the lounge. Then she and I came back here to the observation car."

This seemed to satisfy Mr. Dutton for the moment. The conductor pointed at the gun on one of the small center tables. "This gun was found in your bedroom."

"It was under the bed," Doug said. "It tumbled out when the train slowed down. As I told my father, I've never seen it before."

"How did it get there?"

"I assume someone put it there. I was in and out of my bedroom during the evening. As you know, those bedrooms don't lock from the outside, unless the porter does it. So anyone could have gone inside."

"True enough," Mr. Dutton said. He looked over at the Pullman conductor. "Mr. Winston, talk with the porter in that car, to see if he saw anything." Mr. Winston nodded and left the car.

Uncle Sean was looking at the gun on the table. "Who else on the train would be carrying a gun? I figure Fontana was, but I don't think I should compromise the crime scene by looking for it."

It was time for Jill to tell them what she knew. "Miss Larch has a gun. She keeps it in her train case, unloaded. I saw it earlier today when I was making dinner reservations." And so had Cora Grant, she thought. "Miss Larch's gun looks like the gun found in Doug's bedroom. At least it has the same sort of wood on the grip."

Doug looked surprised at this revelation. "I wasn't aware that Miss Larch had a gun. But if you think her gun is the one you found in my bedroom, there's an easy solution. Knock on Miss Larch's door and see if she still has the gun."

"I agree," Mr. Dutton said. "It's time we got her version of what happened this evening."

Pamela Larch looked sleepy, her blond hair tumbling around her shoulders of her green bathrobe. She peered at Jill from a two-inch opening in her bedroom door, then frowned as she saw the two men behind Jill. "My goodness, Miss McLeod. And Mr. Cleary and the conductor. It's quite late, isn't it? What's the matter?"

"This is Mr. Dutton, the conductor. We'd like to talk with you."

"Why?"

"I'm afraid something has happened to Mr. Fontana. He's dead."

Miss Larch gasped. "Dead? How?"

"He was shot," Mr. Dutton said. "Miss Larch, I understand you have a gun."

"Oh, my goodness. You can't think that I would... I don't even keep it loaded. I told Miss McLeod that. I shouldn't have brought it with me in the first place."

"May we see your gun?" the conductor asked.

"Of course. It's in my train case." Miss Larch backed away, opening the door wider. Her beige train case was on the floor next to her bed. She opened it and took out the top tray, makeup spilling out as she set it on the bed. She pulled out her lacy brassiere and silk panties, tossing them onto the blanket. Then she held out the case so they could see what was inside.

Sean pulled his handkerchief from his pocket and removed the gun from the case, swinging out the cylinder. There were no cartridges inside. Sean sniffed the barrel. "Interesting. It's essentially the same gun as the other. Both are Smith and Wesson thirty-eight caliber revolvers. Model Thirty-Six, also called the Chief's Special. They're small, easy to conceal, with a short barrel. And they both happen to have wood grips."

"But the one we found in Doug's bedroom was darker, almost black," Jill said.

Sean nodded. "Yes, it is. That gun has what's called a blued finish. It's a protective coating to prevent rust and it gives the metal that blue-black look. Miss Larch's gun here is nickel-plated, a shiny finish. More importantly, the gun we found had been fired recently, and this one hasn't. This probably isn't the murder weapon. But we can hang onto it and give it to the sheriff's deputies when we get to Wendover."

"Please, take it," Miss Larch said. "I don't want it anymore."

Sean complied, removing the box of cartridges from the case as well.

"Can we talk further, Miss Larch?" the conductor asked. "We'd like to ask some questions about what happened this evening."

"Of course. Just let me get dressed. I won't be long."

When she emerged from bedroom C a few minutes later, Pamela Larch was wearing the same soft green dress she'd worn during the day, her blond hair falling to her shoulders. She sat down in one of the observation lounge chairs and answered questions, confirming Doug's account of what had happened earlier that evening.

"I did have a drink with Mr. Fontana on the first night out," she said. "But he couldn't keep his hands to himself, so I left. Tonight he wanted to buy me a drink but I said no. He just wouldn't leave me alone. And then he said something quite nasty. I don't think I could bring myself to repeat it." She shuddered. "Then Douglas, Mr. Cleary, came to my rescue. They almost came to blows, but that didn't happen. After that Mr. Fontana and his friend left, and we stayed in the lounge there in the buffet car. I hadn't met Mr. Cleary, Douglas's father, until then, so I was glad to get acquainted."

"Me, too," Sean said. "Now, after that I went to the coffee shop to get a piece of pie. Where did you and Doug go?"

"We came back here, just sat in my bedroom and talked. Ordinarily I supposed we'd have gone to the buffet or back here to the lounge. But I was afraid we might encounter Mr. Fontana in the buffet."

"You would have, ma'am," Lonnie Clark said. "Like I told the conductor and Mr. Cleary here, Mr. Fontana and Mr. Geddes were in the buffet, all right, drinking."

The conductor nodded. "Quite heavily, you said."

"On my last walk-through of the train," Jill said, "before we got to Salt Lake City, I came back here to the Silver Crescent. I saw Mr. Fontana and Mr. Geddes in the buffet. Then they left. Let's see. Rachel Ranleigh was here in the observation lounge, along with Miss Margate and Miss Grant. Miss Ranleigh left. When I left, I saw Mr. Oliver walking back through the transcontinental sleeper. I spoke with Miss Margate a short time ago. She woke up when you and I knocked on Doug's door," Jill said, looking at her uncle. "She told me when she left the car to go back to bed, she saw Mr. Oliver entering this car. Mr. Clark, did you see him?"

The porter shook his head. "No, ma'am, I didn't. I was in the buffet and the kitchen cleaning up at that time. I did see Miss Margate walk by. But I didn't see Mr. Oliver. I must have been in the buffet."

"Henry Oliver?" Sean's expression changed. "We'd better talk with him."

Chapter Twenty

A T THE CONDUCTOR'S REQUEST, Mr. Winston, the Pullman conductor, left the lounge, heading for the Silver Falls to ask Henry Oliver if he would join them. Then the brakeman appeared, waving at the conductor. "I'll be back," Mr. Dutton said. The two men huddled together at the foot of the stairs leading up to the Vista-Dome. As the brakeman left, a man in a dark blue bathrobe appeared. It was Stanley Carson, his hand on his cane as he walked back to the lounge to join the people gathered there.

"I woke up and heard voices," he said. "There seem to be a lot of comings and goings, and the train is slower than usual. Has something happened?"

"This is Mr. Carson," Jill said. "He and his family are traveling in bedrooms A and B in this car. We've slowed down because of a freight train derailment up ahead."

"As to the comings and goings," the conductor said, "Mr. Fontana is dead, murdered. This is Mr. Cleary, a retired detective from Denver. We're trying to gather information."

"Mr. Cleary. Yes, I met you today, up in the Vista-Dome," Mr. Carson said. "I also met another Mr. Cleary, who's been spending a lot of time with Miss Larch in bedroom C."

"That's me," Doug said.

"My son, Douglas," Sean added. "Mr. Fontana was shot, probably sometime after we left Provo. Did you hear anything?"

"No, I didn't. I'm usually a sound sleeper. Perhaps the noise of the train muffled the shot." Mr. Carson sat down. He stretched his legs in front of him and rubbed his right leg, as though it was giving him some discomfort.

"Mr. Carson," Jill said, "when I was making dinner reservations, you asked for the name of the man traveling in the drawing room. When I told you it was Mr. Fontana, you said you'd heard the name before. In what context?"

"In a criminal context, Miss McLeod." Stanley Carson looked around the lounge. "I'm an attorney with the California Department of Justice. We moved to Sacramento in 1946. Before that, I worked for the Illinois Attorney General's Office." He pointed at the cane. "I was injured during the war and sent back to the States for rehab, and then discharged. I went back to Illinois because that's where my family was, and my wife's family. Early in 1945, my office was involved in a joint operation involving the Office of Price Administration. It concerned the theft and illegal sale of gas rationing stamps."

Rationing. Jill remembered her dinner conversation about the war, and rationing.

Where there were restrictions there were also people trying to get around them. People traded or sold rationing stamps, even though they weren't supposed to. Things could be had on the black market, though that was definitely illegal. And there was a "red market" as well, with people selling lower-grade meat for higher-grade prices, or selling meat that contained more fat or bone than was allowed.

Couldn't get a tire for your car? Someone might sidle up to you at a service station and whisper, "I know where you can get one." And some people followed through on that offer, no questions asked, just the quick exchange of money, or coupons.

During the war people had even resorted to rustling, helping themselves to cattle on Colorado ranches. That had prompted Jill and her brother, Drew, to devise a security plan for the chicken coop in Grandma's backyard. It must have worked, because they didn't lose any chickens, or eggs.

Sean Cleary nodded. "We had our share of problems in Denver during the war. Trucks filled with goods that got hijacked before they got to their destinations. We'd find the trucks later, empty, and whatever was inside was long gone, for sale on the black market. We also had a rash of robberies, thieves breaking into homes and taking ration books. And there was a break-in at the OPA in Denver. The bad guys took gas rationing coupons and C stickers. They were already counterfeiting the stuff. Then they got a big haul of the real ones to sell on the black market."

"It was the same in Chicago," Stanley Carson said. "And it was a very lucrative business."

"Was Victor Fontana involved in the Chicago investigation?" Jill asked.

"Yes, he was. So was an associate of his, Charles Holt. But Fontana and Holt were slippery. We never could pin anything on him."

Jill looked at her uncle. "Mr. Fontana and Mr. Geddes were on their way to San Francisco to finalize a business deal with a man named Charles Holt. That's what I overheard them arguing about, when I was in the corridor. Mr. Fontana said he and Holt had made a lot of money during the war."

"Yes, they did," Carson said. "Most of it illegal. But they were very good at hiding their tracks. Anyway, the investigation my office took part in involved a ring of mobsters who were stealing gas rationing stamps from OPA offices around Chicago. They were selling them on the black market and they operated out of a nightclub in Chicago, a place called the Bell Tower."

The Bell Tower? Jill looked at Doug, remembering their earlier talk about the nightclub.

"Hey, I know that place," Doug said. "I went there, before the war. Good food, terrific band, a great singer."

"Yes, the club was very popular," Carson said. "Plenty of customers. And they came not only for the food and the band, but for the gas ration stamps. In the course of our investigation, we learned Victor Fontana and Charles Holt owned the nightclub. We knew Fontana was a liquor distributor. When we dug deeper, we found out about his mobster past. He was working for the Smaldones in Denver, and when he moved to Chicago he forged ties with Frank Nitti's operation."

"The old Capone mob," Uncle Sean said.

"That's right. Fontana's wife is the daughter of one of Nitti's lieutenants. And Holt is connected, too. He worked for the Chicago Outfit, Capone's organization, in the thirties, which is probably how he and Fontana met. Holt also knew Mickey Cohen."

"The mobster in Los Angeles?" Uncle Sean asked.

"Cohen's in jail now, for tax evasion," Carson said. "But we're keeping an eye on his associates, like Holt, who recently set up shop in San Francisco. So whatever deal Fontana and Geddes were cooking up with Holt bears looking at. I'll be contacting my office as soon as we get to Sacramento."

"How come you weren't able to catch Fontana and Holt?" the conductor asked.

Carson shook his head. "We raided the Bell Tower. But someone—I suspect one of the Chicago cops—tipped off both men before the raid. We didn't catch them. But we found a stash of stolen coupons and stickers, and arrested several nightclub employees who were involved in the ring."

"Married or not, Mr. Fontana liked the ladies," Jill said, her expression thoughtful. "That's what everyone says. He forced his attentions on two women during the trip. Miss Larch and someone else."

"Fontana had a mistress," Carson said. "Several of them, over the years. At the time we were conducting the investigation, he was involved with a woman who was a singer and dancer at the nightclub."

"Belle La Tour," Jill said.

"That's right." Carson looked at her with curiosity. "How did you know that?"

Jill glanced at Doug. "Her name came up when Doug was telling me about the Bell Tower. Whatever happened to her?"

"She went to jail," Carson said. "She's one of the nightclub employees who was involved in the ration coupon ring. Belle La Tour was a stage name, of course. Her real name was Elsie Gomulka. She was a local girl, grew up in a Polish neighborhood called Bucktown."

Jill mulled over what Carson had revealed about the rationing scam, and how it ended. Fontana had no doubt masterminded the whole thing. But he hadn't gone to jail for it. Someone else had. Was that someone Cora Grant?

They looked up as Henry Oliver walked into the observation lounge. "Miss McLeod. I thought you would have turned in for the night. I don't think I've met everyone."

"Stanley Carson, Sacramento." Mr. Carson remained seated, but offered his hand.

"Douglas Cleary," Doug said. "I believe I met your wife earlier. This is my father —"

"Sean Cleary," Oliver said. "I thought I recognized you when I saw you in the dining car."

"And I recognized you. Henry Oliver. You have a farm northwest of Arvada."

Oliver frowned as he looked over the people assembled in the lounge. "So why did you get me out of bed in the middle of the night?"

"I'm the one who asked the Pullman conductor to get you out of bed," Mr. Dutton said. "I'm Bill Dutton, the conductor. We're conducting an investigation, and we'd like to ask you some questions. One of the passengers, Mr. Fontana, is dead."

Something flickered across Oliver's face, then he masked it. "Why me? What's that got to do with the price of wheat?"

"You and Fontana were friends," Sean said.

"I knew who he was." There was a wary undercurrent in Oliver's laconic voice. "I wouldn't call that being friends."

"Business associates, then." Sean fixed him with a stare. "During the Depression, you had a still on your property."

Oliver hesitated. "It wasn't my still."

"It was on your land, and you were paid to ignore it. The still belonged to the Smaldones, and Vic Fontana was the guy who handed you the money."

Oliver gave a derisive snort. "You're free with your accusations, Cleary. Especially when you can't prove them. Lots of people had stills. Besides, it's ancient history. Prohibition's been gone twenty years."

"What happened at the bank in Arvada in nineteen thirty-seven isn't ancient history. It's as fresh in my mind as if it happened yesterday."

"A bank in Arvada?" Jill looked at her uncle. "What happened?"

"Somebody died," Doug said. "I remember. You went to the funeral."

"That's right," Sean said. "A good man died. His name was Tom Kendrick, and he was a friend of mine, a Denver cop. He was a uniform, working a Denver beat. But his salary didn't go far enough, so he moonlighted as a bank guard in Arvada. Then one day in the spring of 'thirty-seven, Vic Fontana and two of his buddies robbed that bank. They got away with a lot of cash. Right after that, Fontana left Denver and moved to Chicago, where he used his cut of the bank money to buy into the liquor business. During that robbery, Fontana shot Tom Kendrick in the head. Kendrick died right there in the bank lobby. The robbers hightailed it out of the bank and went west. They hid out on Oliver's farm."

"You can't prove that," Oliver said.

"I notice you don't deny it," Sean shot back. "You were an accessory to that murder."

Oliver scowled. "The hell I was. I knew nothing about it. You were a Denver cop. The Arvada bank job wasn't even your jurisdiction."

"Kendrick was my friend. That makes it my jurisdiction." The two men glared at each other.

Doug put a hand on his father's arm. "Now I remember where I heard Fontana's name. You talked about him, back when Tom Kendrick was killed. You blame Fontana for Kendrick's death. And you think Oliver helped Fontana after the fact. But that's in the past, Dad. We need to figure out what's going on now."

"I agree," Mr. Carson said. "Let's stay focused on Fontana's death."

Jill looked at her uncle, nodding. "That's what Mr. Geddes was implying earlier, when he said you had it in for Mr. Fontana, because of something that happened in the past."

"And that means whatever you're doing here," Oliver said, "this so-called investigation, is tainted."

"You can call it tainted if you like," Sean said. "But I didn't kill Fontana. I didn't like the man and I sure as hell blamed him for Tom's death. But I didn't kill him. I went to bed after you saw me in the coffee shop, Jill. What about you, Oliver? Where were you?"

The farmer shook his head. "I didn't kill him either. And I was in my bedroom with my wife."

"But you did walk back here, to the observation car," Jill said. "I saw you in the transcontinental sleeper earlier, before we got to Salt Lake City. You were headed this way. Another passenger saw you enter this car. But the porter didn't see you, and he was in the buffet kitchen. So you must have gone into one of the bedrooms, or the drawing room. I don't think you visited the Carsons or Miss Larch. So that leaves the drawing room. You were going to see Mr. Fontana. Why?"

Oliver looked at her through narrowed eyes. Finally he spoke. "All right. I did go see Fontana. Just don't say anything about this to my wife. There's no reason to involve her in any of this. She doesn't know anything about...what went on in the past."

Jill suspected that Trudy Oliver knew of, and chose to ignore, her husband's past involvement with Victor Fontana and the still that was supposedly hidden on the Olivers' farm. As for the present, that was another matter.

"I didn't know Fontana was on the train," Oliver continued, "until I saw him in the dining car earlier today, when my wife and I were having lunch. I recognized him, even though it had been fifteen years since I'd seen him. And he recognized me. He came up to me later in the day and said he wanted to discuss a business proposition. I tried putting him off. But he's persistent. He wouldn't take 'no' for an answer. Finally he wore me down. He told me to come back to his drawing room later in the evening. It was before we got to Salt Lake City. That must be when you and that other passenger saw me."

"What sort of business proposition?" Jill asked.

"It wasn't illegal, if that's what you're thinking." Oliver's voice held a challenge as he looked at Jill and Sean. "Fontana wanted to buy some of my land. You see, the town of Arvada has grown out to my farm. Fontana wanted to put up a warehouse, get into the liquor distribution business in the Denver area. I told him I wasn't interested. I had no intention of selling him the land. But he kept pushing. Finally I told him I'd think about it. Then I left. And I'm telling you, Vic Fontana was alive when I left that drawing room."

"Did you see anyone else when you left?" Jill asked.

Oliver shook his head. "No. I didn't see the porter. And I didn't see anyone back here."

Jill thought about this. Miss Grant was still in the lounge when Henry Oliver arrived in the Silver Crescent, but she must have returned to her own car while he was in the drawing room.

They looked up as Mr. Jessup, the porter from the transcontinental sleeper, entered the lounge. "Miss McLeod, I went looking for you and Mr. Winston told me you were back here. We need your first-aid kit. That lady from England, Miss Brandon, she fell and hit her head."

"Oh, no. I hope she's not too badly injured." Jill reached for her first-aid kit. If Miss Brandon's injuries were more serious, she would send the porter for Dr. Ranleigh.

Jill and the porter headed up the corridor past the bedrooms and went through the vestibule into the Silver Rapids, the transcontinental sleeper. Edith Brandon stood in the doorway of bedroom C, wrapped in a warm wool robe the color of sherry. She held a cloth to her right temple.

"Miss Brandon," Jill said. "The porter says you fell and hurt yourself. Let me take a look."

The Englishwoman pulled the cloth away from her head. The cloth was stained with blood and so was her gray hair. Jill looked closer and saw a small abrasion on the skin just below the hairline.

"I'm sorry to be a bother," the Englishwoman said. "I got out of bed to answer a call of nature. When I came out of the WC, I stumbled, tripped over my own feet, and bumped my head. I feel a bit silly about the whole thing. It's bled a bit, as you see. I put a damp cloth on it. It's probably nothing, but I thought I ought to have someone take a look at it. So I rang for the porter and asked him to fetch you."

"It's not a bother at all," Jill said. "Any time you hit your head, it's good to have it checked out. Now, if you'll go inside and have a seat, I'll take a look at this. And if it is more serious, we do have a doctor on board, and I'll send for her."

Miss Brandon backed into the bedroom and sat down on the bed. Jill followed, setting the first-aid kit on the floor. She examined the wound. Fortunately, the abrasion looked minor. "When you hit your head did you lose consciousness at all? Or see stars?"

"No, to both questions," Miss Branson said.

"Good. I don't think you have a concussion," Jill said. "Please tilt your head upward." Miss Brandon did so, then she winced a bit as Jill cleaned the abrasion with some antiseptic.

"I notice the train is moving quite slowly," Miss Brandon said.

"We've had a slight delay up ahead, a freight train derailment. It will be cleared up soon, and we'll make up some time."

"No matter. I'm sure I'll sleep well once I get back to bed."

Jill dabbed Merthiolate on the abrasion and covered it with a small bandage. "That should do it." She put the supplies back into the first-aid kit.

Miss Brandon looked up at Jill. "Thank you, Miss McLeod, for all you do looking after the passengers. It's greatly appreciated. By the way, I had a lovely dinner in the dining car. The Rocky Mountain trout was every bit as delicious as I'd been told. I was at the same table as your uncle, Mr. Cleary. He's quite an interesting fellow. He was telling us about some of the cases he investigated over the years."

"Yes, I know he was."

"I found his stories fascinating, and so did Monsieur Rapace, the young Frenchman. When he was paying attention, of course." Miss Brandon smiled. "He's quite taken with that young woman named Lois, and we were seated right across the aisle from her. She was making eyes at him all through dinner. If I'm not mistaken, she's a good deal younger than he is. I'll bet her mother finds her a handful. In fact, later in the evening, I saw her sneaking out, no doubt to join him."

"Sneaking out? How did she do that?" Jill asked.

"I'd been up to the Vista-Dome in the lounge car. It was after nine, after we left that town called Provo. Once we were away from the town, the stars were marvelous. I got a bit sleepy and decided to go to bed. So I walked back here to my car. I was going through the next car up, the one with all the curtained berths, and that's when I saw her. A lot of the folks in that car had gone to bed already, and the lights were rather dim. But I saw Lois quite clearly. She came out of a lower berth, all wrapped in her bathrobe. She took it off and I saw that she had her clothes on underneath. She put on her shoes and when she saw me, she held her finger to her lips. Like this." Miss Brandon demonstrated the familiar signal for keeping one's mouth shut. "Then she went haring off in the direction of the lounge. I assume she was meeting the young Frenchman."

"What time was this?"

"I think it was around nine-thirty," Miss Brandon said. "It was definitely before we got to Salt Lake City. I was in bed by then. And I should get back to bed now. A good night's sleep will cure what ails me."

When Jill left Miss Brandon's room, she gave Mr. Jessup, the porter, an update. Then she stopped in the corridor, thinking about what Miss Brandon had told her about Lois Demarest. Jill had seen Lois and Florian in the coffee shop during her last walk-through. That was after the stop in Provo.

I really do need to talk with Lois, Jill thought. The girl had been moving around the train during the time Mr. Fontana had been shot, and during the time someone hid the gun in Doug's bedroom. It was possible she had seen something during her after-hours perambulations, something that could point to the killer.

"Mr. Jessup," Jill said to the porter. "Would you keep an eye on my first-aid kit? There's someone I need to talk with in the next car."

He nodded and took the bag from her. Then Jill turned and walked forward, heading for the Silver Maple.

Chapter Twenty-One

WHEN SHE ENTERED the sixteen-section sleeper, Jill counted curtains and found the upper berth where she'd seen Patty Demarest, fourth from the end. She tweaked the edge of the curtain and peered inside the lower berth. Was the occupant Lois, or her mother?

Her mother, as it turned out. Milly Demarest was asleep, lying on her side, with her mouth slightly open and one hand tucked near her face. She wore a high-necked flannel nightgown and her hair was sticking up from her head.

Jill touched Mrs. Demarest's hand and whispered, hoping that she wouldn't wake anyone else in the vicinity. "Mrs. Demarest. Please wake up."

Mrs. Demarest's eyes opened and she stared out at Jill. "What's the matter? We can't be to Winnemucca yet."

"I'm sorry to wake you. I need to talk with your daughter Lois."

Milly Demarest struggled to a sitting position and squinted at Jill. "Lois? What's she done?"

"Could we please go into the ladies' room? That way we won't disturb anyone else."

Mrs. Demarest swung her legs out from the bed, pushing the curtain aside as she stuck her feet into a pair of carpet slippers. She reached for the green flannel robe that had been bunched into a heap next to her pillow. Then she stood, putting on the robe and tying the belt around her waist. Once she was upright, she went to the lower berth to her right and opened the curtain.

"Get up, Lois. Into the ladies' room. Now."

Inside the berth, Lois sat up, wearing a shimmery red nightgown that revealed a lot of her bosom. She opened her mouth to argue, but her mother cut her off. "Not a word out of you. Get moving."

Lois looked mulish, but she did as she was told. She put on her slippers and a robe that matched the nightgown, and got to her feet. Her face looked sulky and a grumbling noise escaped her pursed lips as she walked past her mother and stalked toward the ladies' room at the end of the car. Mrs. Demarest followed.

Just then, Patty pulled aside the curtain in the berth above her mother's. Then she too exited her bed, clambering down the ladder in her pajamas and socks. She scampered toward the ladies' room, with Jill close behind.

"Now what is this about?" Mrs. Demarest said when they were all inside.

Jill turned to face the older daughter. "Lois, I need to ask whether you saw anything unusual this evening. You were in the buffet-lounge car when I did my walk-through, before we got to Salt Lake City. And you were seen later, in the Silver Falls, the next sleeper car."

"Wait a minute." Milly Demarest glared at Lois. "We went to bed right after the train left Provo, about a quarter after nine. I saw you get into that berth."

Lois didn't say anything. She refused to meet her mother's angry gaze. Instead, she smoothed a hand through her dark hair, her lips clamped shut in an unrepentant pout, her arms folded over the front of her red robe.

"She wasn't sleeping," Patty said from the doorway. "As soon as Mama went to bed, Lois got up. I saw her. She had her robe on over her clothes. She took it off and sneaked out. She made the pillows look like she was still in the bed."

"You little rat." Lois raised her hand and directed a slap at Patty.

But her mother was quicker. Milly grabbed Lois's hand with her own, shaking her daughter hard. Her words came out in an angry hiss. "I have just about had it with you, and your behavior.

You have some explaining to do. Where did you go? Who were you with?"

Lois tilted up her chin, her voice defiant. "I was with Florian."

"Who the hell is Florian?" her mother snapped.

"He's a Frenchman," Lois said, tossing her head. "Very sophisticated."

"I'll sophisticate you." Mrs. Demarest shook Lois's arm again. "What the hell were you thinking? Or were you thinking at all? Leave it to you to throw yourself at some French roué. You're only sixteen, for God's sake."

Patty looked alarmed now, looking from her mother to the closed door of the women's restroom. "Mama, be quiet. People will hear you."

Jill said in her most placating voice, "To be fair, I wouldn't call Monsieur Rapace a roué. He's a graduate student at Northwestern. He seems to be a very nice young man, probably twenty-three, twenty-four at most."

"I don't care how nice he is. He's still too old for her," Mrs. Demarest said, her voice low and angry. "I swear, when we get home, I'm going to lock you up until you're twenty-one. Then you can go catting around all you want. But not until then."

Now Lois looked as though she was about to cry. "I wasn't catting around. We sat and talked in the buffet-lounge car, and then we went up to the Vista-Dome in the Silver Chalet. To look at the stars. After that we went to his roomette." She tilted her chin, unrepentant. "He kissed me, but other than that, he was a perfect gentleman."

Milly Demarest looked as though she was about to explode. "A perfect gentleman does not entertain a sixteen-year-old girl in his roomette in the middle of the night."

"It wasn't the middle of the night. Besides, I told him I was eighteen."

Mrs. Demarest opened her mouth, ready to lob another salvo at her daughter, but Jill raised her hand. "This is something you'll have to figure out for yourselves. I really need to ask Lois some questions."

"Why?" Mrs. Demarest released Lois's arm and now looked protective.

Jill started to answer, then stopped as the door of the women's restroom opened. A passenger came in, a girl about Patty's age, looking rumpled in her pajamas. She glanced their way, then went into one of the toilets. When she was finished, she flushed, came out and washed her hands. Then she left the restroom.

"There's been an incident in one of the sleeper cars," Jill said. "A crime. Lois, I need to know if you saw anyone or anything while you were walking through the train. Anything out of the ordinary."

"What kind of crime?" Mrs. Demarest asked. "A robbery? Or worse?"

Lois looked at Jill, alarm on her face. "Is somebody dead?"

Jill nodded. "Yes. That's why it's important."

"How did you know that?" her mother asked.

"That older lady," Lois said. "The doctor. Ranleigh, that's her name. I met her and her niece in the dome-observation car earlier this afternoon. Then later, I saw her walking toward the back of the train. She had her doctor's bag with her. I wondered if one of the passengers was sick. But now you say someone's dead."

"A passenger was killed," Jill said. "Murdered."

"Murdered." Mrs. Demarest ran her hand through her untidy hair. "Good God, a murder. What else did you see, Lois? Start from the beginning."

Lois looked pleased with herself. She was enjoying being the center of attention instead of the object of her mother's censure.

"Well," she said, drawing out the word. "After dinner, Florian asked me to meet him in the buffet-lounge car later in the evening. I knew you wouldn't let me go with him. So I had to figure out how to get away." She glared at her younger sister. "Like Patty said, when we got ready for bed, I just kept my clothes on and put my robe on over them. As soon as Mom fell asleep, I got out of bed. I didn't think anyone saw me. Except little tattletale Patty."

"So you left this car and walked forward to the next car, the Silver Falls," Jill said. "That's where Florian is, in roomette ten."

Lois nodded. "I didn't stop at his roomette, though. He was already up in the lounge car, so I went there."

"Did you see anyone in the passageway?" Jill asked.

"Not then," Lois said. "We had some coffee in the lounge,

then we went up to the Vista-Dome. But I did see someone later, when we left the dome and walked back to his roomette."

"Before or after you saw the doctor in the hallway?"

"Before. We were walking back through the sleeper cars. When we got to Florian's car, I saw a woman come out of one of the bedrooms. Then she went into another bedroom."

"Do you remember which bedroom she came from?" Jill asked.

Lois thought about this, taking her time before answering. "We had just walked into the car, so we were at the very end, just about to walk down the aisle in front of the bedrooms. I think she came out of one of the rooms in the middle of the car, you know, down where the aisle jogs to the right and goes down between the roomettes. It was probably the first bedroom. Florian says that one is where Mr. Cleary stays. I've seen him in the lounge. The blond guy. He's not bad-looking, for a man that's middle-aged. I was surprised. I thought if anyone would be coming out of his bedroom, it would be that lady from Mississippi, Miss Larch. He's been spending a lot of time with her."

"After the woman left the bedroom, where did she go?"

"She started walking toward us," Lois said. "So Florian and I backed up, toward the door we'd just come through, so she wouldn't see us."

Jill pictured the layout of the Silver Falls, and the area near the door leading into the car from the front of the train. The clean linen locker was immediately to the right. Lois and Florian would have turned to their left, heading into the aisle in front of the bedrooms, lined up on their right, with the windows to their left. When Lois and Florian backed up, they were out of sight of the person who'd exited the bedroom. And it appeared that person had been coming out of Doug's berth, which was at the far end of the row.

"Did you see where this woman went?" Jill asked.

"I peeked around the corner," Lois said. "She went into another room right away. So it must have been the one right next door, or the one next to that."

A woman coming out of Doug's room at the end of the row, Jill thought. The person next to Doug, in bedroom B, was Avis

Margate, with Cora Grant in bedroom C. The next berth was oc-cupied by Mrs. Warrick, and Jill doubted that the retired professor was poking around in Doug's room, or that she had a reason to kill Victor Fontana. At the other end were berths occupied by the Olivers and old Mr. Poindexter.

"Did you recognize the person? Are you sure it was a wom-an?"

"Of course I'm sure it was a woman," Lois said. "She was wearing a dress."

"Can you describe her?"

"I wasn't that close," Lois protested.

"Young, old," Jill prompted. "Tall, short."

"She was old, like Mom."

"Old." Mrs. Demarest snorted. "I'm in my forties. That's not old."

"You know what I mean," the girl protested. "Older than me. Not as old as Grandma. Anyway, she looked like she was tall. The dress, it was nothing special. Dark. She had her purse with her. A great big purse. I didn't recognize her. But maybe Florian did. He's traveling in that car."

"Yes, maybe he did." Jill consulted her watch. Nearly one in the morning. Should she knock on Florian's door?

The door to the ladies' room opened and an older woman in a bathrobe entered. She swept past them toward the toilets. When she had closed the door, Jill said, "Thank you for answering my questions, Lois. You've been very helpful." With that, she excused herself and left the restroom.

She headed forward, toward the Silver Falls. The door to the porter's tiny compartment was closed and Jill guessed that Frank Nathan had gone back to bed. She walked up the aisle between the roomettes and stopped at roomette ten, Florian Rapace's berth. She tapped on the door, but the Frenchman was evidently a heavy sleeper. He didn't respond.

Had it been Avis Margate who went into Doug's bedroom? Or Cora Grant? Both women were tall. Miss Margate had been wear-ing a cranberry red dress, while Miss Grant's dress was brown. In the dim light of the train corridor, both dresses would have looked dark. Both women carried large handbags, large enough to conceal a gun. Avis Margate had told Jill she'd gone to bed and hadn't awakened till Jill and Sean appeared at Doug's door. Was she lying? Or was it Cora Grant who had paid a visit to Doug's bedroom?

Jill turned from the roomette and walked forward, going around the corner to the corridor in front of the bedrooms. She stopped at the door to bedroom C. All she wanted to do was ask a question. She raised her hand, then hesitated. Then she knocked. No answer. Well, it was late, after all. Jill's weariness tugged at her.

Just as she turned to leave, the door opened. Miss Grant was wrapped in a sky-blue terrycloth robe, with matching slippers on her feet. Her brown hair was loose on her shoulders and she wasn't wearing the harlequin glasses. She looked younger without the glasses and the tightly wrapped hairstyle.

"What is it, Miss McLeod?"

"I want to ask a question," Jill said.

Miss Grant frowned. "At this hour? It must be after midnight. Well, come in." She held the door wider and Jill entered the bedroom. It was configured the same way as Doug's bedroom, with the bed on the wall opposite the door. Miss Grant's large handbag sat on the floor next to the bed, along with a big carpetbag, its beige fabric decorated with a cabbage rose pattern. Both the purse and the carpetbag were open.

Miss Grant remained standing, her hands stuck into the pockets of the robe. "Has something happened?"

"Yes. One of the passengers is dead."

"Really? Who?"

"Mr. Fontana. He was traveling in the drawing room in the Silver Crescent. Someone shot him." Jill looked at Miss Grant, checking to see if her face revealed anything.

But Miss Grant's expression remained closed and wary, as it had during most of the journey. She shrugged, a tiny movement of her shoulders. "I don't recall having met him. But then I keep to myself. Any idea who shot him?"

"Not yet," Jill said. "But I have some ideas. A gun was found earlier in bedroom A."

"That's Mr. Cleary's room," the other woman said, tilting her

chin downward. "I understand he had an altercation with someone earlier. One of the other passengers mentioned it. So did Mr.
Cleary shoot Mr. Fontana?"

"I don't know. It's possible the gun was planted in Mr. Cleary's
room. You see, someone saw a woman coming out of Mr. Cleary's
room earlier this evening. A tall woman in a dark dress."

Miss Grant allowed herself a tight smile. "There are lots of tall
women on the train, and certainly lots of dark dresses."

"True enough," Jill said. "However, the person who saw the
woman coming out of bedroom A saw the same woman enter
another bedroom just a few doors down. So that makes me think
the woman was Avis Margate. Or you."

"Or me?" Miss Grant frowned. "What possible reason would
I have to plant a gun in Mr. Cleary's bedroom?"

"It could have something to do with what he said when he
met you earlier today," Jill said. "He was sure he'd seen you before,
in Chicago in nineteen forty-one. He told me he thought you
were a woman named Belle La Tour, who performed in a nightclub called the Bell Tower. And I think you heard him say that.
The porter said you were listening to us."

"I'm a librarian from Aurora, Illinois," Miss Grant said, with a
tight little smile that didn't extend to her eyes.

"A librarian who doesn't know where the main library in
Aurora is located," Jill said. "You seemed a bit confused about
that during lunch, when Avis Margate was talking about growing
up in Aurora."

"I was distracted," Miss Grant said.

"All the same, I think I'll tell the conductor," Jill said. "He'll
want to ask you some questions."

Jill turned. She reached for the door handle. From the corner of her eye she saw Miss Grant's hands come out of her robe
pockets. One hand was empty, but the other held something. She
grabbed Jill's arm. Suddenly Jill felt a prick at her throat. She realized it was a knife.

Chapter Twenty-Two

"Y OU THINK YOU'RE so clever," Cora Grant snarled.

She pulled Jill away from the door and pushed her back onto the bed. Then she locked the door and stood in front of it, facing Jill.

"So clever. So observant. So damn nosy. You've got it all figured out, or so you think."

Jill's heart pounded and she struggled to slow her breathing. She stared at the woman holding the knife. When she spoke she hoped her voice didn't sound as frightened as she felt.

"You killed Mr. Fontana. Then you planted the gun in Doug's bedroom. Yes, I figured that out. But I don't know why you did it."

Cora's mouth twisted in a bitter smile. "I'll tell you. It's an interesting story. It starts back in Chicago, nineteen-forty. That's when I got my big break, a job in the chorus at a nightclub called the Bell Tower. You heard me singing earlier and told me I have a lovely voice. Yes, I damn well do. And I have long legs and a terrific figure. So it didn't take me long to move from the chorus to featured performer. That's when I changed my name to Belle La Tour. It sounded so much better than Elsie Gomulka, from Bucktown. That's one of the Polish neighborhoods in Chicago."

"So Doug was right, when he said he'd recognized you."

"I wish he hadn't. I didn't want anyone to realize I was on the train. That's why I disguised myself as the dowdy librarian. You see, my journey from the chorus to headliner wasn't just a matter of talent, or luck. The owner of the nightclub took a shine to me. He loved me, or so he said." Cora spat out the last words, her voice sour with bitterness.

"Victor Fontana," Jill said.

"The very same," Cora said. "I was young and ambitious. He was good-looking and free with his money. So I fell for his line. He was married, of course. But I loved him, or so I thought. And I liked the life he provided. He set me up in a fancy apartment, bought me nice clothes, a fur jacket, expensive jewelry."

"What went wrong?" Jill asked.

"Vic's a gangster. He even married into it. His wife's the daughter of one of the Chicago Outfit hoods."

"I know Fontana was a bootlegger in Colorado during Prohibition. And that he was involved in gambling in Chicago."

"That's not all he was doing in Chicago." Cora fingered the knife she held. "When the war started, so did rationing, and the black market. Vic was right there in the thick of it, making money hand over fist, and none of it legal. Vic and his partner, Charley Holt, they had a gang of hoodlums knocking off OPA offices all over town. You know, the Office of Price Administration, the places that issued ration books and gas coupons. They stole coupons and C stickers, the kind that gave you more gas than the regular stickers. Then they sold them on the black market."

"And the place to go if you wanted black market gas coupons was the Bell Tower."

"Bingo," Cora said. "You get the prize."

"How did you figure into this?" Jill asked.

"I didn't," Cora's mouth tightened. "I didn't have a clue what was going on. Oh, I knew something was dicey with the food coming out of the kitchen. You could get a steak without having to worry about using all your food coupons. Hey, everybody was doing that. But I didn't know about the gas coupon scam. Not until we got raided. That was nineteen forty-four. It was a joint operation, the Feds, the Illinois Attorney General's Office, and the Chicago cops. Somebody tipped off Vic and his pal Charley. I figure that was one of the Chicago bulls. Vic always had cops in his pocket."

"So Fontana got away," Jill said.

Cora sneered. "Slick as a whistle. Him and Charley Holt both."

"Someone got left holding the bag."

"You're looking at her, Miss Zephyrette." Cora's brown eyes smoldered, showing her anger. "I took the fall. Vic and Charley were storing all those stolen gas coupons in my dressing room, behind a false panel. I got hung out to dry. I went to trial, early in 'forty-five. They didn't believe me when I said I had nothing to do with it. The fix was in and I'm sure someone got to the prosecutor. They found me guilty and sent me to prison. The Oakdale Reformatory for Women, in Dwight, Illinois. That's where I got this." Cora pointed at the scar that marred her face. "Some bitch came at me with a knife."

"So you decided to get back at Fontana," Jill said.

"You're damn right I did." Cora's eyes flashed with anger and she waved the knife. "Vic could have gotten me out of the jam, but he didn't. He let them have me, to save his own hide. So I swore I'd kill him. After I got out of prison a couple of years ago, I went back to Chicago. I changed my name. I've been waiting, biding my time. I've been keeping an eye on him, sometimes even following him around. He never saw me. I got really good at slipping into the shadows. Somebody I know from the old days tipped me off that Vic was going to San Francisco on the *California Zephyr*. So I bought myself a ticket."

"I'm surprised he didn't recognize you." Jill looked at Cora, who was waving the knife for emphasis as she talked. Jill took a deep breath and gauged her chances of making it to the door before Cora could use the knife. If I could distract her somehow, Jill thought.

"I made sure he didn't recognize me." Cora smiled, taken with her own cleverness. She was becoming more agitated as she talked, the knife moving in wider arcs. "I dyed my hair and bought those big glasses. The clothes worked, too. And I kept out of sight. He was surprised to see me, all right." She laughed. "I waited, back there in the observation lounge, till everyone left. You, the porter, Avis Margate, even that man who went into Vic's room. Then I knocked on his door. I told him I was Avis. The way he was making a play for her, I figured he'd be happy to hear that."

That would have worked quite well, Jill thought. After sending Avis the threatening note earlier in the day, Fontana would have expected her to respond in some fashion. She pictured him opening the door to the drawing room, sure he was going to see Avis Margate, surprised to see Cora Grant.

"What did he say when he opened the door and saw you?"

"I said Avis sent me, that she wanted me to give him something." Cora looked pleased with herself. "I walked right in and opened my handbag. Then I took out the gun. He still didn't recognize me. I had to tell him who I was." She laughed again. "It felt good to see the look on his face, when the other shoe finally dropped."

"Then you grabbed the pillow, to silence the shot," Jill said.

Cora nodded. "Just in case the sound of the wheels didn't cover the noise. I didn't want anyone to find him until morning. By then I would have been long gone. I checked all the train timetables. I figured I'd get off this train during the night, at Elko, then catch the next eastbound train that comes along."

It would have worked, Jill thought. The *California Zephyr* and the Southern Pacific's *City of San Francisco* went through Elko daily, on eastbound and westbound runs. Jill wasn't sure about S.P.'s schedule, but it was just possible Cora could have left the *Zephyr* in Elko at 1:58 A.M., or whenever they got there, after this delay, and caught the eastbound *City of San Francisco* a few hours later.

That was the reason for the open carpetbag on the floor beside the bed. Cora was packing, getting ready to leave the train at the first opportunity.

Jill shifted on the bed as they talked, moving slightly to her right, closer to the purse and the carpetbag, both sitting open on the floor. She looked inside, wondering if there was anything inside she could use to distract Cora. The carpetbag contained neatly folded panties and a nightgown in the same sky-blue shade as the robe. There was a brassiere and a small cloth bag that might have contained makeup. And the harlequin glasses, which no doubt had clear lenses, intended just for disguise.

Jill glanced inside the purse. Here was a possibility—the metal vanity case that Miss Grant had been using earlier that day. If it was like the one Jill's mother had, it was heavy.

"But you found him, sooner than I expected. How did you know he was dead?" Cora demanded.

"You didn't latch the drawing room door when you left. The porter saw it and went to investigate. Then he came and got me. Fontana was still alive when I got there."

"But he died, before he could tell you anything. That's why you're nosing around, trying to find out what happened."

"Especially after you planted the murder weapon in Doug Cleary's bedroom. Someone saw you."

"How did they know it was me? Miss Margate's as tall as I am."

Jill shrugged. "I'd already talked with her. Besides, you were the last to leave the observation lounge. I know that because someone saw her leaving. So that left you."

"Not for long," Cora said. She untied the robe. She was wearing the brown dress she'd worn earlier in the day. She transferred the knife to her left hand and slipped the robe off her right shoulder and arm.

Jill leaned over and reached into the handbag. She slipped her right hand through the handle of the vanity case. Then she stood in one swift movement, swinging it at Cora Grant's head. The corner of the case hit Cora's forehead, drawing blood.

She screamed with rage. "You bitch!"

Jill dodged and put her left hand up as Cora slashed at her with the knife. The blade nicked the palm of her hand, drawing blood. She ignored the pain. With the vanity case dangling from her right wrist, she unlocked and opened the bedroom door.

Cora came after her. The two women tumbled out into the corridor and smacked hard against the window on the opposite site of the corridor. Jill swung the vanity case again, this time connecting with Cora's hand.

"I'll kill you, bitch," Cora snarled.

Avis Margate opened the door of bedroom B. "What the hell's going on out here?" she demanded, her eyes widening as she saw Cora holding the knife.

Then Frank Nathan rounded the corner, followed by Doug, both of them talking at once.

Jill kept her eye on Cora as she backed toward Avis and the others. All down the corridor, bedroom doors were opening. She saw Mr. Poindexter peer out of bedroom F, then Trudy Oliver at the door of bedroom E. Trudy backed out of sight. Then Jill saw Henry Oliver emerge, in his pajamas.

"It's her," Jill warned. "She killed Fontana. Be careful, she has a knife."

Doug moved to Jill's side, then dodged back as Cora jabbed at him. Behind Cora, the door to bedroom D opened and Geneva Warrick poked her head out. Then she disappeared. When she returned, she had something in her hands. It was the coffeepot that the porter had delivered to her room earlier in the evening.

Mrs. Warrick raised the pot and brought it down hard on Cora Grant's head.

Chapter Twenty-Three

"IT'S JUST A SCRATCH. Thank goodness I'm right-handed." Jill sat at a table in the lounge of the Silver Chalet, looking at the cut on her left hand. Doug, Sean and the conductor stood nearby, concerned expressions on their faces.

Dr. Ranleigh examined the wound. "It's more than just a scratch. Fortunately it isn't very deep and you don't need stitches. But we don't want it to become infected. Have it looked at as soon as you get home."

The doctor cleaned the cut with a damp cloth, then swabbed it with alcohol. That stung a bit. She treated the wound with an antibiotic ointment and wrapped Jill's hand with a gauze bandage.

"I got worried when you didn't come back to the dome-observation car after you looked in on Miss Brandon," Doug said. "So I came looking for you. The porter in the Silver Rapids said you'd gone to talk with someone in the next sleeper, the Silver Maple. When I went back there, I ran into a woman with her daughter. They said you'd probably gone to talk with Miss Grant in the Silver Falls."

"I wish you'd come to get me first," Uncle Sean said. "You could have been seriously hurt. Your mother would never let me hear the end of it."

"I did go talk with Miss Grant," Jill said, looking at the bandage on her hand. "She admitted killing Mr. Fontana. She said he'd left her holding the bag for that rationing coupon business in Chicago. She went to prison for it. She's been planning revenge ever since."

"So you've solved another murder," the conductor said. "This is getting to be a habit, Miss McLeod."

"Not one I'd intended." Jill smiled ruefully. "I let my curiosity overrule my common sense."

Sean smiled. "I've been known to be single-minded in the pursuit of a lead." He looked at the conductor. "What did you do with Miss Grant?"

"As soon as she regained consciousness," Mr. Dutton said, "we locked her in the baggage car. With the baggage man and the brakeman for company. They'll keep an eye on her for the time being."

He looked out the window. The *California Zephyr* had reached the area where the freight train had derailed. Lights outside illuminated the scene, giving the salt flats an otherworldly look. Several freight cars had tumbled down an embankment, falling on their sides, and the track crew was working to set them upright. The *CZ* was stopped on a siding, awaiting permission to continue its journey.

"Once we're past this mess, it won't take us long to get to Wendover. Then we can turn Miss Grant over to the authorities. I'll be glad to see the back of her, and an end to this situation." The conductor pulled his pocket watch from his vest and looked at it, frowning. "This has put us way behind schedule. I hope we can make up some time once we get rolling."

───

Two deputies from the Tooele County Sheriff's Office were waiting at the station in Wendover when the *California Zephyr* made its unscheduled stop. They boarded the Silver Crescent and examined Victor Fontana's body and the crime scene. Then the body was removed from the drawing room in the Silver Crescent and loaded into a waiting ambulance.

Cora Grant was taken into custody, escorted from the baggage car by two deputies. The conductor gave the deputies the gun that Cora had used to kill Fontana and subsequently hidden in Doug's bedroom, as well as the knife she'd wielded against Jill. He'd also turned over the roll of film shot by Rachel.

After the deputies talked with the conductor, they interviewed Jill and the others. The Wendover stop stretched longer, putting the *CZ* even farther behind schedule. Mr. Dutton went to the station, where he telegraphed ahead to Elko and Winnemucca, advising those stations of the reasons for the delay.

Art Geddes also left the train at Wendover. His voice was tired and subdued as he spoke to Jill on the platform, taking his suitcase as the porter handed it down. "I gotta send some wires back to Chicago. Vic might not have been the straightest arrow in the bunch, but he had a wife and three kids. Somebody's gotta tell them. I guess it's gonna be me." He sighed as he tipped the porter. Then he turned and trudged wearily toward the station.

The *California Zephyr* finally rolled out of Wendover, crossing the state line from Utah into Nevada. The engineer hoped to make up some time during its early morning journey across the Silver State, but it looked as though the train would be late getting to its next scheduled stops. It would take the *CZ* more than an hour to reach Elko. This was a crew change stop, where the train would take on a new engineer and fireman. From Elko, it was two hours to Winnemucca, where the train crew would change, with Mr. Dutton and Mr. Mooney turning the Silver Lady over to a new conductor and brakeman.

Jill went to her compartment. She knew she should work on her trip report, but fatigue had set in long ago and she couldn't face it. She went to bed instead. She'd asked Uncle Sean to wake her before the train got to Winnemucca. She wanted to say goodbye to him, and say hello to her cousin Teresa.

Jill had been sleeping for about three hours when Sean tapped on her door and awakened her. She got up, feeling somewhat rested, and quickly dressed.

It was a quarter after five in the morning when the *California Zephyr* slowed, approaching the outskirts of Winnemucca, Nevada. The train was more than an hour late, though the *CZ* had, as Mr. Dutton hoped, made up some time as it sped through the Nevada desert.

When she went to the vestibule of the Silver Quail, Uncle Sean and Joe Backus, the porter, were there. As the train drew closer to the lights of the town, Doug joined them.

"I thought I'd see Dad off. And I haven't seen Teresa in quite a while. The last time was when she and Fred were living in Leadville. I was skiing up in Aspen, so I went to visit them. They only had two kids then. Now they have four."

"The youngest one sure looks like your mother," Sean said.

Doug nodded. "Yes, she does. Thanks for showing me the picture." He hesitated, looking at his father. "Do you believe in love at first sight?"

Sean chuckled. "Of course I do. The first time I laid eyes on your mother, I knew she was the one. Does this have something to do with that young lady from Jackson, Mississippi?"

"It might," Doug said.

"Have you said anything to her?" Doug shook his head, and his father laughed again. "Better get a move on. Only a few hours till you get to Portola."

Teresa and Fred were on the platform as the train pulled into the station. Sean and Doug got off. When Teresa saw Doug, she whooped and threw her arms around him. "Well, if it isn't my big brother, the traveling ski bum! No ski slopes in Winnemucca, so what are you doing here?"

Jill got off the train as well. She had time to say hello to Teresa, since this was a crew change stop. Down the platform, in the direction of the locomotives, she saw Mr. Dutton and Mr. Mooney conferring with the new conductor and brakeman. Several passengers were leaving the train here in Winnemucca, including Milly Demarest and her three children. Jill walked quickly toward the Silver Maple, intercepting them.

"Thanks for your help, Lois," she told the girl. "We did catch the person responsible for the murder."

The teenager rolled her eyes and leaned closer. "Was it that Miss Grant? I overheard a couple of the porters talking about it."

"They said you got hurt." Mrs. Demarest looked at Jill's bandaged hand. "I hope it's not too bad."

Jill smiled. "Yes, it was Miss Grant. And this is just a scratch."

Robby tugged at his mother's sleeve. "C'mon, Mom. There's Aunt Darlene. I hope we go get breakfast right away. I'm hungry."

"You're always hungry," Patty said, hoisting a suitcase.

A rangy woman approached, wearing faded dungarees, her hands stuck in the pockets of an old brown car coat. She had a red woolen scarf wound around her neck. She greeted the Demarests with hugs and took the suitcase from Patty. "So you're finally here. How come the train's so late?"

Milly Demarest ran a hand through her frizzy hair. "Oh, my word, Sis, you're not going to believe it."

Jill retraced her steps back down the platform, chatting for a moment with her cousin Teresa. Then the new conductor called, "All aboard!"

Doug kissed his sister on the cheek, then turned to his father. "Keep well."

"Thanks, son. It's been good to see you." Sean hesitated, and then he stuck out his hand. "Don't be a stranger."

Doug shook his father's hand. "I won't."

Jill and Doug climbed back into the vestibule. The *California Zephyr* moved out of the Winnemucca station, heading across the northwestern Nevada desert.

"What time does the dining car start serving breakfast?" Doug asked. "I'm not that hungry right now, but I could drink a gallon of coffee."

Jill looked at her watch. "At six, about forty minutes from now. But I think if we throw ourselves on the mercy of the dining car crew we might be able to get some coffee."

Doug laughed. "Lead the way."

They walked forward into the dining car, where the tables were already set for breakfast service. All six of the waiters were gathered at two of the tables, finishing their own breakfast. Mr. Gaylord stood up as Jill and Doug approached. "You're up early this morning, Miss McLeod. We heard it's been quite a night."

"It has," Jill said. "And we're desperate for coffee."

Mr. Gaylord laughed. "So was the new conductor. He was in here a minute ago. Took a pot back to his office. Have a seat. I'll bring you a fresh pot right now."

Jill and Doug sat down at a nearby table for four, taking the window seats. Mr. Gaylord returned a moment later with the coffeepot and poured each of them a cupful. He left the pot with them.

"Thank you." Doug raised the cup to his lips and took a swallow. "Hot black coffee. Nectar of the gods."

Jill stirred cream into her coffee and took a sip. They sat in companionable silence for a while, listening to the waiters as they cleared the tables where they'd eaten breakfast and set them up for passengers. The chefs in the kitchen were talking as they banged pots and pans. At the steward's counter, Mr. Taylor was humming to himself.

Jill looked out the window. It was another hour until sunrise, but here and there the early morning darkness was pierced by lights from ranches or vehicles on the roads.

"Maybe we'll make up some more time as we cross the desert. We won't once we get into the mountains." She took another sip of coffee. "You're getting off the train in Portola. Why such a small town? What have you got up your sleeve? A couple of aces?"

Doug laughed. "I don't have to cheat at poker, cuz. I'm good. As to why Portola, I'm meeting a friend. His name is Eric. His father's a Western Pacific engineer, so Eric grew up there, and he's living in Portola, temporarily. He and I met when we were skiing a couple of years ago, up in Squaw Valley. We've got a business proposition to investigate, buying into a ski resort near Lake Tahoe."

"That's wonderful news," Jill said. "My ski bum cousin is settling down."

"I guess so. Strange prospect, after my heretofore nomadic existence. I've been to Sugar Bowl up by Donner Pass so I know there's great skiing in the Lake Tahoe area. And casinos in Nevada, of course. So two of the things I like best in the world. Skiing and gambling. I'm hoping that —" He stopped. "Well, just hoping."

Jill smiled. Love at first sight, was it? Doug's relationship with Miss Larch seemed to be moving fast into serious territory. "That Pamela Larch might be part of that future? As your father said, you'd better get a move on."

"It's early to be knocking on her door. Though we talked a lot last night. We'll see if anything comes of it." He picked up the pot and topped off their coffees. "What about you? Teresa wrote me when your fiancé died in Korea. Then she said you'd taken this Zephyrette job. Are you going to ride the rails forever?"

"I don't know. Forever sounds like a very long time. I don't know what I'll be doing next month, let alone two or three years in the future. I enjoy being a Zephyrette, for now. It's been good for me. I get to travel, meet people from all over the country, and other countries. And make new friends." Jill smiled. "I have met someone. His name's Mike. He was a passenger on the train last December, and now he's in school at the university in Berkeley. I've been seeing a lot of him."

"Great. I'm glad for you. You've got to stop getting involved in murders, though. I understand this wasn't your first effort at crime-solving."

"Well, I didn't set out to be a detective. But it's in the nature of my job to keep an eye on things while we're on the train. That's why I do walk-throughs every few hours. I'm supposed to observe and be ready to help the passengers. Then there's my natural curiosity."

"Natural nosiness," Doug added.

"Stop teasing." She smiled at him. "Who knows what will happen in the future. I wish you the best of luck with your ski resort. I'll come up and visit you."

"The ski resort hasn't happened yet, but if it's everything my friend says it is, I think it could work. I'll let you know. Maybe it is time I settled down and stayed in one place."

He raised his cup then he stopped, setting it down again. He looked past Jill, a grin edging its way across his face. Jill turned and saw Pamela Larch, her blond hair loose on her shoulders. She wore a silky blue dress with a scooped neckline. The gold chain she'd worn around her neck was not in evidence.

"I went to your room in the Silver Falls, but you weren't there. I do hope there's some coffee left in that pot," she said.

Doug stood and pulled out the chair next to him. Jill poured a cup for Pamela.

"I got up early to see my dad off in Winnemucca," Doug said, sitting down again. "And say hi to my sister and her husband. They were there to meet him."

"I'm so glad you're all right," Pamela said to Jill, pointing at the bandage on her hand. "Doug woke me up and told me what happened, how you caught that woman who killed Mr. Fontana. I'm so glad it's all over."

"Is it?" Doug asked. "All over?"

Pamela smiled at him. Then she glanced at Jill. "Doug and I talked quite a bit last night. Just talking, although there might have been some kissing involved! I've thought about it and I've made a decision." She reached for Doug's hand.

He grinned from ear to ear and squeezed her hand. Pamela turned to Jill. "Miss McLeod, would it be possible for me to get my checked bag from the baggage car? You see, I'm not going to San Francisco after all. I've decided to get off the train in Portola."

Jill was smiling, too. "I think that can be arranged."

Chapter Twenty-Four

THOUGH IT WASN'T QUITE six o'clock, passengers were fil-
tering into the dining car in search of breakfast. Mr. Gaylord
returned to the table with a fresh pot of coffee. "We're going to
start serving, so you folks go ahead and mark your meal checks."

"Suddenly I'm ravenous," Doug said, reaching for a menu
and a check. "Bacon-and-eggs ravenous."

"I know what I want," Pamela said. "The railroad French
toast."

"Same here," Jill said. "With bacon."

"Crisp, but not burned." Mr. Gaylord smiled as he took their
meal checks.

They had a leisurely breakfast, then Jill asked Pamela for her
luggage check. "I'll go up to the baggage car to see what I can do
about your suitcase."

"Oh, thank you." Pamela dug around in her purse and gave
the check to Jill. "I appreciate your doing this, Jill. May I call you
that?"

"Yes, Pamela, you may."

It looked as though Pamela might become a member of the
family. Jill hoped this onboard romance would work out. Of
course, Jill had an onboard romance of her own.

She pocketed the baggage claim check and left Doug and Pamela at the table. She walked forward, heading for the chair cars
and ultimately the baggage car. But she had a stop to make first.

The new conductor's name was Barney Spicer. He and the
brakeman, Edgar Higgins, were in the conductor's office on the

Silver Mustang, drinking coffee, when Jill dropped by to introduce herself.

"I read the wire Mr. Dutton sent from Wendover," Mr. Spicer
said, "and he briefed me when he got to Winnemucca. I do have
some questions for you, Miss McLeod."

He got the details about what had happened. Then he
changed the subject, talking about their delayed status. "We're
still running late. I think we'll be able to make up time between
here and Gerlach, but once we get into the Sierra, we certainly
won't be running at top speed."

After she left the conductor's office, Jill headed for the baggage car, where she retrieved Pamela Larch's suitcase from the San
Francisco checked baggage. It took her a few minutes to do so.
That done, Jill headed back through the train to the Silver Crescent. Pamela wasn't in her bedroom, so Jill left the suitcase just
inside the door. Then she returned to her compartment to update
her trip report. This is going to be a long one, she thought, adding
another sheet of paper.

The *California Zephyr* made up some time during this leg of
the journey, stopping briefly for passengers in the small Nevada
towns of Gerlach and Herlong. Then it crossed the Nevada–California border and entered the six-thousand-foot-long tunnel at
Chilcoot. When it emerged, the train went through the tiny town
named for a famous mountain man, James Beckwourth, who had
established a trading post in that area.

By the time the Silver Lady rolled into Portola, California at a
quarter after eight, it was about thirty minutes late. The cars were
no longer silver. They were covered with a layer of grime collected
during the run from Chicago. It was here at Portola that the *CZ*
went through the train wash, a series of curved pipes that sprayed
water on the cars, clearing the dirt from the Vista-Domes for the
scenic trip down the Feather River Canyon. When the weather
was good, as it was today, watching the train go through the wash
racks was a popular sight in the small railroad town. As the train
pulled into the station, Jill saw a line of spectators approaching
from Portola's small business district along Commercial Street.

Doug and Pamela stood in the vestibule of the Silver Crescent, their luggage at their feet. "I've written a letter to Earl," Pamela said. "I'll send it to him special delivery, along with the engagement ring. Doug and I are going to get married at Lake Tahoe. I understand we can do that right away in Nevada."

"Sure can," Doug said. "Now that I've got you, I'm not letting you get away."

"You're really going to do it?" Jill asked. "So soon?"

Doug and Pamela looked at each other and laughed. "Strike while the iron's hot," he said.

"It feels right," Pamela added.

"So you're not going to see San Francisco," Jill said. "Not this trip, anyway."

"We need to have a honeymoon sometime," Doug said. "As soon as my friend and I sort out this business deal, we'll head down to the city by the bay. It'll be nice to see Aunt Lora and Uncle Amos. Jill and her fellow can show us the sights. Besides, I have to meet this guy Mike, to see if I approve."

"I approve," Jill said. "And that's the important thing."

The train came to a stop. Pamela pulled several bills from her purse and handed them to Lonnie Clark.

"Thank you, Mr. Clark," she said. "You've been a great help during the trip and I do appreciate it."

"Thank you, miss," the porter said, taking the tip. "Best of luck to both of you."

Jill followed Doug and Pamela down to the platform, to say good-bye. Then she reboarded the train. They weren't in the station long. After going through the train wash, the *California Zephyr* continued its westward journey, 116 miles down the Feather River Canyon, then into Oroville. It would take approximately two hours and fifteen minutes and encompassed some of the most beautiful scenery on the route.

Right now the train was on the North Fork of the Feather River. The next sight was the Clio Trestle, looming 172 feet over the Mohawk Valley, with glorious views of the surrounding mountains. Then the train went through the Spring Garden tunnel, 7,344 feet long. It emerged on the Feather River's Middle Fork, then descended into the Williams Loop. This was a complete circle that gave the train a one-percent grade as it headed toward Quincy Junction and the Keddie Wye, a towering Y-shaped trestle. Past that, the train would cling to the river's banks as both meandered down the curving canyon, going past the Tobin and Pulga Bridges.

Now that the train was out of Portola, Jill headed for the dining car, which was full of breakfasting passengers and busy crew. Jill saw Mrs. Warrick and the Ranleighs at one table, the Carsons at another, and Miss Margate talking with Miss Brandon. She smiled as she passed them, heading toward the dining car steward's counter and the public address system.

"Join us for some coffee, Miss McLeod," Miss Margate called.

"I will, but first I have to make an announcement." Jill picked up the microphone and launched into her familiar spiel.

"Good morning, ladies and gentlemen. This is Jill McLeod, your Zephyrette. I hope you all rested well." She smiled, thinking of her own restless night. "We are now in the famous Feather River Canyon. The Feather River received its name from Don Luis Arguello, the Spanish conquistador who discovered it in eighteen-twenty. He was intrigued by the vast quantities of wild pigeon feathers that floated on its ripples. He called it *Rio de Las Plumas*. In Castilian, that means River of the Feathers.

"Back before the Gold Rush, a trailblazer named James Beckwourth found the pass through the Sierra Nevada Mountains that still bears his name. It was a better place to cross the ridge than the route the emigrant wagon trains were using, as it was about two thousand feet lower, but the country on the west side of the pass was very rugged. It was not until the eighteen-sixties that pioneer Arthur W. Keddie surveyed a practical railway line down the various forks of the Feather River. The line was not built until nineteen-nine, when the Western Pacific Railroad was completed.

"Gold was discovered at Bidwell's Bar on the fourth of July in eighteen forty-eight, just a few months after James Marshall made the strike that started the big California Gold Rush. Millions were panned from the shining sands of the Feather River. There's still gold there, too. Most likely you'll see a prospector or two today, working down at the river's edge."

Jill replaced the microphone and joined Miss Brandon and Miss Margate at their table. Mr. Gaylord appeared, pouring coffee for her.

"Miss Margate's been telling me about your adventures," Miss Brandon said, raising a cup of tea to her lips.

"It's over now. I'm just glad to have things back to normal."

Jill looked out the window at the beautiful canyon. The April sky was blue, and the morning sun bathed the tall pines and the gleaming rocks of the surrounding mountains. It looked like a golden day for the Silver Lady.

AFTERWORD

A FEW YEARS AGO I was in the lobby of the Hotel Colorado in Glenwood Springs, looking at photographs of notables who had stayed there, including President Theodore Roosevelt—and Al Capone. Yes, Al used to vacation in the Colorado Rockies, along with a lot of other gangsters. And most people who grew up in the Denver area, as I did, have heard of Colorado's own crime family, the Smaldones. The three brothers—Eugene ("Checkers"), Clyde ("Flip Flop") and Clarence ("Chauncey")—dominated organized crime in the Mile High City for years, starting in the 1930s. There was also organized crime in southern Colorado, in the Front Range city of Pueblo, and farther south in Walsenburg and Trinidad. Italian immigrants who came to work in the coal fields brought with them the Mafia and the Black Hand.

Both the books in the *California Zephyr* series required research, not only into organized crime in Colorado, but trains as well. When writing about a historical period or a particular subject, I strive to be accurate in conveying information. I may have tweaked facts from time to time for the sake of plot, characters, and a good story. Any errors are my own.

Many thanks to two of the Zephyrettes who worked aboard the historical streamliner known as the *California Zephyr*. Cathy Moran Von Ibsch was a Zephyrette in the late 1960s and rode the Silver Lady on her last run. Rodna Walls Taylor, who died recently, rode the rails as a Zephyrette in the early 1950s, the time period of the book. I greatly appreciate their generosity in answering my many questions. I couldn't have written this book without them.

We are fortunate to have railroad museums to preserve the remaining artifacts of this country's rail era, particularly the streamliners like the *California Zephyr*. Both the California State Railroad Museum in Sacramento and the Colorado Railroad Museum in Golden have excellent research libraries as well as rail cars and locomotives. The Western Pacific Railroad Museum in Portola, California, is a treasure house of rolling stock.

I recommend the *California Zephyr* Virtual Museum, at: http://calzephyr.railfan.net. Here I found old timetables, menus, and brochures, as well as information on the Zephyrettes.

The Amtrak version of the *California Zephyr* is not the same as the sleek Silver Lady of days gone by. But it's great to ride a train through most of the same route, getting an up-close look at this marvelous part of the country. The journey may take longer, but the scenery is spectacular and the relaxation factor is 110 percent.

The *California Zephyr* story, and that of railroading in America, is told in books and films. Some of them are listed below, along with other sources I used in writing the *California Zephyr* series. Many of these books are full of photographs and first-hand accounts of working on and aboard the trains.

Publications about the *California Zephyr*,
rails, and rail travel in the United States

Portrait of a Silver Lady: The Train They Called the California Zephyr, Bruce A. McGregor and Ted Benson, Pruett Publishing Company, Boulder, CO, 1977. Full of beautiful photographs, lots of history and technical information, and firsthand accounts of what it was like to work on this train.

CZ: The Story of the California Zephyr, Karl R. Zimmerman, Quadrant Press, Inc., 1972. Excellent overview of the train's history, with lots of old photographs.

Zephyr: Tracking a Dream Across America, Henry Kisor, Adams Media Corporation, 1994. An account of Kisor's journey westward on the Amtrak *California Zephyr*.

Waiting on a Train: The Embattled Future of Passenger Rail Ser-

vice, James McCommons, Chelsea Green Publishing Company, 2009. A thought-provoking account of the author's travels on various Amtrak routes and his interviews with passengers, employees, rail advocates, and people in the railroad business, with discussions about the future of passenger rail in the United States.

A Guidebook to Amtrak's California Zephyr, Eva J. Hoffman, Flashing Yellow Guidebooks, Evergreen, CO, 2003, 2008. There are three volumes: Chicago to Denver, Denver to Salt Lake City, Salt Lake City to San Francisco. I discovered these courtesy of a railfan while riding the Amtrak *CZ*. A detailed milepost-by-milepost guide to what's outside the train window, with history and anecdotes thrown in. A useful resource for finding out how far it is from one place to another and how long it takes to get there.

Rising from the Rails: Pullman Porters and the Making of the Black Middle Class, Larry Tye, Henry Holt & Company, 2004. There is also a PBS video. The book discusses the history of the Pullman Company, African Americans working on the railroad, and their legacy.

The Pullman Porters and West Oakland, Thomas and Wilma Tramble, Arcadia Publishing, 2007. A look at the lives of porters in Oakland, CA. Full of wonderful photographs.

PUBLICATIONS ABOUT ORGANIZED CRIME
IN COLORADO, AL CAPONE AND PROHIBITION

Mountain Mafia: Organized Crime in the Rockies, Betty L. Alt and Sandra K. Wells, Dog Ear Publishing, 2008. A look at the Black Hand and the Mafia in Colorado, including the Smaldones and their predecessors and rivals, through the twentieth century, and the Colorado crime syndicates' links to organized crime in other areas of the United States.

Smaldone: The Untold Story of an American Crime Family, Dick Kreck, Fulcrum Publishing Company, 2009. A history of Denver's own crime syndicate, active from the 1930s to the later twentieth century.

Get Capone: The Secret Plot that Captured America's Most Wanted Gangster, Jonathan Eig, Simon & Schuster, 2010. The rise and fall of Capone, America's most notorious gangster, with a look at his vast illegal operations in Chicago.

Last Call: The Rise and Fall of Prohibition, Daniel Okrent, Scribner, 2010. A detailed overview of Prohibition, the reasons for its enactment, the crime that rose from it, and the aftermath.

Information on the 10th Mountain Division can be found at: http://www.drum.army.mil/AboutFortDrum/Pages/hist_10th MountainHistory_lv3.aspx

Much of the information about World War II rationing and crime that arose from it comes from various sources on the Internet.

FILMS

The California Zephyr: The Story of America's Most Talked About Train, Copper Media, 1999

The California Zephyr: Silver Thread Through The West, Travel-VideoStore, 2007.

The California Zephyr: The Ultimate Fan Trip, Emery Gulash, Green Frog Productions, Ltd., 2007.

American Experience: Streamliners: America's Lost Trains, PBS Video, 2006

Promotional films from the *CZ* and other trains are viewable on YouTube.

The original *California Zephyr* appeared on film in the 1954 movie *Cinerama Holiday*, as well as the 1952 noir *Sudden Fear*, starring Joan Crawford and Jack Palance. During the train portion of that movie, a Zephyrette comes to Joan Crawford's bedroom to tell her it's time for her dinner reservation. That Zephyrette is Rodna Walls, whom I interviewed for this book.

I hope you enjoy *Death Deals a Hand*. Now go ride a train!

About the Author

Janet Dawson is the author of the Jeri Howard PI series, which includes *Kindred Crimes*, winner of the St. Martin's Press/Private Eye Writers of America contest for Best Private Eye Novel, and *Bit Player*, which was nominated for a Golden Nugget award for Best California Mystery. The most recent series entry is *Cold Trail*. Two of Dawson's short stories were nominated for a Shamus and another won a Macavity.

In addition to a suspense novel, *What You Wish For*, she has written *Death Rides the Zephyr*, the predecessor to this book. A past president of NorCal MWA, Dawson lives in the East Bay region. She welcomes visitors at www.janetdawson.com and at her blog, www.getitwriteblog.wordpress.com.

More Traditional Mysteries from Perseverance Press
For the New Golden Age

K.K. Beck
Tipping the Valet
ISBN 978-1-56474-563-7

Albert A. Bell, Jr.
PLINY THE YOUNGER SERIES
Death in the Ashes
ISBN 978-1-56474-532-3

The Eyes of Aurora
ISBN 978-1-56474-549-1

Taffy Cannon
ROXANNE PRESCOTT SERIES
Guns and Roses
Agatha and Macavity awards nominee, Best Novel
ISBN 978-1-880284-34-6

Blood Matters
ISBN 978-1-880284-86-5

Open Season on Lawyers
ISBN 978-1-880284-51-3

Paradise Lost
ISBN 978-1-880284-80-3

Laura Crum
GAIL MCCARTHY SERIES
Moonblind
ISBN 978-1-880284-90-2

Chasing Cans
ISBN 978-1-880284-94-0

Going, Gone
ISBN 978-1-880284-98-8

Barnstorming
ISBN 978-1-56474-508-8

Jeanne M. Dams
HILDA JOHANSSON SERIES
Crimson Snow
ISBN 978-1-880284-79-7

Indigo Christmas
ISBN 978-1-880284-95-7

Murder in Burnt Orange
ISBN 978-1-56474-503-3

Janet Dawson
JERI HOWARD SERIES
Bit Player
Golden Nugget Award nominee
ISBN 978-1-56474-494-4

Cold Trail
ISBN 978-1-56474-555-2

What You Wish For
ISBN 978-1-56474-518-7

TRAIN SERIES
Death Rides the Zephyr
ISBN 978-1-56474-530-9

Death Deals a Hand
ISBN 978-1-56474-569-9

Kathy Lynn Emerson
LADY APPLETON SERIES
Face Down Below the Banqueting House
ISBN 978-1-880284-71-1

Face Down Beside St. Anne's Well
ISBN 978-1-880284-82-7

Face Down O'er the Border
ISBN 978-1-880284-91-9

Sara Hoskinson Frommer
JOAN SPENCER SERIES
Her Brother's Keeper
ISBN 978-1-56474-525-5

Hal Glatzer
KATY GREEN SERIES
Too Dead To Swing
ISBN 978-1-880284-53-7

A Fugue in Hell's Kitchen
ISBN 978-1-880284-70-4

The Last Full Measure
ISBN 978-1-880284-84-1

Margaret Grace
MINIATURE SERIES
Mix-up in Miniature
ISBN 978-1-56474-510-1

Madness in Miniature
ISBN 978-1-56474-543-9

Manhattan in Miniature
ISBN 978-1-56474-562-0

Matrimony in Miniature (forthcoming)
ISBN 978-1-56474-575-0

Tony Hays
Shakespeare No More
ISBN 978-1-56474-566-8

Wendy Hornsby
MAGGIE MACGOWEN SERIES
In the Guise of Mercy
ISBN 978-1-56474-482-1

The Paramour's Daughter
ISBN 978-1-56474-496-8

The Hanging
ISBN 978-1-56474-526-2